BACKSTITCH

BACKSTITCH

MARIAN MITCHELL DONAHUE

galiot press

BACKSTITCH
a novel

First published in 2026 by Galiot Press

Copyright © 2026 by Marian Mitchell Donahue
All rights reserved

Copyright laws prohibit reproducing, scanning, or distributing any portion of this book without permission. Furthermore, Galiot Press does not grant permission to any person, organization, or corporation to use any portion of this book for the purposes of training artificial intelligence technologies or systems.

Galiot Press
PO Box 1406
Arlington, MA 02474

www.galiotpress.com
@galiotpress

This is a work of fiction. Names, characters, places, and incidents either are the product of the author's imagination, or are used fictitiously. Except where actual locations or historical events are described or referred to, any resemblance to actual persons, living or dead, events, or locales, is entirely coincidental.

ISBN: 979-8-9989547-6-4

Design by Euan Monaghan
Printed in the United States of America

Present Day

Nothing had prepared her for the eyes. Violet knew she'd see little pieces of herself as a child on banners and bus stops when she went to her mother's retrospective at the National Museum of Women in the Arts. Her sister had warned her they'd used one of their mother's early works for the promotional materials, from the years she hid herself away in their house and all she'd painted were the girls. But there was no warning Marigold could have issued that would have readied Violet for the way her own brown eyes followed her as she walked from the parking garage on Constitution Avenue through the soupy summer day to the doors of the museum. Once seen, they couldn't be unseen. Her own eyes, rendered first in small dabs of oil paint all those years ago, now re-created in high-resolution printer ink, the rest of the image cropped out and left mutilated on some graphic designer's desktop.

Violet tucked her head down and pressed her sunglasses high up on the bridge of her nose to keep from meeting her painted gaze. She couldn't understand why, out of everything, they had picked this early work, and her eyes, to represent her mother's show. Why her own dark set and not her little sister's objectively more interesting hazel one? She was in that painting, too. Why not hers? Violet didn't believe she had any illusions about herself. If anything, the years she had spent as her mother's art object had given her a greater than usual awareness of her own aesthetic truth. Her eyes were a dark brown that almost looks black, which some found off-putting. In a good mood, her mother would deem them only "serious" or "haunting." In worse moods, they became inhuman. Violet suddenly had dolls' eyes or dogs' eyes. The feature—the scrap of an incomplete story—was meant to pull people in further and further. You were supposed to want to know what happened next, but Violet already knew what had happened, and she didn't want to be pulled in. She was already a half hour late meeting her sister at the exhibit.

The last time she'd been in D.C. had been for her mother's burial and now, seven years later, she was back for her resurrection. Violet stubbornly maintained her ignorance of the internet-based cultural spiral that had transformed Alice Snyder from a marginal character in the D.C. fiber arts scene to a "rediscovered" minor feminist icon. Marigold had tried to fill her in on the major developments. It had all started, as it always seemed to, with Gabriel Grant, their mother's only ex-boyfriend from the few short years in undergrad before she'd run off with their father, Arthur Snyder. Grant had been a college dropout from the kind of failproof Annapolis family that took all of life's disappointments with the patience of the wealthy. Sometime during his L.A. years, Grant had sold a photograph of their mother titled *Ophelia* to a private collector, who hosted a dinner party where an up-and-coming musician saw it and used it for a new album cover. Had that little exchange between men not gone anywhere, had the album not been a wild success—spreading that old photo of their mother's half-dressed, semiconscious, twenty-year-old body to every screen it could reach—then someone, some other someone on the internet, might not have finally taken a longer look at that photo and tried to find the woman in it. And what did that person find but the dark and twisted life of Alice Snyder and its burned end when she died from a studio fire in 2017.

A Twitter thread became an opinion piece became an open petition to have the album art changed, or at the very least, to have Alice

Snyder correctly credited as the girl in the photo. Because everyone was supposed to know better than this. They weren't supposed to consume women like this anymore, swallowed and digested in a single, uncritical gulp. Shoved down so fast the world was already on the verge of forgetting her before someone bothered to ask her name. Everyone was supposed to care that she was probably unconscious when that photo was taken. They were supposed to care that she never signed over the rights to her image to be sold and resold. That photographer and his muse were just twenty when that photo was taken, and let me tell you about his history with women, and let me tell you why you're wrong not to care.

Two months ago, Violet hadn't known any of this. She'd been safely numb in her own world in Baltimore, not keeping up with the internet meltdown, not knowing the songs of the summer. It appeared Marigold, on the other hand, had been waiting for something like this. She kept Violet out of it, while still stoking the interest enough to successfully pitch a retrospective of their mother's work, something she'd been pitching to Violet since the summer after their mother had died and they'd packed all her work away in storage units. The summer their father agreed to teach his graduate students at his school's satellite campus in Chile to help deal with his grief and then never came back. The last summer Violet spent in D.C. before she moved north to Boston for grad school and tried to forget everything that came before. Violet had always taken after her father and in grief she was no different. Marigold hadn't run. She had stayed. She'd gathered up the broken pieces of their life and built a new one with it. It was a skill from their mother—one Violet wanted but had never learned. Violet knew her sister was inherently better than her, and so, so much stronger, and it was for her and no one else that Violet had come back to the place where everything had fallen apart.

Violet could have gone her whole life without seeing another one of her mother's works. She'd been there for the process, why would she need to see the product? But following all her mother's work, in the final gallery, would be a new piece from her sister. Something digital and immersive. A daughter's tribute to her mother. Violet didn't need to see her mother's work again, but she had never missed a single one of Marigold's shows and, no matter how painful it was, Violet was going to get through this retrospective.

Inside the museum, underneath a large standing poster that announced "The Life and Work of Alice Snyder," was another set of Violet's printed eyes. Finally, she was forced to meet them. Standing alone in the pink marble lobby, Violet felt the fabric of time start to crease and draw in around her, like a gather in a skirt, and the little girl she'd been at the time of that painting's creation stepped forward through time and space and took her place at her hip. Violet remembered feeling so big when her mother was painting her, but looking back at it from here, she seemed unbearably small. The little Violet kept staring and the grown one wanted to turn away. To close her eyes. To insist that wasn't her anymore, that all the years between now and then meant the death of her old selves. But denial just brought the truth of it into clearer focus. That little girl had always been there, staring out from the painting, waiting for Violet to come to this exact place in the story and deal with the facts of her life.

A docent posted at the entry to the exhibit passed out maps and curated guides. There were two options: audio or visual. Violet chose the visual guide and stepped back into the past.

MARIAN MITCHELL DONAHUE

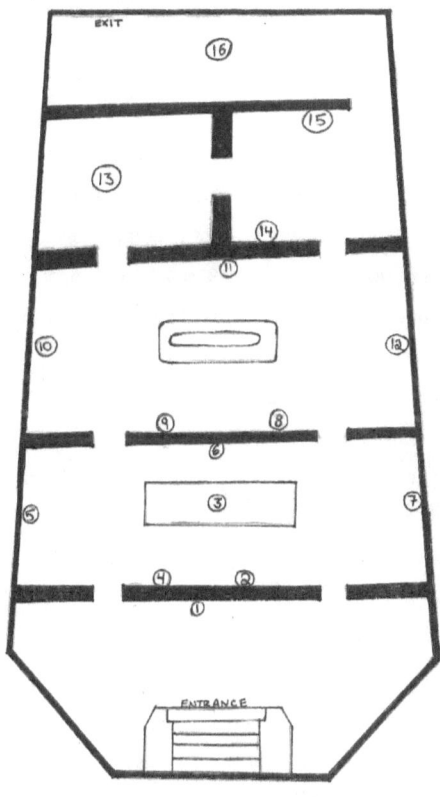

Selected Pieces

1. Two Girls with Fruit
2. The Work of Painting
3. Line Drawings
4. The Missing
5. The Rose of the Winds
6. The Escape
7. Veiled Seascape
8. Red/Blue
9. The Present Past
10. Thresholds (little failures)
11. The Two Faces of Janus
12. Portrait of the Artist in Four Parts
13. The Lives and Fates of the Dioscuri
14. The Fire at Artemesia Drive
15. The Alice Tapestry
16. What It Was Like To Be There

Early Work: The Home, the Girls, and the Still Life

From 2004–2010, Snyder produced hundreds of sketches but pursued only a handful of ideas to completion. Even fewer have ever been shown to the public until now.

This period of work is marked by two things: the common setting and the repetitive visual language. For these six years, Snyder's eye was trained solely on her domestic life. We see it as she sees it. Each painting takes place within the confines of her home studio, with the greatest distance being some rare scenes painted in her backyard. The composition of these pieces is tight and purposeful. Still life elements are arranged, portraits are posed. There is a stunning lack of physical movement that demands the viewer's undivided attention on the captured subject.

The reward for our scrutiny is depth of meaning. For Snyder a rose was never just a rose, but also a symbol, and a name, and a direct reference to another rose painted by another person hundreds of years ago. In each painting, take note of what you deem important or familiar and look for it again in the following pieces.

Two Girls with Fruit

2004

Alice Snyder
American, 1974–2017
Oil on canvas

In her home studio Snyder paints her two daughters in the style of the Flemish Primitives, posed side by side surrounded by halved fruit. The standing figure with fig is Violet, approximately nine at the time of painting, and the sitting figure with pomegranate is Marigold at age seven.

Notable for its traditional influence and anachronistic details, e.g., the girls' elastic hair ties, *Two Girls with Fruit* is a prime example of Snyder's fascination with visual narrative. She plays with the viewer's engrained visual vocabulary (the fig is associated with the Christian doctrine of original sin, and the pomegranate is a symbol of the Greek goddess Persephone), but the painting never commits to telling a simple narrative that would explain the relationship between them. In doing so Snyder makes us aware of the associations we bring with us into her constructed world and warns that she is not interested in providing a simple story.

BACKSTITCH

Violet felt her mother's insistent hand rock her awake in the dark hours before dawn. She rolled over to face her, but her mother had already moved on to Marigold, who was sleeping below in the bottom bunk. Violet dragged herself upright, climbed down the ladder at the foot of the bed, and rubbed her eyes. Marigold was putting up a bit more resistance. Whispers damp with sleep of *you said* and *school* and *last time was the last time*. Violet couldn't make out their mother's responses. She had never heard her mother's reasons because she never objected. Violet obeyed. As soon as Marigold had been coaxed upright, their mother handed them their muslin shifts, clicked on their bedside lamp, and left them to dress without another word.

The girls sleepwalked through all the necessary preparations. They slipped into their loose, sweat-creased dresses and helped each other with the ties. Marigold went to her dresser on the opposite wall and grabbed her hairbrush and a hair tie, handed them to Violet, and turned around to allow her sister to brush and braid her hair. Violet had taken to sleeping in the twin French braids her mother wanted for this painting. She found the tightness of her wrapped hair soothing. When they were done, she took Marigold's hand in her own, clicked off the lights, and led her out of the room.

Violet could smell the rotting fruit from down the hall.

Their parents' bedroom was just across from theirs. Violet could hear their father snoring through the wall. She led Marigold down the hall, hopping from one spot to the next to avoid the squeaking patches in the floor. Past the closed doors and the family photos, through the dark parts of the house to the studio, still awake and alight. No one called it the living room anymore. For the girls, it had only ever been the studio. Heavy canvas drop cloths covered the whole floor, old bookcases they'd pulled from other people's trash piles were packed with paint cans and tools, while freshly primed canvases dried on the far wall. The low, white staging platform was set up in front of the dark blue velvet curtains that smothered the bay window. The set was simple. A wooden chair screwed into the platform at an angle, just right of center, surrounded by halved fruit sliced and glued into place five days ago.

The thick, sweet smell of decay perfumed the upper floor. Bananas browning. Melons molding. Apples yellowing to mush as the days dragged on. Marigold had asked if they could throw away the food after the first few days, once their mother had mixed the right colors for the fresh cut insides, but she was denied. "I like them there" was all their mother offered as explanation. Even their father had become uncomfortable with the smell, making their mother promise: no more permanent placings for impermanent materials.

The girls moved carefully into position. Marigold: sitting slouched down in the chair, feet dangling. Violet: upstage right of the chair, with one hand on its back. Violet fit her toes into the pencil outline her mother had drawn on the first day. Right leg forward, left leg bent and a bit behind. The pose of a step just taken.

Alice began adjusting her lamps and Violet watched the fruit flies take wing, a hazy, swirling cloud of black dots stirred up by the direct white light. When the light was right, the girls' mother began fussing with them. Marigold, lucky girl, only had to sit and hold a halved pomegranate in her lap, ruby seeds spilling out across her skirt. Her prop didn't ooze or stink, it just dried out. Alice went to the fridge and selected a newish sliced fig for Violet to hold. It was so soft it took a considerable portion of Violet's concentration to keep from squishing it between her thumb and ring finger. She held her fig out to her side and her mother tapped her, arm up and hand out, until she was perfectly in place. Violet could feel the lines of tired muscles ache once more as she forced them into a familiar, painful shape. She reached out to take Marigold's hand just as her little sister did the same and, joined, they faced their mother as a complete picture.

The artist took a step back, scanned the scene, and, finding it acceptable, went to take her place behind her easel. It always surprised Violet how quiet her mother could be when she wanted. When she worked during the day there was no end to the noises. Percolator humming, paint cans pried open or hammered shut, scraping, stirring, and often single exclamations of curse words the girls were not supposed to repeat. But in times like these, when she was very clearly doing something they all knew she'd promised to stop doing, Alice was quiet as a stalking cat.

Violet began counting in her head slowly from one to eight. The sweet decay wasn't as bad if she took it in slow. Marigold stared out at a picture of a hastily drawn smiley face their mother had Scotch taped to the opposite wall at exactly the line she wanted Marigold's eyes to fall in the picture. Violet didn't have a picture. She supposed at nine she was too old for one. Instead, her mother occasionally reached out to a point to the right of her head and wiggled her fingers to get Violet's eyes back where they should be. Violet had considered asking her sister what she did with her mind when they spent hours frozen, but that would create a smaller secret inside the bigger secret and Violet didn't want to carry more silence inside her.

Eyes ahead, body already aching from the weight of her own lofted limbs, Violet tried to focus on the world around her. Out of her periphery, she saw a puff of flies find her hand and set about inspecting the terrain. Flies on her hand, flies on the fig's skin, flies flying around to the wet, red insides of the flesh and seeds. Violet knew she couldn't really feel them—they were too small and light—but the thought of all those little black insects crawling on her made the muscles in her back tense and the hairs on the back of her neck prickle. Violet refocused on her counting, eight in, eight out. She fought her body and kept still.

When they posed during the day Violet watched the backyard through the glass-paned French doors in the dining room. She saw the ivy climbing up the trees flutter in the breeze and the growing leaves detach and dance through invisible currents before they floated to rest on the ground. She felt rather than saw the frenzy of brown squirrels chasing each other up and down trees. But at night she could barely see past the column of light she was in.

Violet calmed as her mother's scraping and brushing sounds fell into a familiar pattern. She must be close to the end. Her mother had declared the painting "almost there" weeks ago. The past two late night wake ups had been "the last time." Violet and Marigold always believed her in the moment of her proclamations but were never surprised when she came back to them in the dark hours and asked for one more time, one more time.

In the end, the girls were back in bed only an hour before they would have gotten up anyway. Violet and Marigold spent it in their respective bunks (silent, together) listening to their mother continue her work down the hall and waiting for the creak of their father's bedsprings to cue their sleep playacting. Violet stared at the cracks in the ceiling, breathing through her simple sadness, a familiar, nameless weight pressing down on her chest and belly. She sometimes thought of peering over the edge of her bed to see if Marigold had found a way to go back to sleep, but that weight kept her pinned where her mother had left her.

The Work of Painting
2005

Alice Snyder
American, 1974–2017
Oil on canvas

In conversation with Vermeer's 1666 work *The Art of Painting*, Snyder's *The Work of Painting* is a meditation on the relationship between subjects and subjectivity. At first, what appears before you is a typical scene in an artist's studio. The painter is turned away from the viewer to face her canvas, there is a dress form wrapped in lace in place of an actual model, and there is an enlarged photograph of a drowned woman tacked onto the back wall. Look closer and we find that the three figures (artist, form, and photograph) are all reflections of the artist herself.

In Gabriel Grant's now infamous photograph, *Ophelia*, a young Snyder is the doomed Shakespearean heroine laid out on a riverbank just after her suicide, re-created here as wall decoration. The dress form is a cynical, almost comical take on the use of models in the studio, and then there is the artist herself at thirty-one supposedly capturing the scene. Study the artist's clothes in this painting. What first seemed like a brown dress is in fact the same white dress pictured in *Ophelia* now shown from the back, caked with mud and bits of grass.

Marigold woke up to a shout, the ghost of it hanging in the air as she shot upright in bed. Her mother cursed once more from down the hall, then seemed to busy herself with slamming kitchen cabinets open and drawers closed. Marigold lay back down and tried rolling over on her side, to tuck herself even tighter in her cocoon to get back to sleep, but the covers went tight and started pulling in the other direction. She scowled in half-awake confusion before remembering she was in Violet's bunk. She'd had another bad night. It had started when the silence of the house had made the small, endless noises come alive: scratching in the walls, water rushing through pipes, Violet twitching in the bed above her. Hours of lying wide-eyed and listening in the dark. Of flipping her pillow over to the cool side again and again. Of raising one limb up in the air at a time until the digits tingled from the blood drain and she let it fall back onto her bed with a *thump*. After boredom came frustration and then tears. Once she hit the crying phase, Marigold climbed up the ladder, poked Violet awake, and asked to sleep with her. At ages nine and eight, they only just fit back-to-back in the twin-size bed.

Another bang. Something slammed down. A curse. Violet groaned and pulled her blanket tighter over her head. Marigold gave up. She sat up and wiped the sleep from her eyes, then ran her hand over the ridge of her French braid. Even a year after *Two Girls with Fruit* was finished, Marigold relied on the braid to help her when she was plagued by strings of sleepless nights. She called it *buzzing*: When the world came at her too loud and too fast. When it was worse than her not being able to sit still, when she was charged from day to night with the electric worry that there was something she was meant to be doing but she didn't know what it was. Violet always seemed to pick up on whatever panicked frequency Marigold operated on and would try to intervene. She'd step in to answer questions addressed to Marigold, get her cold water to drink, make excuses for her to step into another room to collect herself. At least now that it was summer Marigold didn't have to worry about getting through a full day at school on just a few hours of sleep. Now she could sleep whenever she got tired, like sometime in the middle of the day when the heat was heaviest.

She looked at the papers Violet had taped up to the wall next to her bed. Marigold mostly had pictures she'd traced out of books and cut-up magazines, either glued into collages on construction paper or taped directly to the wall in no particular order. Violet's wall had, from left to right: a piece of computer paper with a list of school assignments and their due dates written in her teachers' handwriting, a loose-leaf page in Violet's own handwriting with her vocabulary words for the week, and a drawing Marigold had done for her birthday. She'd traced the image out of the book *Ginger*. In the original tale, a large orange cat is upset when her family gets a new black kitten and she suddenly has to share all of her things. In the end they are happily curled up together, squeezed in a single cardboard box. Marigold had traced the picture of the two cats in the box, but she'd switched the colors so the big cat was now black and the kitten was orange—just like them.

She strained over her sister's sleeping figure to check the time. 6:10 a.m. She considered trying to ignore it but, finding herself now fully awake, she disentangled her legs from the blankets and crawled down the ladder. She went to the window and pushed down a single blind. Still dark outside. If she hurried, she could watch the sunrise from the front bay window, the only place for her to hide and still see morning light change. Then at least she could distract herself as time passed instead of being stuck inside her own head, feeling worse with every minute. She crept out into the end of the hallway just in time to see her mother storm away from her easel and into the kitchen. Marigold took her chance without another thought, leaping ballerina-light from one quiet place to the next down the hall. As she approached the doors to the kitchen, she heard her mother open and slam shut drawer after drawer, little swears with each hit.

"Shit. Fuck. Fucking. Damnit."

With her back to the wall, Marigold peered around the doorframe to the kitchen. Her mother was standing at the counter in her work clothes: baggy jeans, sweat-stained sports bra, cooking apron crusted with paint splatter, bare feet, hair tied up into a frizzy topknot.

"Why does no one in this house ever do the fucking dishes? Living in a fucking pigsty..." she ranted as she pulled a spoon out of the pile of dirty dishes and ran it under the tap. Marigold crouched low at the hallway entrance as she waited and planned her route. To her right were the walled-in kitchen and dining rooms and to her left was her mother's studio, which had been rotated ninety degrees for the new work. The set was now against the wall, and the right half of the curtains was pinned back, permanently parted to mimic the light falling the same way as the piece she wanted to reference. Though her mother didn't say "reference" anymore. She said, "in conversation with." Marigold didn't quite get the difference, but it seemed important.

Her mother turned to get her coffee can from the bottom shelf of the microwave cart. Marigold shot out from her hiding place and darted across the studio. She skirted the crinkly plastic tarp and kept to the thick canvas drop cloth that covered most of the floor. She tiptoed onto the set, risking the most explosive place in the house for a piece of morning light, and slipped behind the undisturbed left panel of the curtain, tucking herself back into the hidden pocket before her mother could catch her.

She closed her eyes to listen better. Hissing coffee maker, clinking ceramic mug, fridge opening and closing for the milk, and the *tatink tatink tatink* of the stirring spoon. Then she heard her mother walk back out to the studio and she froze, expecting to be caught. But after half a minute a knife scraped as it mixed oil paint again on a palette, and Marigold relaxed just a bit.

Her feet were cold. She pulled her nightshirt out to tuck her knees into it and leaned her hot head on the glass so she could look up her street as the sun rose. Her mother's brushstrokes started, stopped, started again, punctuated by slurping as she drank her coffee. Marigold took a deep breath and strained to smell it through the curtain.

From outside a familiar mechanical *rat-a-tat* interrupted the morning. Marigold smiled. It was their minivan, or Das Crapwagon as their mother liked to call it. She slowed her breath as the car rounded the corner onto their street and pulled in front of their house. Marigold now only focused on the car, thrilled to see her father without him seeing her. He'd been working a lot of nights. She didn't know exactly what he did, only that it had to do with science and it took a lot of time.

The car shut off, and then nothing. Marigold waited. Seconds. A minute. Marigold started to buzz. Her stomach coiled up tight like a snake. She shouldn't be watching him. He wasn't ready to be watched. But moving now would reveal her position and she couldn't be yelled at when she was like this. She would crumble, and that would make the yelling worse. She was trapped.

The car door opened, and her father swung himself out. Tall, barrel-chested, tired, like a sleepy golden retriever. He was wearing his casual lab clothes with his nicer teaching clothes draped over his arm. Briefcase in one hand, backpack slung over the other shoulder, and a milk crate of binders and papers under one arm. She watched him fumble in his pocket for his keys as he walked to the side of the house and disappeared. He often used the side door to slip in and out of the house when their mother was working like this. He'd even scared Marigold once by coming upstairs when she hadn't realized he was home.

Marigold closed her eyes and listened again. The metal screen door clattered shut. The door to her father's downstairs office opened and closed.

"About fucking time," her mother said to herself.

"No, no," her mother's voice turned mock sweet. "Come home whenever you want. I'll just raise our two kids by my fucking self and feed them and clean up and shop and squeeze in my work whenever I find time..."

Marigold pressed her hands over her ears. Her father always tried to get their mother in their bedroom or to usher her downstairs when they were fighting about something. It didn't change much. Even the harsh stage whispers and low voices they used didn't stop her from being able to hear half their words through the walls. She wasn't sure which was worse, half hearing the fight and knowing it was happening, or not hearing it and letting her mind make up what might be in the secret places she could not know.

Marigold began dismantling herself, turning the whole into a series of neatly laid out pieces. She started with her toes. Unscrewing them one by one, lefty loosey. Popping them off and leaving them in a pile. She unhooked her knees and unlatched her hips. She twisted the screws at her neck. Her head was a problem. If she could detach it just a little, she hoped her ears would go deaf and her eyes blind, and then she might be free from the ache of feeling so much all the time. Tempting, but scary. She tried to loosen only that part. To dull but not fully numb.

Her mother went into the kitchen and dropped her mug on top of the pile of dishes, causing an avalanche of metal and ceramic.

"Fuck!"

Loud enough to get through the curtain and the hands and Marigold's loosened head. Her hands were not enough. She tucked her head between her knees; her face pressed against the thin fabric of her nightshirt like a mask. She dug her fingernails hard into her shins, letting the sharp edge of pain relieve her building pressure. A sudden breeze of cold air cut through the stuffy room.

She shouldn't be here. Wasn't supposed to hear this.

Crashing getting worse. Now ceramic plates breaking on the floor. The tang of something metal. The empty *pong* of plastic cups bouncing off the floor. There was no way Violet could be sleeping through this. She'd be frozen in her bed, alone in their room, wondering where Marigold had disappeared.

Finally, the door to their father's office opened with a bang. Marigold heard his three giant steps up as he skipped stairs and the creak of the railing trying to hold its place against the weight of his charge. Two more steps and then the voices took over.

"What are you doing?"

He always tried to whisper but the strained voice still carried.

Marigold stuck her fingers in her ears and scratched to drown out the sounds.

"Not here," her father said in full voice. He sounded sad. Pleading.

Every time her mother began speaking Marigold scratched again to keep it out. She wasn't nice when she was like this. She wasn't really her mother.

Swatting, slapping, shoving. Clumsy steps. A *thud*. Marigold imagined her father's back hitting the wall.

She shouldn't be here, shouldn't be here, shouldn'tbehere.

"Alice, the girls, you'll wake them up."

Hissing and a stumbling jumble down the stairs, then the slam of the door. Marigold counted to thirty to make sure it was safe to uncoil. She counted to thirty again to *really* make sure. She pulled her head up one inch at a time testing the air, listening. There was movement downstairs, voices rising and falling, but nothing solid. Nothing specific enough to add to the pile of things that would burrow its way into her head and keep her up at night.

Marigold began reassembly. She raised her eyes fully and focused them. She held her breath until dots danced at the edges of her vision and then took a giant breath to feel the blood rushing to her face. She wiggled her butt, stretched her legs out even though her feet poked out from behind the curtain, pointed her toes. She looked at each piece of her and thought: *That is my leg, that is my knee, that is my toe.* She ran through the whole inventory of her until the space she'd made between Marigold and Marigold's body was small enough to press the two pieces together.

She peeked out from behind the curtain and slid back into the studio. Bright light fell in behind her, warmth across her back like a hand pushing her forward. Marigold had always liked the easel's shape. The angle of the legs, elegant as they extended from their meeting point, the short width-wise lines, one to hold the long legs out and the other to cup the work in progress. It looked flimsy, but she knew the force of her mother's hand on its face. She knew how much it could take.

Marigold took up her mother's place in front of the canvas and tried to identify what still needed work. The reference photo was printed out and stuck with painter's tape to her cart. Across the bottom in her mother's handwriting: *Vermeer "The Art of Painting"*

1666. She'd used the same composition but different content. Centered: an artist seated at an easel, back turned to the viewer, painting a figure. A messy table with props and fabric on the left. A large map hanging on the wall on the right.

In the new painting, her mother had replaced the model with a foam-headed dress form whose shoulders were draped in old lace curtains. The map on the back wall was now a blown-up photograph of her mother when she was young. Marigold had seen this picture before, framed and hung in her mother's office. In it, a young version of her mother was lying on the banks of a rushing river in a white dress, drenched with water. Marigold thought she looked peaceful in that photograph, like she was sleeping. Her mother had replaced the artist's figure with her grown-up self. She was turned away from the viewer, as in the original, but now she was standing barefoot. Instead of depicting herself in her normal work clothes she wore a dress similar to the young version of herself in the photograph, but in place of the lovely pale white of its lace, all the viewer could see from her turned figure was the back, ruined with mud, hair hanging dark and limp as dredged kelp.

Marigold reached out and touched the image of her mother's back, freezing when she met wet paint. She jerked her hand away but a speck of the brown paint from her mother's lank hair had kissed her fingertip. She rubbed it between her thumb and middle finger, seeing streaks of brown, green, and red inside.

Voices rose. Her mother saying her father's name. A *damnit*. A *Jesus Christ*.

Marigold went to the top of the stairs, but her parents' voices ebbed again.

A family portrait used to hang on the wall there, one of those shopping mall ones they took at Christmas one year when Marigold had still been a baby. Her mother had needed the wall to tape up reference photos and notes, so she took it down. Threw it out, Marigold assumed. Her mother had often complained about it when she had people over to look at her art. On the day it was taken her mother had kept referring to the photographer as "the kid," and sighed loudly every time his strobe light glitched. Violet wouldn't stop picking at her eyebrows and their father kept tickling her to try to get her to smile but that just made her pick harder. Her mother said they needed to get it replaced with something better, but they never did.

At first the wall looked fine. Marigold looked closer. Her stomach coiled again. There was a sliver of a crack snaking up the wall two feet above her head. She reached up to touch it but paused when she heard a squeak at the end of the hallway. It was Violet—messy hair, rumpled pajamas, rubbing the sleep out of her eyes.

The sounds of their parents' fight reached Marigold, traveling through the vents and into the girls' room. Violet stomped down the hall, knees high, stepping hard on every loud spot on the floor as a signal.

Creak. Creak. Creak. I'm up. Shut up. Stop fighting.

Violet peered into the kitchen and Marigold mirrored her. Large pieces of broken ceramic, scattered silverware, and an overturned mug of coffee dripping from the counter to the floor. Marigold glanced back to Violet for a reaction, but her older sister just sighed.

"Did you hurt your feet?" Violet asked.

Marigold shook her head. Her face started to flush.

"It's okay. It's okay." Violet scooped her into a hug. Marigold gave her a tight squeeze. They walked together back to the windowsill. Marigold slid back to her former position. Violet unhooked the right side of the curtain and let it fall behind her as she hopped on the ledge. She pulled the curtain close so they could hide there together on the bright side.

Line Drawings

2001–2007

Alice Snyder
American, 1974–2017

Graphite, charcoal, and pen on paper

Encased here is a selection of sketches pulled from Snyder's extensive catalog of line drawings from her pre-graduate work. This selection traces the evolution of the artist's hand and eye from amateur to professional. While the earliest images still possess some rudimentary appreciation for the elements of art, they clearly show a hesitation on the artist's part to take a direct approach to her subject. Overrun with settings and crowded marginalia, these early sketches devolve into crude, almost cartoonish figures for the sketches' point of focus. Compare these to her later work, where the main subject is fleshed out first, and the setting is addressed second. Here you see the power of her line, the weight and signature of her hand. The figures in these late sketches are drawn more realistically, and the artist's eye is upon them unflinchingly.

    We thank the Snyder Family for contributing these sketchbooks.

Every great discovery begins by gathering scattered remnants of important evidence, followed by a single jolt of truth when they are all assembled, finally, in the right order. For Violet, her first great discovery took years, and began when she was six years old and learned about heliocentrism. It was late April, there was a small art opening just off campus Alice had promised to attend, and Arthur was hosting an observatory night for the students in his upper-level astronomy class on the roof of the physics building. She'd stood silently by her parents' knees while they bragged to other couples that the benefit of having stopped at two kids was that at any moment the family could cleanly separate into any combination of duos. Tonight, it was decided Violet would go with Dad and Marigold with Mom.

To kick off the evening, the family of four had an early dinner on campus at Kenning University, where Dad worked. The girls had gone to the campus cafeteria and gathered the feast while Dad taught his final class for the day. Then, at the crest of a hill on the west side of campus, they set up a picnic. As their mother whipped the comforter open a fine cloud of sawdust and plaster rose for a second, suspended in the sky, then drifted with the wind away from them. Violet unpacked the bags of food. Marigold was in charge of handing out forks and knives. They'd gotten a bit of everything. Two pizza slices, a pile of noodles and veggies from the stir-fry station, a cold turkey sandwich, a selection of mini-chip bags and individually wrapped cookies, and a few cans of semi-chilled sodas, caffeinated for the parents, ginger ale for the girls. They didn't have plates, so they passed the plastic containers around and around, sticking forks into shared bowls and biting off each other's bites.

Their mother was wearing her favorite long brown dress she said made her look like "a very stylish paper bag" and had put Marigold in one of her least frilly special occasion dresses. Marigold had loudly fought to wear her preferred outfit of leggings, sneakers, and a T-shirt, but all her leggings were going thin at the knees. Her T-shirts were stained at the armpits, and her sneakers had a little patch of duct tape keeping the sole attached to the top. If the reception had been just a week later, they could have found something better at Goodwill. They just had to make do, their mother explained, until their father's next payday.

Violet was allowed to wear her ideal evening uniform of denim overalls, a T-shirt with a cartoon on the front from a cable show they'd never seen, sneakers, and an extra sweater tied around her waist for when it got cold that night on the roof. Their mother liked to dress her to match their father, with him having changed from his teaching clothes to a much more casual set of jeans, a NASA T-shirt, and a dark green cardigan she'd knitted him for their five-year anniversary. Once he'd changed in the physics building bathroom, her mother had them stand next to each other to appreciate her handiwork. She called them her "matching set."

They ate without talking, but not in silence. Foam containers squeaked, plastic bags were ripped open, soda bubbled and fizzed, everyone chewed and made nonverbal exclamations of "um," for the disappointing turkey sandwich, and "mmm!" for the surprisingly good noodles.

Once she was full, Violet stood and shook out her legs, sore from sitting cross-legged for so long. Her father stretched out on the comforter, hands beneath his head, and watched a high wind push the clouds away to an uninterrupted sky that would soon be dark enough to reveal the stars. Her mother sat next to him and squinted into the sunset.

"Say 'bye-bye sun!'" she prompted Marigold.

"Bye-bye sun!" Marigold called.

Violet turned to look in the same direction but didn't call out like the other two. Their father sat up and scooted over to her.

"You know it's not really going anywhere," he said.

"I *know* that. I'm not a baby." She huffed.

"Of course you aren't, my apologies." Her father hid a grin. "What I *meant* to say is, you know it's not the sun that's moving."

She turned to him to check if this was a joke and, seeing that it wasn't, attempted to correct him.

"Um, yes, it is." She gestured out to the sunset.

"Nope, it just looks like it's moving. But really we're the ones that are moving."

"Revolving?" she asked. She'd heard him use that word before and tried to see if this is where it fit.

"Yes, we are revolving, but we are also rotating. Revolution makes the years, but rotation makes the days."

She squinted back at him.

"Here," he said. "Do this." He repositioned himself so he was close behind her, kneeling to make him eye level with her. Then he extended his right arm straight out and kept his palm to the sky. Instead of mirroring him directly, Violet laid her small arm straight over her father's, palm up.

"Now watch the sun," he spoke quietly. The sun was a perfect circle. Then a moment later it dipped below the tree line and was interrupted.

"Now I want you to think about the sun staying still, all the way out there in space, and we are here on this planet turning away from it. So the sun isn't going down, your hand is actually moving up."

"But I'm standing still," she said, struggling.

"It feels like you're standing still, yes, but the planet, the Earth we are standing on right now is moving, so everything on it, including you, is moving, too. That's the center"—he pointed to the sun—"and we are turning away from it. We are going back and back and back."

Violet shifted her feet in agitation as she tried to grasp his words. She thought of herself as a little stick on the big circle of the Earth turning away, away, away until she faced nighttime. She thought of those standing roller coasters she'd seen when they'd gone to an amusement park for their mother's birthday. Of a ballroom competition she'd seen in the middle of the afternoon on PBS where ladies in long feathered dresses spun tight to their men as they traced large ovals on the floor. Violet had tried to spin like them, tight around herself but gliding across the floor, but she'd fallen. All she'd seen when spinning was a blur of color and then the floor jumped up to hit the side of her body.

A few moments earlier Violet had been sure of something. There had been a belief, solid and still, then her father spoke, and it began to shift and slide out of perfect alignment. She was on the other side now, reaching out, feeling the edges of the new idea in her mind, tracing its shape to understand it better, learning the movement of the universe, yes, but also the pleasant pain of learning something. There was the whole universe, then the planet, then her family, and then her. Little stick on a rounded line turning away, going back, back, back.

Violet learned the importance of going backward again when she was eight. The school she and Marigold went to started requiring uniforms. They had gone to a little storefront in a strip mall she'd never seen before and a grandmother-like lady had fitted the girls for stiff khaki kilts, starched collared shirts, and hard plastic shoes. It only took one day of school for Violet and Marigold to realize their skirts weren't right. All the other girls' mothers had hemmed their kilts so that they lay just over their knees instead of mid-calves. Some lucky ones inherited skirts from their older sisters and cousins, the cotton softened and pen marked with their original owner's initials at the kick pleats. Violet's and Marigold's skirts were too new, too long, too stiff. The first thing Marigold said to her sister when they met outside their school to wait for pickup was:

"My skirt's not right, is yours?"

Violet asked their mother at dinner. The air in the house had been thick since they'd gotten back from school, their mother's mood alternating between long periods of suspicious silence and sudden explosions of curse words and movement in her studio. Under normal circumstances, Violet wouldn't have risked the request, but she knew it couldn't wait another day.

"I think my skirt needs to be hemmed," she said after recounting the names of all her new teachers and the meager first-day news. They all looked over to her mother.

"The skirt is fine," she said.

Marigold shot Violet a panicked look from across the table. The girls in their classes may have let them get away with the wrong length skirt as a first-day blunder, but leaving them that way was unthinkable. Practically an invitation to be excluded.

"I can do it myself," Violet offered. "If you show me how."

"If I have to show you how, then you're not doing it yourself," her mother snapped.

Violet looked at Marigold, apologetic, then let it drop.

Then their father picked it back up.

"What if I do it?" he asked, voice low and hesitant. "I'm sure I can figure it out."

"Fine." The girls flinched as their mother dropped her silverware with a clatter on her plate. "If it's such an emergency I can get you started after dinner, but I am *not* doing it all for you, okay?"

Violet nodded, smiled a thank-you to both her parents, and stayed silent out of gratitude for the rest of the meal.

They set up at the dining room table. They turned their chairs to face each other, the tools they needed spread out between them. Alice held Violet's skirt and Violet held Marigold's. Violet watched her mother fold back the hem and pin it in place with her large yellow-headed pins, and she did the same. Her mother threaded her needle, Violet copied her double thread, did the same looping knot, raised her hands in readiness, and paused.

"What you need here is a backstitch," her mother explained. The dinner had softened her. "The backstitch is the strongest stitch you can make by hand. I like to hold the fabric on its side like this so I'm sewing the line backward. I don't know if that's correct or not, but that's what works for me. First, we need to pull the needle through to start. You'll need to start right in the middle of where the first stitch will be."

Violet pierced the edge of her sister's skirt, hesitated, then held it out to her mother to check that it was right before she pulled the thread through. Her mother looked, then nodded.

"Good, now you want to pull it all the way through. Good. Now bring the needle back, go down and under your first knot, and come back up on the other side. Good!"

Her mother smiled. Violet felt her shoulders drop.

"Now you start the real stitch. Push the needle back in where you started, go down and under the end of the last stitch, come back out, pull through, and there. That's a backstitch. In the fabric it's a tight loop. You go forward underneath, then loop back on top. Try not to think about it too hard. Let your hands do what they think is right."

Violet did another, then another. Pushing forward, then pulling back. It felt like walking backward.

"Loosen your grip," her mother corrected her. "Your stitches are too tight; those will take you all night. It's khaki, not silk."

Violet pushed the needle farther and made each new section bigger.

"Good," her mother said. "That's right."

They hemmed both skirts this way. Sitting side-by-side, giving and receiving notes. Even though her mother had said she wouldn't do the whole thing, she still sat there and led Violet through the stitches until both skirts were hemmed.

The assembly of evidence started for Violet at eleven when she answered a question wrong in biology class. They were starting genealogy and practicing the scientific method. She'd been prepped by her tutor that summer—Punnett squares, dominant and recessive genes of pea plants. But instead of plants, Ms. Black started asking questions about human inheritance. Tracing traits back up the line. Can two redheaded people have a brown-haired child? Can a grandfather with a pronounced widow's peak affect the likelihood that his grandchild will have a widow's peak?

Ms. Black asked if dimples were recessive or dominant. Violet answered, *recessive*. And Ms. Black said no and went to another student. But Violet knew she wasn't wrong because she had dimples but neither of her parents did, so it had to be recessive.

Violet took her notebook with her to the library at lunchtime to get a second opinion from the internet. She found a website right away. It was designed for pregnant mothers, to help them imagine what their new baby might look like. She put in her mother and father, and she got Marigold. She clocked through the other options and all she saw was Marigold with slightly darker eyes, Marigold with slightly blonder hair. No Violet anywhere. Violet leaned back in the chair in frustration. She couldn't see what she was doing wrong. There was some order or operation she was skipping, some issue with her method. Violet needed it to make sense, to push and shove and work at it until the facts slid into place and made a nice, neat little answer. So she filed the unknown error away and waited to get more information.

Violet asked about her grandparents for the first time the next day when her mother was out and her father had a rare evening at home. He'd made one of his go-to thirty-minute dinners: pork chops with Mrs. Dash, instant potatoes, and canned green beans.

"What did your mom look like?" Violet asked as her father laid her plate in front of her. He lowered himself into his own chair and pursed his lips. The pursed lips meant he was thinking.

"Well, she looked kind of like me," he said. "But much prettier."

"I think you're pretty, Daddy," Marigold chimed in.

"Thank you, Goldie, I think you're pretty, too." He ruffled her hair.

"Then what did your dad look like?" Violet asked.

"You know what Grandpa looked like, his picture's on the mantelpiece. Grandma's in that one, too. I think it's from their last anniversary party."

Violet knew the one. They were already old in that picture, white hair, eyes hidden by glasses, and they weren't even really smiling so she couldn't assess the presence of dimpled cheeks.

"But what did they look like when they were young?" Violet pressed.

"What's with all the questions, Lettie? Do you have a school project or something?"

"No," she said. Her father was staring at her harder than she liked. It wasn't a mean look, just a very steady one.

"It's not for school," she lied. "I got paired with someone new in biology class and she saw Mom pick me up one day and she asked if I looked more like you and I said no and so she said I had to be adopted."

Her father listened. He took another bite of pork chop, chewed, swallowed.

"Well," he said slowly, "she sounds like a very mean little girl."

"I hate her," Marigold said solemnly.

"Marigold, *hate* is a strong word. You *strongly dislike* her."

"Okay, I strongly dislike her."

Their father nodded and went back to his meal. Marigold mouthed to Violet, *I hate her*. Violet grinned despite the tightening knot in her stomach. She didn't understand the specifics of his job, but she knew he was a scientist. So he had to have the answer that would make everything clear and neat again. He had to know the detail she was missing that would make it all make sense.

"But what—"

"Lettie, your dinner is getting cold," he interrupted. She started sawing at the meat.

"I still don't understand—"

"Violet, please," he said, louder and low enough to silence her. "I'm very tired and I don't want to answer any more questions right now, okay? Goldie, you had your presentation in history today, right? How did it go?"

Marigold launched into a recitation of her day. Unsure of what else to do, Violet set to cutting her pork chop into many small pieces, then mixing together everything on her plate into a mushy, salty pile she could just shovel in without much chewing. She couldn't file it away. That void, the spot where the answer should be, sat at the center of her growing heavier and heavier.

Violet's mother took her to a special lunch at the National Gallery of Art for her twelfth birthday. There were several things that struck Violet as weird. First, her birthday was a whole week away, on October 26, and they'd never celebrated early before. Second, they were going to an art museum when she'd specifically asked to go to the Museum of Natural History that year. Third, Marigold was being excluded even though Violet told their father she wanted her little sister to come. And fourth, and most concerning, no one would explain to her why things had to be this way. She asked and prodded but all she got were vague workaround answers. Left with no other option, Violet went along and waited for something to start making sense.

Her mother rushed ahead, looking back every once in a while to make sure Violet was behind her. Like they were late for something. It was supposed to be fun, but everything felt a bit too forced. Her mother's smile was tight, her eyes frenetic, skipping from wall to wall, from face to face, without really landing. It all felt familiar but wrong, one shade removed from what it should be.

By the time they stopped in the East Garden Court, Violet was happy just to be allowed to sit. Her mother told her to wait on the bench while she made a call. Violet made her breaths long and slow, like they'd learned in gym glass during their unit on yoga. She was sweating from the walk and the humidity of the room. She shrugged off her coat, folded it, and laid it on the bench. The plants seemed aggressively green. It would be winter soon and this place would still be clinging to its greenery and heat.

Violet studied the fountain at the center of the room, drawn by the sound of the delicate trickle of water. The centerpiece was a statue of two winged cherubs strangling a swan. The child angels were smiling as they played, one pulling the bird's plumage, one twisting its delicate neck. The metal body and neck of the swan had aged, rusting into a reddish hue, while its wings and the angles had stayed the same greenish-gray. The reddish-brown was beginning to leak onto the cherubs where they touched. Violet wondered if the red would keep moving, if it would one day take over both of the murderous angels. Was the red because of the air, the metal, or the water? She would ask her father when they returned home.

"Violet!" her mother called. Violet startled and stood. Her mother walked over to her and smoothed her hair.

"I'm sorry, sweetie, I didn't mean to scare you." Her mother's voice sounded high and light. "I was just making that call and I ran into an old friend of mine from school. Is it okay if I introduce you?"

Violet couldn't keep the suspicion off her face. Her mother was looking at her, speaking to her, like she did when they were in front of strangers and Marigold started acting fussy. It was a silent electric current transferred in a stare, halfway between a plea and a command, to behave yourself or else. But Violet wasn't doing anything at all to deserve it.

"Okay," Violet said slowly, watching for the cue of how she was meant to behave. Her mother stepped to the side and revealed a stranger standing behind her. He was about the same height as her mother. Dark hair, dark eyes. Violet felt trapped, unsure of the rules, unsure of everything. He took a step closer, his hands in his pockets.

"Hello, Violet, I'm Gabriel." He glanced between her and her mother. He dropped his voice low and bowed at the waist like the whole exchange was a joke for her mother's entertainment. Violet refused to give him the smile he was clearly searching for. The scientific part of her was beginning to understand. Putting together pieces, ordering the information. The horrible implication of Gabriel's existence was curling itself tight at the base of her skull.

But, she reasoned, *a lot of people have brown hair and brown eyes.*

Violet held out her hand and smiled hard at the man. He took her hand and shook it, and smiled reflexively in response. He had dimples.

So, she was right. Her father, her biological father, had the answer she was looking for, and the line she had traced back from herself had been correct, even if it hadn't been right.

They ended up drifting to a nearby room with four large paintings on each of the walls. Violet pretended to study them as she tracked her mother and Gabriel in the edges of her vision. Gabriel came up beside her.

"These were my first favorite paintings. Back when I was a kid. Well, not as young as you but your mother tells me you're pretty smart, so maybe you can handle it, hm?"

He knocked into her with his hip, but she was unprepared and stumbled to the side. Gabriel sent an apologetic look over her to her mother.

"Can you tell me what they mean?" he asked.

Finally, with a test in front of her, Violet was able to start focusing. The four giant paintings all pictured the same man at different ages riding down a river on a boat while an angel dressed in white watches over him. The wall told her it was titled *The Voyage of Life*.

"It's about the voyage of life," she said flatly, hoping that would be the end of it.

"Yes, and? Can you tell me what it's about?"

Violet felt irritation spark. The title of the thing tells you what it's supposed to mean. And this wasn't even the type of art she didn't understand, like those modern rooms of giant colored blobs with names like *Untitled Five*.

"It's about life. His life?" She pointed to the man in the painting closest to her as a young man reaching toward a giant city in the distance. "He starts as a baby and grows old and then dies."

"But he never leaves the boat."

"No." She hadn't thought that was important. "No he doesn't."

"Why doesn't he leave the boat?"

"Because he can't." The irritation was sparking more now. She wanted out of this conversation and out of this room and far away from the man next to her. She couldn't think of how to do it. She looked over to where her mother should have been, but she'd been replaced with an elderly couple in visors. Violet looked around the rest of the room, through the doorways into the other galleries for a sign of red hair but there was none. Her mother had left her alone.

"Why can't he?" Gabriel's voice was starting to sound irritated, too, like her answers weren't good enough.

"Because the boat is always in the middle of the water. If he leaves the boat he—he dies, right?"

"Yes!" Gabriel finally looked away from her and back at the paintings. With the weight of his stare gone, fear began to creep in. How long would her mother be gone? If she walked off now to find her would she get in trouble? Get lost? Would she be able to find her way back?

"I came to the same conclusion," he continued. "He's stuck in the boat, away from everything he wants, because the water is time. If he tries to leave it he'll die. So he can only drift past and want things he can't even touch."

"So it's sad?" Violet asked. A dash of red hair caught her eye off to her right. She turned her head so fast she heard a small *pop* in her neck. Her mother was walking back toward them. Relief flooded through her. It would be over soon. Gabriel hadn't seemed to notice yet.

"It can be sad. But at least his angel is always with him, right? Even when he turned away from her. At least that way he isn't ever alone."

The Missing

2007

Alice Snyder

American, 1974–2017

Acrylic on patchwork backing

Her first surviving experiment with handmade backing, *The Missing* is an exception to the typical rules of Snyder's early work. It is a simple scene: Three huddled figures are shown from the back, presumably the artist and her two daughters, kneeling on the grass in front of a Celtic cross gravestone. It does not directly reference any historical work from the canon. It is not obviously self-referential, and it is one of her few monochromatic works, relying solely on white paint and its black fabric.

Luckily, Snyder's daughters were able to provide more context for this outlier. Marigold Snyder explains:

[The Missing] happened right around the time our mother's father died. She never talked about her parents, but she at least created pieces about her mother. Her father was nowhere. Not in her life, not in her art. I don't think I ever heard her say his name. Our father bought us funeral clothes, but we never went to the funeral. I don't think any of us noticed they'd disappeared from our closets until we saw them all torn up on a canvas in the studio. This time she references here, this trip to the cemetery, was the first and last time we went.

One Thursday in the early spring of 2007, the girls were picked up from school by their father before the regular dismissal time. Violet saw the note from the principal's office arrive with a student aide during her English test. Saw the teacher read the note, look right at her, whisper something to the aide, and look at her again. She finished her test early, only checking her answers once instead of her usual twice before turning it in.

"What's going on?" she asked her sister as soon as the office aide dropped her off in front of the principal's office.

Marigold just shrugged.

Their father stepped out of the office, and they sprang to their feet.

"Early dismissal today!" he said. His smile was too hard, a smile he used for strangers.

Out in the parking lot, settled in their seats in Das Crapwagon, winter coats unzipped but still on, he turned to address them.

"Your grandfather died," he said simply.

The girls looked at each other, confused. Their father's father had died when they were little, in third and second grade. All Violet remembered of the funeral were the itchy black clothes, eating sweaty cheese cubes, and people talking above their heads.

"We knew that," Violet said, trying not to sound like a brat.

"Mom's dad, not mine," he clarified.

This did not ease the confusion.

"Mom doesn't have a dad," Marigold explained. "She told us she didn't have one."

"Everyone has a dad, it's just that some people don't have relationships with them. Sometimes they don't even like them."

Violet felt her father's eyes in the rearview mirror snap to her, so she kept her eyes on her shoes until Marigold passed her the water bottle from her lunch sack. There were small, unbearable times like these when Violet felt a thunderstorm building inside of her. Pressure rising around her temples and the back of her throat. She had to fight to keep her breathing slow. She felt the tickle of sweat as it beaded and ran down her sides. The only thing she could compare it to was the feeling when the sky turned dark in the middle of the day and she began instinctually looking up to see when lightning would shatter the clouds. In these times she silently commanded herself: *Don't look, don't look, don't look.*

Violet felt the pressure ease when her father's eyes moved off her. As long as she didn't make eye contact, as long as he didn't make her talk about the thing they *never* talk about, the thing Marigold didn't even know about, then she didn't ever have look straight at the blinding light. She didn't belong to him, not the way Marigold did. And somehow, in her usual day-to-day life she managed to forget about that light. But forgetting entirely was impossible.

She sometimes fantasized about taking all that ugliness inside of her, the not-belonging, and pushing it into one part of her body, like a toe or a finger, and then cutting off that part of her with a single, brutal cut so she didn't have to carry that swirling shame inside her all the time. But she did carry it. And her one relief was that as long as no one named it, or looked too hard at it, she was allowed to pretend it wasn't real.

"Did she ever know him?" Marigold asked. "How long have they been . . . not talking?"

"Since she was a young lady. For the whole time we've been married, actually. I've never even met Mom's dad."

Even Violet was surprised by this. She was so used to her father being her mother's handler it seemed hard to believe there were things about her even he didn't know.

"Is Mom okay?" Marigold asked.

Their father sighed and stared out over their heads through the rear window.

"Mom is in pretty rough shape," he began slowly. "Because, well, when her dad's lawyer called to let her know he had passed, he also shared some information about her mother... that she didn't know before."

Their father shifted in his seat and brought up one leg to better twist around to face them.

"When Mom was very young," he began again, "like, a little kid, her mom died suddenly, and her dad had to raise her on his own and he wasn't very good at that. He never told her what happened to her mom. He never took her to visit the grave. And he got people to help raise her, but it wasn't the same as having her mom. So she was very sad and very lonely for a long time."

"When did it get better?" Marigold asked.

Their father gave a short laugh Violet didn't understand.

"Well, that kind of sad doesn't really go away—but!" their father rushed to say. "But things did start getting better when she was in school. Mom was always really good at school."

"Was she still sad about her mom when you got married?" Violet asked.

"Yes, but she wasn't sad all the time. When she had you, Vi, when she first became a mom, she thought about her own mom a lot and that made her sad. But she was also happy because she was excited to meet you and—" Their father shook his head suddenly. "Anyway, the point is that Mom might need some extra help from us. She might need extra hugs or extra alone time. We just need to give her what she needs for right now."

The girls nodded.

"Okay good." Their father turned back around in his seat and put on his seat belt. "Right now, we need to go meet Mom at the graveyard and then after we can pick up a treat for dinner."

"Wait." Violet sat up straighter in her seat. Thoughts spun away in different directions. She tried to remember which black clothes they both already had that they could wear to a funeral. When would they get their homework done if they had to stand in a parlor for hours while strangers talked about a man they hadn't even known existed? Could Marigold get by on just cheese cubes tonight?

"Don't we need to change?" Violet asked. "Goldie can wear my old Christmas dress, I know it's navy blue, not black, but it's dark at least, and I have pants and a sweater, but I don't know if pants are okay to wear—"

"Hold on." Their father cut her off, hands waving. "The funeral's not *now*. Sorry I—I didn't explain this right."

He stared off again, right hand moving in line with his words as he spoke. "She found out from her father's lawyer, the person that told her about her father's passing, that her father is going to be buried next to her mother in a cemetery in the city. Mom didn't ever know where her mommy was buried because she was so little when she died. And then she and her dad were fighting so she never found out from him as an adult. So *now*"—here their father turned back to look at them again—"now Mom wants us to come meet her at the cemetery where her mother is buried."

"Do we need to . . . *do* anything at the cemetery?" Violet asked.

"No. Just be there. She might want to tell you about her mother. She might want to just be quiet. Whatever she does, we do, too, okay?"

The girls nodded. Their father put the key in, and the car was filled with the rattling engine and the radio—traffic and weather together on the eights. Violet and Marigold settled into their seats, staring out their respective windows, both trying to imagine what it would be like if their mother died suddenly like that.

The girls sat up in their seats when their father pulled off the main road under a wrought iron entryway. They knew this place. St. Ann's Catholic Cemetery was in a cluster of old cemeteries northeast of D.C., not far from Kenning University. They'd passed it a hundred times as their parents drove them to and from campus. Sometimes they'd even played the graveyard game, struggling to hold their breath until they were fully past the manicured lawns and rows of old headstones. It was supposed to be a sign of respect, an attempt not to brag about their working lungs and beating hearts in the presence of the dead, but they'd never taken it seriously. Usually, they'd hit a stop sign or a red light somewhere along the way and sputter out the last of their air, gasping and giggling while they debated which one of them had held out the longest.

As they wound their way from path to path, the girls' breathing shallowed, their movements in their seats became more subdued. Violet was worried about her clothes. They were still in their uniforms, which was at least better than being in their regular clothes. A little more formal. She realized as the car started to slow that they didn't even have flowers. People on TV always brought flowers with them when they visited cemeteries. They wore black and had flowers and they cried. She didn't have the first two, and she didn't think she could produce the third.

She was also worried about their mother. Would she be crying? Would she be in one of her angry-quiet moods? Would she yell or ignore them or do something completely new? There was no way of anticipating which kind of mother might be greeting them anytime they woke up, anytime they walked in the door. Which name would her father use? Would she be Mom or Alice or Allie or Al or Sweetheart or Please?

The car pulled over to one side and shuddered off. The girls unclicked their seat belts and waited while their father heaved himself out of his door and slid open their own. They hopped out one at a time and braced against a freezing wind.

"Ah, duck that's cold," their father said. He never cussed. He said things like "duck" and "mother trucker" and "sugarhoneyicetea." Their mother said the real words, their father said the kinda versions, and the girls knew both versions but didn't repeat either. Their father bent to button up his coat.

He set off across the street and the girls followed. They kept their heads bowed against the wind but high enough to track the back of their father's shoes. They wound through the uneven rows, past obelisks and angels, past moldy forgotten tombstones and flat markers dimpling the ground, until their father came up short in front of a thick stone cross. Next to it was a spray-painted outline of the next grave. Their grandfather's grave. And standing in front of the cross was their mother.

She was dressed for a special occasion: a black-and-white print dress she'd altered from Goodwill, black tights and boots, and a large black men's cardigan she'd taken from their father's closet. Her hair was pinned up in a lopsided twist at the back of her head.

Violet felt something off in her mother. Not loud-wrong, but quiet-wrong, sleep-all-day and refuse-to-eat wrong. Her mother didn't shift her feet or even shiver when another wind rushed by. She just stood and stared at the stone cross, letting her open coat flap in the breeze, blinking slowly. It was her father who couldn't stop moving. Stepping in to read the engraving, rubbing his hands together to keep his fingers warm, and watching, constantly watching, his wife and the girls and the cross. Eyes darting between the three like one of them might spring up and bite him.

Violet studied the gravestone. A flat-faced bottom portion engraved with information and an ornate cross with a circle around it, all carved out of the same pale stone. The cross was filled with looping knots and in its center, where the lines met, was a lily. Violet leaned in like her father had to read the inscription.

Rose Miller
1951–1982
Wife and Mother

Frederick Miller IV
1982–1982
Wished for Child

Violet risked her own sideways glance at her mother, but there was nothing there for her to hold on to. Her mother's body was there but there was no light in her eyes. Violet didn't feel the usual thrum of anticipation she always felt in her mother's presence. She didn't have to worry what might happen next, or if they were wearing the right clothes, or that they didn't have flowers. Violet knew the weight of her mother's eyes on her, but this was the first time she felt the terrible weightlessness of being present and still unseen. It was worse than invisibility, it was like not existing at all. But just as Violet began to let the thought creep into her mind, her mother spoke.

"Take a picture of me and the girls," she commanded. She pulled a disposable camera out of her coat pocket and handed it off to their father.

"From back there," she directed him. He got into position.

"Farther." She swept her hand back like she was brushing him away. And once he'd backed up enough, she signaled for him to stop. She turned back and kneeled at the foot of the grave. The girls kneeled beside her, one on each side, and their mother tucked them in close.

"This was my mother," she told them. "She died while she was trying to give birth. That's my brother's name there beneath hers. He died trying to be born."

Marigold tried to look up at the engraving but her mother's grip around her shoulders was growing tighter, and her head was forced down at an odd angle, vision nothing but grass and the edge of the gravestone. Violet managed to keep her head up, but the wind was blowing right in her face from this angle. Her eyes welled. She blinked hard and let the tears fall. So she did manage to cry, even if it was the wrong kind.

The Rose of the Winds
2009

Alice Snyder
American, 1974–2017

Oil and gold leaf on wood

Premiering in 2010 at the Suki Gallery in Old Town Alexandria, *The Rose of the Winds* features Snyder's younger daughter, Marigold, at about age eleven dressed to recall Lord Frederic Leighton's 1895 *Flaming June*.

The girl's figure seems at first a direct reference. Both feature a sleeping redheaded figure curled into a ball, wrapped in sheer orange fabric. But if you were to hold Snyder's piece side by side with the original you would see Leighton's *June* has her body tucked in, arm under her head, whereas Snyder's *Rose* has her body twisted, arms splayed out. Snyder has replaced Leighton's romantic Mediterranean background with her rendering of the Milky Way and an elaborate compass rose design.

Despite this piece being her first critical success, Snyder soured on *The Rose of the Winds*. In an interview with the *Hyattsville Sun* years later, Snyder said:

I loved that piece [Rose] right up until everyone else started loving it, too. It catches the eye. I get that. But I painted it to capture how love, romantic or maternal, can screw with your head. It was meant to be figurative. But all anyone cared about after it went up was how pretty it was. How lush and vibrant. But that was all just technique. People were so happy with the prettiness, they got lazy in their analysis.

By 2009 the girls had their own house keys. Or, more correctly, Violet had a set of house keys and Marigold went wherever her sister did. It had taken a few years but, by Violet's eighth grade and Marigold's seventh, their parents had managed to get them into a carpool. Yes, that meant they had to drop off and pick up six kids instead of two, but at least it was only on Tuesdays. All the other days of the school week the girls were dropped off at the curb in front of their house and let themselves in, always turning back to wave at whichever parent had driven them to let them know they were alright. On this Wednesday in April, Violet and Marigold only had a half-day at school. They came back home at noon, waved, closed the door, and then hesitated as the scent of the house stunned them to a standstill.

What was usually a musk of dust and burnt coffee undercut by the sweet oniony smell of the kitchen garbage can had been replaced by the sting of bleach and the reek of lavender. The dust bunnies at the corners of each step leading to the top floor were gone and the white tiled foyer they stood on shone. Violet dabbed a finger on the wall, expecting a new coat of paint, but it came back dry. No one had ever, to her knowledge, cleaned the walls before. Yet some signs of life remained. The stairs were still worn in their center from years of traffic, and the wooden hand railing was lightened in two sections where the family's hands always reached out to steady themselves as they went up and down.

Violet was confused, thoughts whirring faster and faster as she tried to identify the why of it. Her parents rarely had parties in the house because her mother didn't want to go through the trouble of breaking down and stashing her entire studio in her office for the day. Occasionally she invited some art friends from school to look over her work and give her notes. Once every few months her agent, Dee, visited to look over finished pieces, but there was always a week of breakdowns and freak-outs leading up to those days. They were easy to anticipate. But today Violet came up empty.

"Girls? Is that you?" their mother cried from down the hall of the upper level. The girls took the stairs together, Marigold holding out her hand at the same moment Violet reached out to take it.

They crested the top of the stairs and again hesitated. Their mother's studio had grown, now consuming the living and dining rooms completely, with her materials and tool carts pushed into the kitchen and blocking access to the stove, cabinets, and oven. The single raised platform in front of the curtains had been replaced by four smaller sets of different scenes. One was a little library with white bookshelves and a table covered in green fabrics. Second was a simple carpet screwed to a platform and an X-shaped contraption with an open book nestled in the top V. The third set had pieces the girls actually recognized, including the old beige sofa from the graduate lounge in the physics building where the girls sometimes took naps when their father was working late. Their mother's old sewing tools framed the picture: a dress form, a broken loom from a yard sale she said she'd refurbish but never did, an old plastic bag with a pile of knit things she usually kept safe in her office that they'd never been allowed to touch. All the way in the back corner was a fourth set with a white wooden bench that usually lived in the basement, plastic leaves and silk flowers duct-taped to frame it.

"There are my babies!"

The girls let go of each other as they spun to face her. She emerged from the end of the hall dressed in her painting clothes, but her hands were still clean, meaning she hadn't started yet. Violet's stomach clenched.

Their mother scooped them into a double hug.

"I've been waiting for you all day!" their mother trilled, kissing one and then the other on the tops of their heads.

"We were at school," Violet said, muffled by her mother's side.

"Well, I knew that, silly, I'm just happy you're home." She held them out at arm's length and took them both in.

"Today's a big day," she said. "Instead of doing one set of reference photos at a time we are going to do a full day of shooting. Isn't that exciting?"

Her grip tightened. Marigold started to squirm, but Violet let the pain from the clamped hand around her arm focus her.

"You'll be, like, real models with hair and makeup and everything! Mommy even invited over a friend to help her assist with the photos."

"Do we have to do it right now?" Marigold asked. Violet froze. There was too much whine in her little sister's voice. And, just as she expected, her mother released them and put her hands on her hips, pouting.

"Yes, it has to be today. What's wrong with you two? I thought you'd be excited."

"I'm *tired*," Marigold whined again. Violet could hear the tears building up in her sister's voice. *Please don't cry*, Violet prayed, *please don't cry*. Nothing made their mother angrier faster than the implication she had done something wrong.

"You're tired?" Their mother raised an eyebrow. "Really? Your half-day in seventh grade was too much for you?"

Violet knew Marigold had had a bad night. That she'd barely gotten any sleep. Same as the night before and the night before that. *She needs a nap*, she wanted to explain. But there was something growing in the room, a manic pull. They'd been here before. The three of them were caught evenly in the snare of this pull. If Violet did nothing, she knew exactly how the next few minutes would play out. Marigold would start to cry a bit. Their mother would get angry, say she was overreacting, say she was too sensitive, and Marigold would end up apologizing for her reaction. Then they'd just do whatever their mother wanted them to do in the first place. Violet knew this sequence like she knew the beat of her own heart. If she said something, put herself in between her sister and her mother, she didn't know what would happen. Probably nothing new, but there was still the possibility that it could make things worse than the bad it already was. The bad she knew she could survive.

Violet stayed silent and waited and wished she could skip to the end.

Crying, mother's defense, mother's offense, sister's apology.

The door to their parents' bedroom shut and the girls jumped.

"My friend was here all day helping me set up and he's agreed to stay as long as he needs to. We don't want to waste his time, do we?"

Marigold shook her head.

"We've been working really hard all day to do all of this." She gestured to the room. "And now all we need is for you play dress-up for a few hours. And then once we're done, we're done. No more having to get up in the middle of the night. No more staying home from birthday parties because I need you to pose. One and done, I promise."

The girls resisted the urge to look at each other. To commiserate in their parallel thoughts.

You've promised before. I've heard this before. It never sticks.

A man came out of the hallway, large black camera in his hands. Longish dark brown hair, almost black eyes, pale skin. Short for a man, just a bit taller than their mother. Dressed in head-to-toe black: T-shirt, jeans, and boots. Violet's face went slack as she recognized him. Half of her wanted to panic and the other half tried shutting down. Her thoughts were a jumble of *nononono* and white noise.

"Violet, you remember my friend? We ran into him at the museum that one time?"

He gave her the same automatic smile she'd seen the day they'd met. The well-behaved part of her said, *Smile back, you're supposed to smile back*. But she was too stunned to react. Luckily Marigold pulled herself together faster.

"Hello," she said quickly, voice balanced and sweet like she hadn't just been crying. "My name is Marigold, but my family calls me Goldie, so you can call me either."

"It's nice to meet you, Marigold." He smiled again and looked back at their mother. "You've raised some very polite kids, Lizzie. They'll do well in life."

Marigold risked a glance over to her sister, eyebrows raised.

Lizzie?

Violet shrugged. No one called their mother Lizzie. Her name was Alice, not Elizabeth. It didn't even make sense.

Marigold cleared her throat and for a horrifying moment Violet thought she was going to ask about the nickname, but what she said was:

"Sorry, but my sister isn't a kid. She's almost a teenager, so she's a *young lady*."

Their mother looked annoyed but Gabriel just grinned.

"In October, right? Your birthday?" His voice was too high and bouncy, like he was talking to a baby.

"Yes," she said. *You know this*, she thought. *You were there. We've already done all this before.*

"Hey, snazzy duds." He reached out like he was going to touch her school cardigan. "Public schools didn't used to have uniforms this nice."

Violet jerked back her shoulder before he reached her.

"Lettie, don't be rude," her mother said. "Apologize to Gabriel."

Violet swallowed her scowl.

"I'm sorry," she lied sweetly. Before he had the chance to try to touch her sweater again, she turned on her heel and walked through the kitchen back to their bedroom, Marigold trailing behind her.

Their mother had set up their parents' bedroom as the prep station. Hot curlers, hair spray, brushes, and combs lined the floor. Costumes, made and/or borrowed, were piled in order on the bed and the tackle box of makeup was open and ready on the closed toilet seat in the bathroom. Once they were dressed in their first costumes (frilly dresses, both with hair pulled up into tight half-up half-downs) their mother moved them into position on the first set. Violet sitting, holding a book in her lap mid-page-turn. Marigold, sitting next to her sister, feet crossed, looking over her shoulder.

It was the same thing they'd done a hundred times. Get dressed, follow direction, hold still. But it all felt different with Gabriel taking their picture instead of their mother. Before, Violet had only ever been a prop, a thing her mother used to create a picture, just like the plastic ferns or silk flowers. It was her face and her body, but it was never really her. The colors of her skin and the shape of her face might be captured on the canvas, but it was as a fairy or an Italian princess or a milkmaid. This new set of eyes wouldn't let her disappear the way she wanted to. The way she needed to. Every time she tried to let herself slide away to whatever daydreams she could conjure, she'd be dragged back to the present. Stuck in her body, feeling her backside go numb, her neck itched from the cheap lace on the high collar. The fact of him kept her there. They had a link, an invisible thread tying them together that was made all the more powerful by the silence it demanded.

The girls suffered through scene after scene. The girls together reading. The girls' portraits against a black backdrop. The girls cross-legged in front of the X-shaped bookstand, reading. They skipped the third set completely, but they didn't dare ask why. They were firmly in the silent-but-pliable portion of the process. Hunger didn't exist. Tiredness didn't exist. Their mother urged them on, getting changed faster, into position faster. Getting short with Gabriel when he took her direction as a suggestion instead of an order.

For the final scenes, Marigold and Violet would be posing separately, with Marigold going first. Violet insisted on going back to the bedroom with them to prep. She couldn't bear if Gabriel said something to her, some sly reference to who they were to each other.

Their mother dressed Marigold in a gauzy orange dress that went down past her feet. She separated, curled, and sprayed section after section of Marigold's hair. When they came out of the room Marigold was so sugared up on the soda their mom had slipped her she ran to the couch on the fourth set and jumped into position, almost knocking the couch off its feet. Their mother hurried after her, reference photo printed out in her hand, laying each piece of hair into place, draping the dress just so.

Violet came out last, wearing a long purple skirt in a stiff fabric, white blouse tucked into its high waist. Her hair was pinned back into a low bun and her shoulders were covered by a white and blue scarf. She kept her back to the wall and tried to stay out of everyone's way while she waited for her turn to pose. She couldn't resist watching Gabriel shoot. He'd just spent hours watching her, after all. She let herself really look at him for the first time since they'd met at the museum and his dimples had given him away.

His hair was a flat brown instead of her own reddish-brown. But there was something familiar in the way he laid out each piece of his equipment in a neat single file on a piece of cloth, and the color-coded tape he used to track his cartridges. But especially the way he always wanted the next thing, the next angle, the next scene. Wasn't that her, too? Wasn't she always saying "when I get to high school," "when I get to college," "when I move out." Something a teacher had said once about her that her mother liked to repeat when she got frustrated learning something new: Violet doesn't want to learn, she wants to already know. And she did. Violet knew.

And after the knowledge came the thunderstorm. It started building from deep within her. Approaching lightning skittering across her skin like static, making her skin prickle, nausea beginning to roil just below her ribs. She sank down to the floor and tried to breathe through it. It wasn't just Gabriel or her father that started it going now. She'd be getting through the day and then something bad would happen, she'd answer a question wrong in class or she'd misread a simple social interaction, and then suddenly she'd feel her whole body start to turn on itself and all she could think of was how bad the next hour was going to be. When she did cry, and it was always a relief when it happened, she'd weep the same two words over and over again to herself. "I'm sorry, I'm sorry, I'm sorry." She didn't think of anyone in particular while she said it, but apologizing to no one for nothing seemed to be the only thing that gave her relief.

Violet tried her usual tricks: biting the inside of her cheek, snapping a hair tie on her wrist, but it wasn't enough. Not this time. Finally, she pinned her eyes on Marigold and tried to focus on that. Her sister was a burst of orange flames in the dim room. She was curled in a ball on the couch like she was sleeping. Their mother was putting the finishing touches on her position, coaxing her finger to lay just so. Gabriel watched, camera at his chest, crease between his brows. A crease Violet recognized from her own face in the mirror. She bit her cheek harder. She wished she had her mother's hair like her sister. As her mother moved Goldie, gently rocking her awake, they blurred together. Two bright twins in the artificial light. Violet couldn't help looking back at Gabriel. *Two bright twins*, she thought, *and two dark ones.*

The final picture was Violet's solo shoot. It was the only exterior shot of the day meant to take place in the backyard. Violet asked what time it was. No one answered.

"Isn't it getting too dark?" she said to the room.

"We were waiting for sunset." Her mother threw the explanation over her shoulder as she started packing up supplies. Gabriel opened the back doors and let the natural light in.

"Timed it perfectly, Lizzie," he said. "Magic hour."

"Get your stuff, let's go," she barked back at him. She checked her wristwatch again. Their father would be home soon. An hour, maybe less. It was hard for Violet to tell which of her fears was worse: that he would come home and there'd be a fight, or that he'd miss the whole thing and she'd have carry yet another lie.

Her mother snapped at Violet. "Big tree in front of the shed," she directed. "Hop to it."

Violet scrambled to her feet and hurried out the back door. She was halfway to the tree before she remembered she wasn't wearing any shoes. It had been a rare nice day after the cold and rain of the week. April had allowed them one day of clear skies and warm sun. But at twilight, the temperature was dropping fast, and the ground was still mostly mud.

Her mother pulled the front pieces of Violet's hair out of her bun to frame her face. She looked at Violet's bare feet, paused, then started scooping up mud and dirtying the bottom of her skirt. Violet looked over her mother's shoulder. Marigold watched from the glass door, still dressed in burning orange in the comfortable warmth of the house.

Violet took her position next to the tree. Her mother showed her the reference photo. It was another old painting she didn't recognize. A girl peering around the corner of a lush trellis holding her scarf in place. Grass tickled her feet, and a point inside the arch of her right foot stung from stepping on a weed. She tried to fluff out her skirt, but the fabric was too heavy to catch the wind. Violet looked over to her mother for guidance, but she'd disappeared behind a large circular reflector. She didn't come to her like she had with Goldie. She didn't place her hands or set her hair. Violet wasn't sure if the thing she felt was disappointment or pleasure.

Gabriel brought his camera up and started shooting, shifting his weight forward and back between his feet as her mother called out prompts.

"Look out. Head up. Now chin down, keep the eyes there. Yes."

She could see clear over three of her neighbors' backyards. She watched low, dead branches begin turning into inky black silhouettes.

"Hold the position."

How does she even know what I look like? Violet thought. Her mother was directing like she was the one behind the camera. Like she was watching Violet through Gabriel's eyes.

The skyline, where the horizon should have been, was broken up by a storage container, a barbecue firepit chimney choking with vines, and two types of fencing. She heard the *rat-a-tat* of Das

Crapwagon pulling into the driveway. She wanted to glance at her mother. A warning, a confirmation that she heard the car, too. To tell without tattling that it was time to stop. Violet couldn't move. Gabriel's camera was on her, pinning her in place.

"Look out to the left now, down, just the eyes not the whole head, yes exactly like that."

The front door of the house opened and slammed shut. Wind in the treetops, wind against dead leaves and dry bark. She was getting colder. The orange glow of her sister disappeared from the glass door. She must be greeting their father. Marigold would tell him everything; no one had told her not to. No one had told Violet not to say anything, either, but she'd known anyway.

Numbness spread from her hands and feet up her arms and legs. She wished the wind would blow harder. Hard enough to break the dry bark. Hard enough to hurt her, to press past her hot insides and whistle through her bones. Hard enough to knock her off her feet and send her sprawling in the mud. Her parents couldn't get mad at each other if she was broken and bleeding. They would have to take care of her then.

"Come on, be a big girl. Stop tearing up, it's not that cold. We're here and we're not too cold. Left hand out behind you, like in the picture. There's a boy there. He loves you. You're happy."

But Violet was cold, and she didn't love the nonexistent boy, so her left hand kept coming back around, wrapping around her waist, the only bit of comfort she had left.

"She doesn't look like she's in love," Gabriel said to her mother. "She looks alone."

Violet saw, in her periphery, the glass door fill with her father's familiar brown suit and the flame of her sister's dress.

"She looks like she's running away," her mother replied.

The girls didn't have to pose anymore after that day of many sets. It wasn't just something their mother promised—their father did, too. Violet didn't exactly remember what happened after her father interrupted the shoot, she only knew what didn't happen. There was no yelling or fighting. No throwing Gabriel out. No explanation. No nothing. Everything just stopped. Violet was let back inside to clean up. By the time she and Marigold had changed into regular clothes and come back out, all trace of the photographer was gone. Their parents were behind the closed door of their bedroom. If they were fighting it was quiet enough not to carry.

A pizza arrived, and they ate on paper plates in the sets. Their father sat on the white bench, their mother on the beige couch, Marigold on the wooden bench from the first shoot, and Violet on the floor, back pressed to the wall.

At some point their father said they wouldn't be posing anymore. At some point their mother said they had done a really good job today. And she said thank you. She'd never said thank you before.

When they went to bed that night Violet heard Marigold crying in the bunk below her. She needed to cry, too, but that need was deep down in the well. She lay awake for hours, in pain from the sudden freedom, afraid of what might happen next, happy—in a way she didn't understand—that her father had come home and seen them like he had. Even if she'd been afraid of it, even if it ruined everything and nothing was ever the same, she was glad he had seen.

The Escape

2009

Alice Snyder

American, 1974–2017

Oil and mixed media on wood

Despite premiering alongside *The Rose of the Winds* in 2010 at the Suki Gallery, its sister work, *The Escape*, was widely overlooked in its time. However, approaching Snyder's career retrospectively allows us to reexamine this supposedly "lesser work."

Initially devised as a reference to Arthur Hughes's 1855–56 piece *April Love*, Snyder's *The Escape* anticipates the major technique and material changes Snyder will make while earning her MFA at Kenning University. The central figure, originally a red-haired lovesick maiden, is replaced with Snyder's older daughter, Violet, at age twelve, brunette and scowling. Vibrant colors are replaced by an ashy, gray-washed palette. And, according to artist's notes, she uses crushed dead leaves and dried mud from her own backyard mixed in with the paint, signifying her early interest in material experimentation.

Unlike the fickle symbols of *Two Girls with Fruit*, *The Escape* invites the viewer into its world, encouraging them to use the clues provided to fill in the blanks of a possible narrative. The girl's feet are muddy, her cheeks and nose pink from the wind. Is she running away from something? What is she running away from? Is she pleased about this decision? Or is she simply escaping a trap?

Marigold would never admit it, would in fact lie if asked directly, but she was doing better once they stopped posing for their mother. She slept more. She finished her lunch at school every day. She still felt like crying most of the time, but at least it wasn't all of the time. And she could tell Violet was doing better, too. The evening they all went to their mother's opening Violet could even have been described as being in a *good mood*. She only barely sulked while their mother filled in her patchy eyebrows with brown eyeshadow and smudged some pink onto her cheeks. And when they got there the parents and the girls separated easily, with Violet walking room to room actually reading the placards for each piece of art instead of finding a hallway somewhere to hide in. Marigold, as always, stuck tight to her side.

The Suki Gallery called the exhibition "Desperate Romantics" and featured work from contemporary artists that engaged with themes of romantic love, obsession, and passion. *The Escape* should have been everyone's first stop in the room, but the orange and gold splendor of *The Rose of the Winds* caught the directed light perfectly and shone out past the room that held it. Visitors came in through the front door and made a beeline past the information desk, even past the bar, through the first two rooms, to begin their journey through the art in the middle. Even those who stuck to the normal gallery rotation, starting at the beginning and going all the way through in order before arriving at the end, kept snagging in between rooms when *The Rose* would catch their eye. Perfectly placed on the farthest wall, it reminded them of what was to come, building their anticipation until they could finally pull in close and inspect it properly.

"If I tell you something, will you promise not to tell?" Marigold asked Violet when they finally got to *The Rose of the Winds*, keeping her voice low to avoid being overheard by anyone in the gallery.

"Always." Violet leaned over to hear her sister better.

"I don't like it," Marigold admitted. *The Rose of the Winds* was hung and lit on the best wall in the gallery. Strangers floated from room to room, looking at it, commenting on it. Some heads even did double takes when they recognized Marigold, standing in the corner in hand-me-down everything, as the figure in the main attraction, a shimmering golden body floating in space.

"I don't like it either, Goldie." Violet sighed and looked back at the crowd. She scanned the room and shook her shallow plastic cup, soda long gone, ice melting to water in her hand. No one recognized Violet because no one was looking at *The Escape*. It was hung in the same room, but in a less desirable place: on the right inside wall next to the entryway from the previous room.

Marigold watched her mother flit from group to group, greeting people, accepting congratulations. Occasionally Dee would pop up and introduce her to someone new before disappearing again. Her father trailed behind her mother, topping up her wine, stepping in to get names whenever his wife gave him the agreed-upon signal to show she had forgotten and should know. He wore his character for the evening naturally, like he'd always meant to be an artist's spouse. He talked her up so she could be modest, brought up the review in the *Post* so she wouldn't have to, helped to sidestep questions he knew she didn't want to answer.

"Did she say why she changed your background but not mine?" Violet asked.

The Escape had been painted realistically. The tree, ivy, mud, shed, all of it exactly as it was in their actual backyard. The shadow of a lover was gone, the love story replaced by a single girl with muddy feet, muddy hem, fighting against the wind. But in *The Rose* their mother had exchanged the white bench and fake foliage for a matte black background. Marigold's figure was hanging in space.

Marigold didn't get it, but she didn't want to ask and look stupid. Especially when everyone else in the room seemed to love it so much.

"I'm not sure," said Marigold. "But she must have had a reason."

Marigold knocked back the rest of her cider, draining the diluted sweetness.

"Do you want another?" Violet asked. Marigold nodded. Her sister took her cup and wound her way away.

Two women in black, bodies bent like parentheses, shushing each other in play, blindly stepped backward from the crowd into Marigold's earshot.

* * *

"Stop! Stop shhhhh stopit."

"Tell me I'm wrong! She's been doing the same shit since forever and not getting anywhere and then Gabriel Grant mysteriously reappears and suddenly she's getting the full red-carpet treatment?"

"I thought you liked her work."

"I do! I just liked it better when she was failing like the rest of us. I guess if you fuck the right people . . ."

"STOP. Her husband is right there. You are so bad."

"Oh come on, he knows. Everyone knows. She paints that girl all the time, you think a physicist can't tell the difference between the daughter that's his and the one that isn't?"

* * *

Marigold wanted to lean in. She wanted to stick her finger in her ears. She wanted to stop existing, she wanted to run, she wanted to cry and run to her parents and make what the women said go away.

But she had to stay still. That was the deal. When Violet left her side, she had to stay exactly where her sister had left her. She always knew where Violet was. She tracked her sister as she walked across the room to the drinks table. She saw the bartender give her a hard time, saw their father come up next to her. Saw her face change. The two of them gestured back to where she was standing in the corner, more words. She recognized the smallest shift in her sister as she was being scolded and felt a pang of guilt. She always seemed to be getting Lettie into trouble. Even when she didn't mean to. Even when she tried her best. If she missed a homework assignment or got a D on a biology paper, they both got in trouble. Marigold for doing poorly, Violet for letting her.

Come back, Marigold prayed. *Come back. Make it stop. Make it right again.*

The women in black had drifted to her right side now. Not bothering to whisper anymore. Having too much fun to care.

* * *

"You're sure? Are you sure-sure?"

"Positive. Yes I'm sure-sure, I saw him! He's here!

Oh my god, this is amazing.

He's right outside. Shhhh—don't look."

"I have to look! Oh my god, do you think he's coming in? Is he gunna say something? What if there's a fight?"

"My money's on the physicist."

"You think?"

"You don't think? Look at the size of him! Even if he is a gentle giant, one swing and Gabe's down."

"Yeah, but Gabriel is crazy. Like, put away the knives crazy. You *know I heard he almost killed Alice when they were in school together. Accidentally almost killed."*

"Wouldn't blame him if he had. You know what she's like."

* * *

"Here." Violet reappeared at Marigold's side, sodas in hand.

"Is Gabriel Grant here?"

"What? No." Violet said, then scanned the room. "I don't think so. Why? Did you see him?"

"No . . . um . . . I just . . . um . . . I overheard someone saying he was here? And it seemed like a big deal." Marigold couldn't repeat what she'd heard, even to Violet. Especially to Violet. Even though she knew, absolutely knew, they had to be wrong. Even if she knew that the second she took her fears to her parents they'd be dismissed. Even that would be giving them too much power.

"Big deal, how?"

"I don't know."

"You're not supposed to be listening in on other people talking—"

"I know—"

"It's not polite."

But Violet couldn't seem to let it go, either. Marigold was fluent in the language of her sister's face. Violet still looked pinched, concentrated. She was weighing options, coming up with a plan.

Just like Dad, Marigold thought. *Did math in her head just like Dad. She'd already decided to be a scientist just like Dad. So what if the coloring was different? Colors didn't mean anything. They were just colors.*

"I need to go to the bathroom," Violet said. Marigold saw their parents across the room, smiling. Her father's arm was around their mother's waist, and her head was tilted onto his shoulder.

Violet handed Marigold her drink to hold and signaled for her to follow. The bathrooms were up near the entrance, tucked behind the front desk.

"Stay here," Violet commanded, placing Marigold just outside the entrance to the ladies' room. "No talking to anyone. No walking around. If someone talks to you, come and get me from the stall." Then she disappeared behind the closed door.

Marigold's hands hurt from holding the cold drinks. She looked around. A young woman with a name tag was stationed at the door keeping the drinks from slipping out onto the sidewalk and the cigarettes from slipping into the gallery. People moved back and forth like waves crashing and receding on a beach. Then one dark figure broke off from the crowd and leaned against the wall opposite Marigold in front of the men's room.

Gabriel Grant looked the same as he did the day he'd taken their photos. Without his camera his hands skittered around him while he waited. Hand in his pockets, running through his hair, to his shirt hem, to his neck. He spoke to no one.

Marigold froze, willing herself invisible, but she needn't have bothered. He didn't even look her way. He was leaning, one foot propped up against the wall, eyes steady on the entrance to the second gallery, waiting.

She saw the flutter of her mother's hair dodging through the crowd and pressed herself harder against the wall. She could hide inside the ladies' room. She could turn away and not see and not hear whatever was about to happen next. But she didn't. She stayed still and waited. If her mother or that man bothered to look around, they would see her, but they had eyes only for each other. He kicked himself off the wall as she approached, already grinning. Marigold's mother came in like a missile, already frowning.

* * *

"What are you..."

"...not allowed to attend a public event?..."

"...Did anyone see you?... You know who I mean..."

"Part of the agreement is that I can see my daughter... whenever I... all that money for Lizzie?"

"...haven't told her, haven't told Marigold..."

"...have rights. Never signed anything..."

"...not on my night, this is my night..."

"...talk tomorrow, usual time, my apartment..."

"...Please..."

"...Fine...Tell me...say it..."

"...love you..."

"...Tomorrow?"

"Tomorrow."

* * *

They flew apart, Alice back to the crowd, Gabriel through the front door. Both of them were grinning.

Marigold ducked into the ladies' room, lightheaded from trying follow the changes in her mother's moods. She dumped the sodas in the trash can and went to study her face in the mirror over the sink. She looked like her mother. Everyone said so. She looked like her mother and no one else.

"Goldie? Did something happen?"

Marigold moved to the side to let Violet wash her hands.

"My hands hurt from the cold, so I had to dump the sodas," she blurted.

"Okay, that's okay. I'll get Dad to get us more."

"Sorry."

"It's really okay." Violet smiled but still looked concerned. Marigold pulled out a paper towel and handed it to her sister.

"You sure you're okay?" Violet asked again, drying her hands.

"Yep, nothing happened. I just got cold."

Veiled Seascape
2010

Alice Snyder
American, 1974–2017

Oil, acrylic, and yarn on canvas. Embroidered tulle

Never before shown, *Veiled Seascape* was considered lost for many years before being rediscovered in the storage facility of Snyder's mentor, local sculptor Soo Lawrence. Consisting of three main parts—the painted seascape, the destroyed backing, and the embroidered veil—this work bridges the gap between Snyder's early work and her more structural pieces in the next room.

While remaining dedicated to examining issues of the female form and identity, Snyder widened her scope to include meditations on memory, history, and death. She graduated from direct canonical references to dynamic imagery. Snyder also underwent a major personal change in this time as well. With her children entering high school and her husband comfortably tenured in the Kenning University's physics department, Snyder enrolled as an MFA student in Kenning's School of Fine Arts. After a self-described "brutal" first year, she destroyed most of her work from her first two semesters and pivoted from painting to sculpture, from the old guard to the new.

Luckily for us Snyder held on to this fascinating early work.

SEASCAPE

Alice Snyder stepped back from her finished canvas. She was trying to paint her oldest memory. Her mother and her alone on a beach in early spring when she was very young. She kept trying to get back to that scene, to become that small girl huddled next to her mother's warm figure as cold salt air whipped her hair against her face. But other, stronger, memories kept crowding around her instead, until Alice was more than just herself at present, the thirty-six-year-old professor's wife and mother of two teenagers; also herself at twenty-three, the pregnant bride; at eighteen, the muse; and at eight, the motherless child dressed in black. They framed her, these other Alices, and assessed the new piece together, the final layer of paint still wet on its face. Present-day Alice sighed and felt all the versions of herself agree on a conclusion: The painting was shit.

She tapped the wooden handle of her paintbrush against the edge of her palette and tried to quell the panic climbing up her back. For their final critique, her first-year MFA Studio Art cohort had been assigned an additional piece just two weeks before end-of-the-year presentations were scheduled to begin. A self-portrait. Something meant to identify her, to encapsulate her, something recognizable as her work but independent from the portfolio she'd been creating with her advisors for months. Something so good the department would be forced to keep her. But today was Wednesday, the final presentations were scheduled for Friday evening, and the one thing she knew for sure was that she could not bring this seascape to the committee.

Kenning University's Graduate Art Program was one of the most difficult to graduate from, an honor easily confused with quality. They accepted ten students each year but typically graduated only seven. Her husband, Arthur, thought the yearly cuts were barbaric. His physics department cut graduate students only in extreme cases of academic failure or plagiarism. But in this program the cuts were treated like a sacred rite, a crucible every surviving student would carry with them for the rest of their lives. Being a graduate of this program would mark her forever as special, as worthy.

Alice turned to her paint cart and cleaned her orange-tipped fine point brush with turpentine. Then she moved on to clean her other brushes, then she began moving around her paint tubes. *It'll still be shit when you turn around,* she scolded herself, *so man up and turn the fuck around.*

The painting was indeed still shit.

It was a seascape broken into rough thirds; blue-gray sky on top, green sea, and pale sand below. She'd originally planned to paint her memory of that day on the beach but when she reached back for images, she wound up with a handful of nothing. She could describe what it felt like: stinging eyes, wind rushing through her clothes, hands sticky from sea spray. The scratch of sand when the front edge of their blanket kicked up and flew over their laps like the wind was trying to tuck them in for the night. She remembered her mother's body heat, her presence, the respite Alice found when she buried her numb face in her mother's side. But there were no images. No color palette, no correct or incorrect details. It wasn't until this moment, when she was on the other side of creation, that she finally saw how wrong it all was.

The memory was intimate, bodily, but she shied away from that feeling, setting the viewer yards away from herself and her mother.

She'd avoided painting their figures until the very end, distracting herself instead by building up details in the setting, even adding embellishments to the area meant to frame the spot where the figures would eventually sit. A brown and gray cliffside off to the left she doubted even existed in real life. Footprints and animal tracks on the sand behind them that took her an entire day to get just right. She'd wasted her entire studio time with her paintbrush tipped with the cobalt of her mother's dress or the orange of her hair, simply staring unfocused at the lines of sky, sea, and sand.

Alice dropped her supplies with a clatter onto her cart, shook out her hands, consulted her watch. She had forty-five minutes left of her scheduled studio time before another painter in her class, John Butler, would arrive and start working with his industrial grade automotive spray paints. The overlap was meant to teach them about mutual respect and sharing spaces, but she found the studio uninhabitable when John was there. She had tried in the first week to power through and had been rewarded with a four-day headache from the fumes and traces of electric blue spray on her uncovered canvases. She had to pick up the girls from school now anyway. By the time she got to Paint Branch to get Marigold and Eleanor Roosevelt to get Violet, dropped them off at home, and drove back into the city, her studio time would be over.

All the graduate students shared two workspaces between them, single room concrete boxes behind the main art building. Each had a row of windows drilled shut along the top of the back wall, a single small vent, and only the front door to offer fresh air. No heating or air-conditioning. They survived winters with old space heaters people pulled out of strangers' trash. They sweated through summers with damp handkerchiefs wrapped around their necks, routinely wetted by the trickling spigot at the back of the main building. Most students left the flickering fluorescent ceiling lights off, preferring instead to design their own light scheme using cheap floor lamps, bare lightbulbs clamped on easels or ladders, and strung-up white fairy lights.

The panic grew, clawing up to Alice's tensed shoulder and clenched jaw. She watched one of the art department's Jurassic cockroaches lumber across the floor between other students' carts. She had a secret affection for the art school cockroaches. They belonged here, often marked with splatters of paint or coated in sawdust from the sculptors' studio. She even saw one once in the undergraduate studios with bits of gold leaf attached to its exoskeleton.

Her assessment the previous week had gone as poorly as all her others. After a full year of chasing the faculty's approval of her favored technique, oils and acrylic paintings with embroidery hidden inside, her resulting portfolio was a Frankenstein's monster of solutions she'd come up with to address the faculty's concerns. When she'd been accepted to the program Alice had felt vindicated. Her years of working from home, painting in the spare moments motherhood allowed during school days and after everyone else had gone to sleep, were finally being recognized by someone other than her husband. She knew that someone in this school must have liked her work to let her in, but some switch flipped the moment she crossed into the school as a student. Suddenly no one on the faculty could manage to find any redeeming qualities in her work. Wave after wave of criticism, all conflicting and confusing. She had to stand next to her work silently, always silently, and listen to person after person miss the point entirely. If she tried to counter or clarify any point they made, she couldn't take criticism. If she was obedient, followed their notes exactly, they would dress her down for her confused voice or lack of stylistic focus.

On and on, critique after critique. Her committee was visibly frustrated with her, and at this point she was beginning to return the feeling. And then she'd really pushed them to their limit with the unfinished version of the seascape. Walter Drood, her seventy-year-old advisor, had groaned when she'd brought it out. And the chair of the art department, Dr. Freeman, had declared it "hotel lobby art" with a derisive laugh and waved it away. *It's not done yet*, she wanted to tell them. *Just wait until it's done.*

Alice rubbed her eyes with the heels of her hands, the tatters of her memory swimming behind her aching eyes. Her chubby, baby-fat cheeks chapped by the harsh wind. Her mother's heat. The soft blanket and scratching sand. She suddenly recalled her mother hadn't worn makeup that day. It was one reason the day was special. No hour-long ritual of paints and powders in front of the bathroom vanity. Alice urged her mind to remember what her mother's face had looked like, but it didn't appear. The desired image dissipated like a drop of ink in water the moment she tried to see it.

Alice held the incomplete memory, looked back at the canvas, and couldn't connect them. One felt real and the other wasn't. This time all she saw was paint. Layers of dried oil whipped into peaks to form wave caps, stippled to imitate shadows on sand. It didn't even look like something she'd make. That was the point that churned her panic into cold, hard anger. The committee had been right. It *was* hotel lobby art. Vaguely pleasing but soulless. In forcing herself into what her teachers seemed to want, she'd managed to prune every part that was recognizably her. She should have done something like her memory. Small, warm, and incomplete.

Tears welled up but she leaned her head back and blinked them away. She didn't have time to cry. She needed to experiment, to confirm that she had, in fact, painted the wrong thing. Alice went back to her cart and built up a dark brown color on a large brush. She took a deep breath and swiped the paint in a diagonal slash across the seascape's face, and then swiped again to make an X.

She stepped away. Nothing. No sense of violation, no ringing peal of loss. If anything, she liked it better now than she had a minute ago.

How had she gotten so far down this road without seeing how wrong it all was? The little figures barely suggested bodies. An ersatz cliffside. Symbols meaning nothing. Something Gabriel had said to her once back in undergrad when they were still together. She'd made the mistake of seeking his approval of her work only once, showing him a rough sketch of a portrait she wanted to try. He'd looked the page over, sniffed, and said, *Well, you're a very good technician at least*. Well-made nothing. It felt like that.

Each time she looked back it got worse. Every single mistake she'd made until then came back to taunt her now. And then her mind would hook into her own intoxicating blend of pity and self-hatred. The familiar spiral. She was a craftsman, not an artist. She had peaked back in her modeling days. Should have just done what everyone wanted her to do all those years ago when she'd gotten pregnant with Violet. Should have taken the honor of being used and abandoned by someone great and gone on with the rest of her small life. What had Gabriel said the last time they'd fought? *You'll be another bored suburban housewife, getting drunk and swearing she used to be interesting.*

She didn't want to file this failure away somewhere in her house. Didn't want another lesson in persistence or patience or any of the other shit failure was supposed to teach her. The seascape should be torched, mutilated, wiped from the face of the earth and blotted from human memory. But this was her last large canvas. If she wanted to try again she could go smaller, but it wouldn't go with the rest of her show. This was it. This was it. This was it.

Alice went to her cart and grabbed a wide palette knife. She stabbed at the cliffside, both hands clutching the handle as she brought it down over and over. Chips crumbled to the floor. She scratched at the remaining stubborn bits of paint, burnt sienna and raw umber wedging under her fingernails. Now she had the reverse problem. Instead of a cliff, she had to deal with the ghost of a cliff. Negative space in the exact shape of the thing she'd tried to destroy. Somehow it managed to hold her eye even more now that it was gone. She pressed her hand flat against the canvas inside the paint crater. Still too intact.

Alice went to her pile of shopping bags in the corner where she'd dropped them on the way in. Violet had her first high school dance in a month. She'd skipped her first homecoming and the back-to-school dance, but now that she was almost done with her freshman year, she finally had some friends to go with. One of the other mothers had taken them all to Macy's last week to pick out dresses, all the popular styles some variation of each other. Strapless, short, babydoll cut, a ruched bodice, and a cascade of ruffles or pickups down the skirt. Alice thought they looked messy, cheap, like someone had rolled around in garish taffeta, tacked it up in random places, and walked out the door. When Violet saw the price tags she demurred, insisting her mother would make her something custom. Alice swore to Violet they'd be able to find something at Goodwill that wasn't too embarrassing. And anywhere that Violet went, Marigold wanted to go, too. If Violet got a dress, Marigold wanted one, too. And, well, Marigold's eighth-grade graduation wasn't too far away. Even Arthur admitted they couldn't expect the girls to share clothes much longer.

One bag held the bridesmaids dress Alice would cut and fit into a cocktail silhouette for Violet and the glittery top Marigold had picked to inspire her graduation dress. The other bags held yards of old curtains she'd bought for their yardage of lace, linen, and voile. They held dyes, matching thread, yards of tulle, and some extra notions. Purse, toolbox, and sewing basket were at the bottom of the pile. She brought all three back to the foot of her easel.

She pulled out an awl from the toolbox and started stabbing in the center of the ghost cliff, holding the top of the frame with her right hand for traction. Even the pointed end of the awl wasn't enough to pierce the gesso-primed canvas. Alice dropped the awl on her cart and pulled out a thick embroidery needle and fabric shears from her sewing basket. She pierced the canvas backing with the needle, fingertips burning with the effort, and widened it with her shears. Alice dropped those tools on her cart as well and investigated the wound. At the exposed inner edge of the rip, threads on the warp line crossed with the tight weave. She scratched at the edge until one was loose enough to pinch and pull out. The hidden weft line rose out, unraveling while the shorn threads still stood straight. She ran a fingertip over the little edge line. The threads felt stiff, but soft, like the edge of a new paintbrush.

Alice looked down at her tool, considered, and continued with the sewing basket. She threaded a large, dull yarn needle with a length of cheap yellow yarn she had in her scraps bag. She used the awl again to make two small holes, then ran the yarn through it. She did it again to make another, smaller, X inside the missing cliff. The yarn left little fibrous clouds at the places she pulled it through, the result of a too-loosely wound thread being forced through a too-tightly woven backing.

Alice went still, waiting to feel something, and did. She couldn't ever explain to others why she made the decisions she did when she was in process. It was impossible to put it into the exact right terms to guarantee the successful transfer of understanding. The closest she got was this: One night in bed with Arthur, as he was massaging her sore hands from hours spent in her home studio, he'd made some little comment about how things seemed to be working for her better today than they had yesterday. And she'd agreed. That piece, the beginning of what would become *Dioscuri*, had been with her all day, and every hour that passed brought the material in front of her closer to the image in her head. It was out there in front of her, a point she felt more than saw, and each step toward that point resonated with rightness the moment she was finished taking it.

The seascape had no final point that she could see and so its failed ending had to become a new beginning. Alice pulled up the scattered memories of that day on the beach again and threw them out in front of her mental path. *For now, we have to keep moving*, she coached herself. *Let's move that way.*

Alice was just finishing scraping away the center of the seascape when she heard a knock at the studio door behind her. Standing in the doorway were her daughters: Violet, fourteen, and Marigold, twelve. They were backlit from the May sun, their shadow figures dressed for school, sagging backpacks at their feet. Violet still had her fist on the door from knocking. She was eyeing her mother, assessing her, maybe trying to read her mood. Marigold hovered behind her sister, nervous, swaying her weight from one foot to the other.

"How did you . . . ?" Alice blinked, trying to catch up.

"You weren't answering your phone, so we called Dad, and he picked us up," Violet said. It didn't sound accusatory, just obvious.

Alice dug into her purse and pulled out her phone. Five missed calls, seven unread messages. She checked her sound settings.

"It was on silent," she explained. She silenced it at the start of every studio session. But she always stopped working when Butler showed up and started spraying.

"The spray-paint guy didn't show up and I just... I didn't realize time was passing."

"Okay," Violet said. "Are you okay?"

"Yeah, I— Wait, your father picked you up?" The girls nodded. "And he brought you here? Why didn't he drop you off at home?"

"Well, he kind of had to leave class to come—"

"Shit."

"—and he got a TA to cover, but he had to get straight back because it was a big lab thing—"

"Shitshitshit."

Alice checked the time to confirm: five p.m. Arthur had mentioned something big today. It was department meetings in the morning and the... What? Final review for the graduating seniors? Or was it for the grad students? Was it an actual exam? She dredged her mind for a reference to a "big lab thing," but she hadn't been listening that closely this morning when they'd discussed the schedule for the day.

It's done, Alice thought. *It's over. You missed it. Can't fix it. Move on.*

"Did you girls eat?" she asked.

Violet relaxed, arms crossing around her chest. *She isn't nervous*, Alice realized. *She'd been bracing herself.*

"No," Violet said.

"Hungry?"

Violet glanced over at Marigold, who, to Alice's eye, made no indication one way or the other. But some understanding passed between them because Violet gave a little nod in recognition. Alice was glad there were two of them. Being able to direct them toward each other took some of the pressure off her.

"Yeah. Do you want us to hang out in the cafeteria until you're done?"

Alice grabbed her purse from the floor and held it out to them. Violet stepped forward, took it, then retreated to the doorframe.

"Take whatever cash is in my wallet and get a snack." Alice turned back to her canvas. The emptiness of the ghost cliff now spread across the canvas in the rough almond shape of an eye. She'd left the little figures of herself and her mother intact, floating in the stripped space. Its presence on the canvas felt good, the ridge of paint around the floating image island was right. But the fine lines she'd initially used to render them weren't right anymore. Too weak to stand up to the space she'd made all around them. Right size, right shape, wrong... what? Color?

Alice pulled her paint cart over but stopped once she realized the girls were still in the doorway.

"What?" Alice asked. Marigold flinched. She always was too sensitive. The same moment Marigold had reacted Violet seemed to grow an inch taller.

"We were wondering what time you might be done?" Violet asked. "It's just that we have some homework we need a computer for, and we were going to do it today at home—"

"I don't know how much longer I'll be." If Butler and his spray paints never showed, Alice could stay here all night if she wanted. "You might have to go home with Dad when he's done."

"But, um, doesn't he have observations tonight?"

Alice remembered now. Arthur was conducting one of the observational portions of his Stellar Astronomy class tonight. Then he would use the energy of his insomnia to grade in his office until dawn, crawl back home, and sleep for four hours before getting up and going to Goddard for meetings.

"Well, then, I guess—" Alice tried to push her daughter's concerns away, push her husband's schedule away, push everything else away. She was getting somewhere now. After months of going in the wrong direction and forcing herself into some half-formed impression of what other people thought she should be, she was finally, *finally* getting somewhere real. If she stopped now, she might lose sight of it. She might never find it again.

"I don't know what to tell you." She turned to face her girls. This time they both flinched. "Daddy has work and Mommy has work. Do you want me to quit? Do you want Mommy to stop painting so she can drive you home right now?"

"No," they said in unison.

"That's not what I'm—" Violet started.

"You aren't little anymore," Alice charged on. "You aren't babies. I can't take care of every little thing you need. You have to start doing things for yourself. Vi, you're fourteen, you should be able to feed yourself by now. When I was your age, I was making myself dinner almost every night *and* getting all my homework done on time. And why can't you just do this homework tomorrow when Dad doesn't have a night class?"

"It's me, it's my paper," Marigold stepped forward, shoulder to shoulder with her sister. "I have a paper to write for history, and Violet is going to help me—"

"Can you do it tomorrow?"

"It's due tomorrow."

Alice threw her hands up.

"Well, why did you leave it until the day before? Christ,

Marigold, if you knew it was due then why the hell—and you." She turned to Violet. "Why did you let her leave it until the night before. Didn't you know it was due?"

The girl just stood there, silent.

"I'm asking you a question, Violet. If you knew her paper was due tomorrow, why didn't you sit down with her earlier and type it out. You're supposed to be in charge, Vi."

"I'm sorry. I—"

Violet cut off and turned to Marigold, listening.

"Speak up," Alice ordered. "I can't hear you."

"I said," Marigold's voice rose, louder but sharp and thin. "If you give us your student log-in info, we can use the computers on campus and—"

"Thank you!" Alice took back her purse and pulled out a Post-it and a pen. "Thank you, Marigold, for coming up with an actual *solution* instead of just complaining about something and then shooting down other peoples' ideas on how to fix it."

"I'm *sorry*," Violet said again. Alice scribbled her log-in and password and held it out to them. At first the room was still. Violet took a single step forward, paused, and when Alice didn't move, she walked the rest of the way and reached for the sticky note just as Alice jerked her hand away. Violet froze, studied her mother, reached again. Alice jerked it away again and broke into a smile. Violet returned the smile. This was supposed to be a game.

"There's my girl," Alice said, letting Violet take the note. "Now, both of you come here and give your mother a hug."

Marigold rushed over and ducked under Alice's right arm just as Violet tucked herself into her left side. They squeezed her tight and she relaxed into the strength of their thin arms. Marigold poked her head up.

"I'm sorry I left my paper to the day before," she said.

Alice gave Violet a little squeeze and Violet turned her face up as well.

"I'm sorry I let her leave her paper to the day before," she said.

Alice kissed one and then the other on their foreheads and released them.

"I just need you girls to be a little more organized, that's all. I'm doing my best and Dad's doing his best, and we need you to do your part, too, okay?"

They nodded.

"You have the cash for food?"

"Yes." Violet patted her jeans pocket.

"Cafeteria, then use the little computer lab on the second floor of the physics building. I'll come and get you there when I'm done. If there's an emergency, Dad's close. Now go, be good."

Alice turned back to the wrecked seascape as the door shut behind her. Color, the figures needed more color. She pulled her cart back to her side and picked up a new paintbrush.

BACKING

It wasn't that Alice was avoiding her husband so much as she had passively given over to the insanity of everyday life, and as an unfortunate result didn't overlap with him at all the day after the missed pickup. Her crime, if there even was one, was that she let Arthur's schedule and her own fail to connect, and she, hapless damsel, did not expend the last of her brain power trying to see him. She wasn't afraid of the confrontation. She just didn't have the energy to pretend to be sorry. There was too much work to do.

She got the girls off to school in the morning and went straight out to hit the Goodwills in the area looking for fabric, in any form, that matched her memory of that day on the beach. She found a girl's tiered skirt made from a similar red-and-black buffalo-check flannel as the original blanket, and a navy blue men's suit that was close to the dress her mother had worn. At her studio she seam-ripped and cut the clothes into their basic materials and draped the pieces over her wrecked painting. She tried bunching the new fabric, folding it into smaller pieces, laying it flat, but no matter what she did with it the fabric overwhelmed the picture. None of the fabric pieces were large enough to paint on and she didn't have the technical skill to build a new canvas in time.

As she touched each scrap, she tried to call up her feelings from that day. She remembered her mother's hand on her shoulder, gently rocking her awake in the morning. The heady smell of her mother's perfume as it lingered in the family car and mixed with the musty smell from the heaters. Alice always used to drop her mittens, so her mother had sewn little cords from each mitten to each jacket sleeve so she'd never lose them. She remembered walking on sand in heavy boots. A completely empty shoreline and salt air so cold it burned. But had that all been from the same day? Or was she confusing things? Her mind seemed eager to make a story where none existed, to make meaning where there were only faded images and forgotten people.

Her phone trilled in her bag. She silenced it and dropped it back in her purse, Arthur's message unread.

And then there were the holes she had punched in the left side, left over from before she'd realized she could move forward with the seascape as it was. Before she found a new path and back when she had still been bent on destroying it. Alice pulled the limp yellow yarn out of the canvas and picked away at the fibrous cloud. She stepped away and considered her options.

The Alice from a week ago would patch it, but that Alice also thought the seascape was a good idea, so her opinion was only worth so much. The last time she'd been happy with her work was before she'd applied to Kenning, when the girls were still posing. She would have hidden the stitches then, tucked them inside hair or clothes, their soft raised lines nestled neatly inside oil finishes. She tried on the image of the same seascape done in her old style, but it hung off her thoughts like an ill-fitting dress.

Why did my mother wear a dress to the beach? Alice thought. *Why didn't she do her makeup? Why then? Why winter?*

She needed to get her hands on it again. Alice took her shears and clipped the edges of the embroidery punctures until they were large enough to run a strip of red-and-black flannel through the opening. Soft skirt fabric caught on the rough inner weave of the canvas. She pulled it back and forth, watching the square checks run over the canvas and disappear, listening to the *shhhtshhhtshhht* of their friction. She skipped back a few steps, took in the whole of it again, and went to her cubby to get her sketchbook. There was a limited amount of fabric, so she'd need to plan out exactly how to sew it before she started cutting.

Her eyes stung from concentration, her back ached from slouching over her lap, her head pounded from hunger, her fingers were red and numb from all the tacking she'd been whipping through. None of it touched her. It was her body's discomfort, her body's problem. Alice wasn't her body, she was a will, and this will wasn't even a little bit tired, not a hint of pain.

"Alice," a man's voice broke through her concentration. Arthur had appeared in the room. Alice blinked. It was already dusk outside, bright yellow day cooling into pinks and blues. She sat up straight on her stool, back and shoulders popping as she moved and swallowed hard as she studied his face. This evening she mostly saw apprehension.

"Hi," she said.

"Hi." His face softened into concern. "How are you doing?"

"I don't have time to do this right now." The words spilled out of her in a rush. "I know we need to talk about yesterday, and we will. But I cannot do it right now, okay? I have to do this. I *have* to do this."

"Okay," he said in a small voice.

"It was one fuckup. And you've done it, too. Remember when you forgot Marigold at the pool after swim practice that one summer? And that wasn't even for work, you just laid down for a minute after lunch and fell asleep. I know you had to leave class to pick them up, but I really think they overreacted, calling you. I mean, Marigold could have just gone to aftercare, and Violet could have, I don't know, hidden in the bathroom or joined a club or something. That high school is fucking huge, no way they would have found—"

"I got a call from the school," he broke in, voice still gentle. "From both schools. We're down to one strike for Marigold and Violet's school has a mandatory study hall for any students not picked up on time. Costs thirty dollars to pick her up."

"Hold on—" Alice jabbed her needle in the navy fabric she'd been working on and draped it on top of her sewing basket. She swung around to face Arthur. "First, there is no way we already have two strikes for Marigold, yesterday was strike one, and—"

"We can talk about this later." He put his hands up to try to slow her down, but she charged forward.

"And since when do we have to *pay* to pick up our own child?"

"Yesterday was strike two," he explained. "Strike one was when we didn't bring her in for that Halloween pageant thing—"

"If it's a *required event* it shouldn't take place on a *Saturday*. They already have them five days a week, why do they need a sixth?"

"And the high school has to pay the teacher who runs after school study hall, so if you aren't signed up for it at the beginning of the year you have to pay to spring your kid."

"Shit."

Alice pressed her palms hard into her eyes until the blackness swam.

"Have you eaten?" he asked.

"I don't have time, Arthur."

"You'll get sick if you don't eat." He walked over to her, hands joined behind his back. "If you get sick, you can't work at all."

"I'm too close to stop now."

He drew up to her side but waited until she leaned against his chest before wrapping his arms around her and kissing her forehead.

She relaxed, hands limp in her lap, letting herself be held. She liked him better at the end of the day, when his cologne had faded enough to let the natural human scent of him through. When his usual crisp button downs were rumpled soft, ashy blond hair wilder from running his hands through it all day.

"How much longer do you need?" he murmured.

"I present tomorrow. Five p.m."

"Do you want me to be there?"

"No," she said quickly. But a moment later admitted in a smaller voice, "Actually yes. But not in the room."

"I can wait with the girls on campus and after we can get food somewhere."

"It may not be a celebration." Alice turned her head up to face him as Arthur slackened his grip to look down.

"Is it that bad?" he asked.

"It's not good. I'd say fifty-fifty chance I'm not invited back next year."

He nodded, keeping his face neutral, but Alice saw some thought pass through him when she'd given him the odds.

"What?" she asked.

"Nothing."

"Arthur." She sat up to look at him more directly. "Say it."

"I think if that happens," he started slowly, "if you aren't invited back, you would survive it. I know this place means a lot to you, and you've been killing yourself all year. But I also know you don't need a degree to make art."

"I need the connections. I need people to vouch for me just to get in the door. People don't know me." Alice broke away from her husband's embrace. He released her but didn't back away. "They only know me from gossip and rumors from fifteen years ago. When they look at me all they see is Gabriel Grant's old, used-up ex-girlfriend. If I want them to see something else, I have to *make* them see it. I can't rely on good luck—"

"You're right, you're right."

"And I know you're trying to be comforting but the 'you can do it' platitudes really aren't cutting it here."

She tried to look up at him again, but he was staring over her head to the seascape. She turned her whole body around again on the stool to face it. She looked back at him, to the piece, then back to him.

"Well?" she prompted.

"Well . . . it's a lot different from the last time I saw it."

"It's getting better."

"I can see that."

"You can?"

Arthur nodded.

"I may not know this world as well as you"—he looked down at her—"but I know you pretty well. You don't get lost like this when things are going poorly."

"What am I like when things are going poorly?"

"You drink too much coffee, start lots of projects around the house that you don't finish, there's usually some bit of crying."

Alice sucked her teeth. He wasn't wrong. She held out her arms, and he stepped into a side hug as they studied the painting together.

"If you can drop the girls off tomorrow morning," he said, "I can pick them up."

"You have class," she reminded him.

"I'll make it work."

Alice looked up at him as he studied the seascape. The dim lighting brought out his round jaw. There was a patch of beard a bit longer than the rest he'd missed when trimming this morning. From this angle she could appreciate the line of his neck and the rise of his cheekbone. He moved to look over at her, but she reached up and held his chin in place. He stilled. She studied the lines, then released, giving him a little nudge.

"I need to get back to work," she said.

"If I bring you something, will you eat it?"

Back in her body, the pain in her stomach was getting worse.

"Most likely," she admitted.

"I'll be back soon. And yes, I will quietly leave it with your things and bow out without disturbing you."

She turned her face up to him and he dutifully gave her a small kiss.

"Good, now go away," she said smiling. He kissed her once more and went.

The next time Alice looked up her stomach grumbled loud enough to break her concentration. It was night and there was a white plastic 7-Eleven bag sitting on top of her sewing basket.

VEIL

Friday felt different from the moment Alice woke. Arthur let her sleep all morning. He got the girls up, fed, and ready for school in almost complete silence. And even when they said goodbye to her they used their gentlest voices. Like nuns in a church, they treated her with a reverence that shone on her like sunlight breaking through gray clouds. It was this constant calm, more than any of her interior confidence, that steadied her throughout the day. Her last day.

When she got to the studio, Butler's bulky pieces had been moved out. Probably already lined up in the main building's gallery space where the critiques would take place. Her bags were in the pile she'd left them in seven hours ago when she'd finally returned home to sleep. The backing fabric application was holding strong to her fresh eyes. She'd run the strips of red-and-black flannel on diagonals at the edges of the canvas. In the center was a patch of navy suiting. She had cut four sections and sewn them together in a rough cross to imitate the waist and side lines of a classic sheath dress. Her last act of the previous night had been stuffing some excess fabric in under the blue sections to imitate the curve of a waist meeting a hip. She was afraid it would look "crafty," and it did, but the craftiness did not bother her, so she kept it.

She could have presented it as is but there was one final image in her mind she wanted to try capturing before she had to defend herself. She dug through her bags and pulled out the yardage of white tulle she'd gotten for Marigold's graduation dress, and the orange embroidery floss destined for Violet's party dress. She'd only ever embroidered on linen in a frame. Attempting to embroider on loose tulle had its own set of challenges. The image would have to be captured in a single fluid line. She couldn't hide knots or mistakes behind opaque fabric. And she wouldn't have any tension in the fabric to hold it in place, so she'd have to weave the needle in and out and pull each line all the way through to keep it from bunching or gathering as she went further along.

First, she needed an image. She found an empty page in her largest sketchbook, compared it to her canvas, then swapped one for the other on her easel. Pencil in hand, blank page before her, she balked. She needed her mother's face but there was nothing there. Her father had purged the house of pictures after her mother's death and Alice's one preserved photo showed her only in turned profile, caught as she smiled down at an infant Alice. She wanted more than anything in that moment to conjure her mother's face, but fear and doubt crowded around her, strangling her movements, stilling her hand.

Soo Lawrence, the sole sculpture teacher on faculty, had given a lecture on materials and form at the beginning of the semester. Alice had been one of the only painting students to attend. Soo had asked, every time she clicked to a new slide in her presentation, the same question as a refrain.

Why did it have to be this way?

So why? Alice asked herself. *Why does it have to be this way?*

Alice flipped open the top of her sewing basket. She took out the top tray and started digging. Under the notions and trimmings, under the buttons for Arthur's favorite tweed jacket still hanging unusable in her closet, color-matched thread for one of Violet's skirts she'd not managed to hem, scraps of yarn from scarves unraveling in her closet, samples she asked for in fabric stores for dresses she'd never make, under all of that was a matte gold jewelry box. She popped off the top. Two embroidered red roses: hers on top and beneath it, her mother's.

The oil on fingertips that keeps the thin skin supple and sensitive is why people are not allowed to touch works of art. Oil degrades. It is why people hold precious photographs by the thin outside edge instead of pinching the corner like they want to. It is why museums hire chemists to scan their priceless pieces of history for the formation of soap under layers of color.

Alice knew all this and touched the roses anyway. She trailed her ring finger along the old, soft thread. The lightest, most insubstantial damage she was capable of.

She drew her mother at a hard angle, like she would have seen it that day on the beach if she had raised her head to look up. The underside of her mother's chin and jaw, the rise of her cheekbone, eyes forward to the sea. When Alice didn't remember some detail of her mother's face, she filled in the gap with what she wanted her mother's face to be. It was like her face but with all the flaws removed. As she drew, other details drifted back to her. Whether they were real or imagined she did not know. The curve of a hip where she'd hide from strangers, strong arms and shoulders when she'd be suddenly plucked off the ground and carried. There was the tight French twist her mother always wore but that detail, though accurate, was not right, so Alice sketched in her own wild mane of tangled curls instead. Each line she drew made her task more complicated, but she felt it was right, so it was what she had to do. She filled page after page with attempts until she could glide from the front of her mother's neck up her face, around her hair, and back down to the other side in a single liquid line.

Alice draped the length of tulle on her sketch pad, threaded her needle, and began to weave the floss through the netting.

At four her phone trilled with an alarm, and she forced herself to stop. It was far from being ready for a general audience, but it was good enough for a department panel. It said something. She could defend it. Only a few seconds spent studying her work before she plucked the tulle off her sketch pad and folded it into a neat package.

There was a knock on the door behind her. John Butler stood in the doorway in his least paint-splattered black clothes.

"I thought I'd see if you needed help moving your pieces," he said.

"Thank you," she said, taken aback by his thoughtfulness. "That would be great."

It took three trips for them to get everything over to the main building. Alice had barely looked at the rest of her portfolio for a week and was pleased that when she did look at it, she didn't feel sick. It was good. Inconsistent maybe, some pieces clearly working better than others, but not the monstrosity it had become in her mind when she'd been avoiding it.

Each student went through their work piece by piece in front of the semicircle of chairs set up in the main gallery space. Art faculty were in the first two rows, clipboards balanced on their knees for their assessment sheets. Dr. Freeman sat front and center, as usual, with his student assistant to his right taking notes for him. He sat low in the seat, arms crossed, muttering, gesturing every once in a while to the piece in front of him while his assistant scribbled furiously. At the end of each presentation the faculty were allowed to give comments or questions as needed to help any floundering students flesh out their ideas. Alice searched the seats for her advisor, but he wasn't there. She tried tapping her feet and shaking out her hands to dissipate the rising anxiety, but it just irritated her seatmates, so she settled into rhythmically clenching and unclenching her hands into fists to keep her emotions in check.

They presented alphabetically. Tee Anders went first. She was a painter involved with the guerrilla art scene in D.C. and her work consisted of community murals of young black victims of gun violence throughout the city. Her self-portrait was a photograph of her mid-spray as she worked on one of her pieces. She presented with a series of high-quality photos of her work and a prepared speech about the effect of art as a form of community memory. Alice knew she would stay in the program. John Butler presented his abstract auto-spray pieces, then Lynne Byron went through her nature studies. The committee interrogated, prodded, and Dr. Freeman sometimes outright demanded a student argue for their position in the program. The closer they got to Alice the tighter her stomach became. Even when one of the students had a meltdown—Samantha Gorski, sculpture—and had to leave the room halfway through her presentation to calm down, Alice only barely registered the woman's overflowing emotions.

Then it was Alice's turn.

She started with one of the earliest pieces she'd made that semester, a version of Cassatt's *Little Girl in a Blue Armchair* with an aged-down version of Violet posing in the home studio. Old style, embroidery in paint. She went through each of her pieces, explaining what compelled her about the image, waxing poetic on themes of motherhood, traditional femininity, and the domestic life, taking care not to look directly at Dr. Freeman as she spoke. She explained for each piece what she felt did and did not work. She retraced her journey through the year, accepting that none of this was where she meant to go in the future.

Then came the final piece. She unfolded the tulle and draped it over the face of the wrecked seascape, letting its long tail tuck under the bottom edge and flow out onto the floor. She placed it on the easel and turned to face the committee.

"This is my response to the final self-portrait," she began. "It is . . . well, as you can see it is a failure." She heard someone stifle a surprised laugh.

"But," she continued, feeling better with the movement of her words, "it is a failure in an interesting way. Once I finished painting the original seascape, I saw what the committee had seen, that it didn't work in any way, so I started taking it apart. I would not show this piece." She admitted this while admiring how the drape of the tulle turned from see-through to solid when it was gathered. She could still see the painted colors of herself and her mother, huddled together far away, beneath the netting and looming face. "I don't think it works in any manner of ways, but there are certain vital things about it that are right, and I believe that sometimes it is better for a thing to be right than for it to be a functional success."

It wasn't the strong ending she'd hoped for, but Alice couldn't think of what to say next. She folded her hands in front of her and nodded her head once, as if to say, *Okay go ahead*. Dr. Freeman was the first to speak.

"So, you think at this point in your time here it is acceptable to present failed work as proof of your value in this program?"

"I think all art fails in some way." Alice didn't know where that came from, but she went with it. "Art can't be about chasing perfection. We have mathematics for that. Art only has to be true."

"And this"—he flapped his hand at the piece—"*this* is true to you?"

"Yes."

He scoffed and turned to his assistant, giving rapid notes.

"I'd like to hear more about your process for this final piece," Soo Lawrence spoke up from the second row. "Why did you choose these materials for this memory?"

Alice's brain went blank. There had been a reason at the time, she'd been following something, but she hadn't thought through how to put it into words.

"Well," she started slowly, begging her mind to catch up to her mouth. "It wasn't really the memory I was trying to capture. Once I saw how wrong the original seascape was, I moved away from trying to capture the day exactly and started capturing what it was like to try to remember something that wasn't there." Alice's thoughts found a bit of traction and started rolling ahead of her. "So, this is less about a memory, and more about re-creating what it is like for me to try to remember the day, and in *that* way this self-portrait isn't strictly a visual representation of my image but a visual experience of my brain."

The moment the words left her mouth Alice forgot what she'd said. *Please let it have been smart*, she prayed to no one. *Please, no more questions.*

A few of the other faculty members lobbed softballs at her. "What is your artist's statement? What are your major influences?" Then the conversation petered out and she was allowed to sit down again. Two more students presented after her, but she was mentally somewhere else, already thinking forward to the dinner she'd have with her family after this. Despite the exhaustion, a part of her mind wanted to spin off into worst-case scenarios: She'd be asked to leave, she'd be laughed at, she'd remain Gabriel Grant's discarded plaything to the art world for the rest of her miserable days. She plucked out each anxiety and redirected it, over and over again, to think about materials she wanted to experiment with, questions she had no answer for, and pieces she wanted to make next.

Present Day

A hand on her shoulder shocked Violet back to the present. She flinched and turned under its light touch. It was Marigold, fighting a smile at her sister's overreaction.

When people in Violet's new life asked what her sister was like, she always started with a physical description. She would tell them to imagine Botticelli's *Venus* but real and clothed. Look at this picture of their mother and father and let their father's chubby cheeks soften their mother's sharper features, and light the eyes with curiosity instead of darkening them with thought. Marigold had been taller than Violet since high school and on this day wore wedges to bump her up even higher. Marigold was light where Violet was dark, in her hair and eyes, but their skin was the same. Marigold shone outward, whereas Violet always seemed caught out to be noticed at all, attention lighting her solitary figure in a dark room. If Marigold was a Botticelli, then Violet was a Vermeer.

"Am I that scary?" Marigold asked.

"Just your face." Violet pulled her sister in for a hug.

"Dickhead," Marigold muttered in her ear. "Why didn't you text me when you got here?"

"You told me you wanted me to see it fresh, so I've been taking it all in."

"You've just done the one room?" Violet didn't hear any judgment in her sister's voice, just surprise and a touch of concern. Violet usually powered through art exhibits at twice this speed.

"It's a lot," Violet said. She tried swallowing but her throat was too dry. "I haven't seen most of this stuff since we stored it, so it's a lot."

"Of course." Marigold backed off. "I've been around it so much I think I've gotten immune. And growing up has helped. It doesn't occur to anyone that those girls"—she nodded to a sketch of them together laid out with their mother's journals behind glass—"are really real. But in any case, I'm really glad you came. You're the person I wanted to show all this to the most."

Violet turned back to look at the room, embarrassed by the flush of tears threatening to spill. The rooms were filling up steadily with strangers. Retired couples, mothers with young children, college-age art students with their large black sketchbooks. No one looked twice at the sisters, the grown-up girls from the painted world.

"Dad is supposed to arrive tonight and see it tomorrow," Marigold said.

That was enough to clamp down on the tears.

"And he's actually coming?" Violet asked, a bit too loud.

"I told you he was coming," her sister said.

"Yeah, but . . ." Too many words tried to march through her mouth at once. He'd promised before and always finked out. He'd missed Marigold's undergraduate graduation and Violet's PhD graduation. He'd missed almost every one of their birthdays since their mother had died, seven years of milestones mostly attended by ghost. He always had excuses. It was a bad time in the school year or travel was complicated. Then it was the pandemic, and no one could travel at all. Then he couldn't afford the rising costs of flights. The only times he'd seen them in person were the few occasions work brought him back to the area, and even then the girls were meant to go find him. They would go eat lunch near his hotel, go see him between his meetings. And he never stayed at the house. Once he'd used the insurance money to rebuild the house on Artemesia Drive, their father had begun renting it out to students and not one of them had spent a night there since.

"He's trying, Vi," Marigold said. "I think it's—"

"Don't say it's different this time," Violet cut her off.

"If he says it's different, I'm going to believe him," Marigold said, her voice turning cool as a breeze in summer. "If you don't want to, that's on you."

"I just don't want to be let down again." Violet hated how young she sounded. When had their roles reversed? When had Marigold become the adult in the room and Violet the petulant child, still mad at Daddy for not being nice enough?

"Well, I can't do anything about that," Marigold said. "Maybe he comes through this time, maybe he doesn't. But I'm still going to give him the chance. Because that's what you do for family." Violet tried turning away but Marigold kept on holding her eye. "You give them a chance to come back, even if they've left you behind."

Violet crossed her arms and silently berated herself. Not for acting like a child, even though she knew she was, but for going down the exact same path that led to the exact same fight and the exact same hurt. Marigold never let her get mad at their father for leaving them that summer without the reminder that Violet had left her sister, too. That for every wound their father inflicted on Violet, Violet had done the same to Marigold. She couldn't understand how her younger sister, doubly wounded, could be functioning so much better. Or maybe it wasn't so much superiority in function as it was in form. Maybe it was simply that Marigold admitted that she'd been hurt, while Violet just carried the pain around with her everywhere and pretended it wasn't there.

"I think the second section will be easier for you," Marigold's posited, her voice artificially brightened. "It's a lot of her work from after she got her MFA."

"The era of self-portraits?"

"Yeah, but they mixed in her more thematic work," Marigold said. "The fabric experiments, the installation pieces, the sculptures. It's more about her early life, too. The stuff before us."

"Good, because if I have to look at my tiny scowling face one more time—"

"Not so different from right now, actually." Marigold nudged her sister, a little forgiveness.

"That is my tired face," Violet explained. "This is my thinking face."

"Well, they both look like they hurt."

"They do." Violet glanced forward into the next room. She saw the large fabric sculptures of her mother's middle age. "So, it gets easier from here."

"For a while, but then . . . you know."

"She dies at the end?" Violet tried to pass it off as a joke. "Yeah, I remember, I was there."

Violet tried for a little laugh, but it just sounded like a cough.

"But that's not really the end though, right?" Violet continued. "Because you have a piece, too, right?"

"Yeah, it's . . . I'll wait for you at the end," Marigold decided. She pulled herself up back to full height, and her professional mask slid back into place. "You keep going in order, and I'll wait for you at the end."

Violet opened her mouth to say okay, but Marigold had already turned and walked away. People churned through the room slowly, like sea-foam at the beach, rocking back and forth, sliding side to side so slowly it looked like they were barely moving at all. Once Violet lost sight of her sister's retreating back, she was left alone again with her other selves, now multiplied from the paintings she'd seen. The first, a small shadow haunted by the smell of rotten fruit. The hunched figure sitting in front of a stranger's grave. The girl in the stiff purple skirt, who couldn't seem to do anything right. She couldn't pick them up the way she'd seen mothers do, couldn't comfort them in her arms, couldn't tell them things would get better because she knew they'd only get worse. She pulled out her guide, found the next spot on the map, and kept going.

Redesigning the Frame: Sculpture, Space, and the Self

From 2010–2016 Snyder drastically altered her approach to her own work. After her success with *The Rose of the Winds*, her interest in historical conversations seemed to cease entirely. She stops painting her daughters and instead focuses on her personal history. Instead of working in oil paints she leans harder into the elements of her early work most reviews deemed "incongruous" and "crafty," namely her fabric arts elements.

Instead of chasing down success with what had worked for her in the past, Snyder threw herself into these new sculptural and textural pieces. Using construction, quilting, embroidery, and weaving, Snyder's work during this period of time focuses on the actual experience of art by the viewer. Instead of simply hanging a flat image on a wall, she begins altering how and when the viewer is allowed to perceive her work. She plays with the limitation of the human eye, plays tricks with opposing colors, and sometimes literally surrounds viewers with her perspective.

These years are also where we can see the influence of her husband, an astronomer, on her work. Snyder begins to experiment with the manipulation of time and the physics of light. She states in an interview with *Art Review* she became "...obsessed with the fact that to trace a source of light back to its origin is to, in fact, move backward in time. It changed time travel from something from a sci-fi movie to a natural, everyday phenomenon."

In this next room, pay special attention to the way bodies move through space, both your own body and the figures of bodies in the following pieces.

MARIAN MITCHELL DONAHUE

Red/Blue

2011

Alice Snyder
American, 1974–2017

Threadwork on round frame

This piece marks several major changes in the life and career of Alice Snyder. Premiering at the Acadia National Gallery in 2011, *Red/Blue* is the first major work Snyder created post-MFA and serves as the prelude to the more philosophical and figurative work she creates during her future sculptural period.

While the pieces may seem wildly different, try to compare this work with *Two Girls with Fruit*. Whereas before Snyder used a shared symbolic language, here she uses a shared scientific language. Red and blue are two primary colors that combine to make purple, in the case of paint, and magenta, in the case of the visible light spectrum. In 3D, red and cyan filters can be used to trick the brain into turning a flat image into a three-dimensional scene or composition.

You may find it easier to study this piece from afar. The central figure of the artist at twenty swirled into a tight fetal position, doubled and then overlapping in red and cyan thread, has been known to create a dizzying effect for some viewers.

In May of 1995, two weeks before her college graduation, two weeks before her life was meant to truly begin, Alice Miller bought herself a pregnancy test with cash at the corner Rite Aid and peed on the stick in the ground floor bathroom of the art building. It was too dangerous to do in her father's house, and she hadn't been back to the apartment since Gabriel had disappeared the previous month. She'd missed a period due to stress before. They'd been pushed around when she was sick or just not eating enough. Periods were inconsistent. She knew this. While four months might seem like a lot, things had been much more intense lately. And it wasn't like she hadn't bled at all. There had been spotting. Beautiful, wonderful spotting that had reminded her that one-time mistakes don't always upend your life.

It's nothing. she told herself. *You're being crazy. You're overreacting. It's nothing.*

But then the three minutes were up, the stick was blue, and all at once it quickened into something.

And in that scene—cold basement, cooling pee on a plastic stick—all that came to Alice's mind was Dante Gabriel Rossetti.

Alice had actually been inspired by the Pre-Raphaelites first. Years before Joe renamed himself Gabriel Grant, Alice had discovered this velvet and satin corner of history one evening in November of 1993 as she was walking through the main stacks of the Shoemaker Library looking for her own inspiration.

She liked the library best at night, when the yellow light poured out of the high curved windows of the Romanesque building and the only sounds were of her footsteps down marble corridors and up wrought iron ladders. When she was too awake to go home but too tired to be around people, Alice would walk up and down the tight aisles of the stacks and wait for something to jump out at her. This is how she found most of her inspiration. A green leather tome about the history of tea spurred on the painting of a domestic scene in a kitchen. A history of the corset in red cloth binding with gold embossed letters resulted in a love scene. This evening, as she trailed her gaze across the spines of history, her gaze snagged on an old brown leather edition of Cecil Y. Lang's *The Pre-Raphaelites and Their Circle*. Alice pulled the book off the shelf, slid down to the floor in a single liquid motion, and let herself be lost in the old world.

Later that night she surprised Joe at his apartment. There was a party starting when she arrived. He never told her about his parties. She got the sense he liked to keep her separate from all that. To keep her to himself. That's why he wouldn't let her sit for the other art students when they asked. Why he waited outside each of her classes, often skipping ones of his own, to walk her from place to place. It felt good, being held that tightly, feeling someone that close. It reminded her, even on her worst day, of who she was and how much she was wanted.

People she knew from their painting class were out on the front steps of his building smoking. A girl she'd seen at the shows, one of the other art department girlfriends, was already puking lime-green into a bush. Alice nodded hello and trudged up the stairs. Joe answered the door, did a double take, and stepped out into the hallway with her.

"What are you—?"

"I'm obsessed. This is what I want to do next," she cut in, voice raising in excitement. Joe plucked the book from her hands and thumbed through to the first image. A sweet self-portrait of the young Dante Gabriel Rossetti drawn like a romantic hero, all soft lips and long curly hair. On the opposite page was a line drawing he'd done years later of his sleeping wife and muse, Elizabeth Siddal. Joe leaned against the wall and kept flipping through the rest of the book but kept one finger wedged between the pages where the young Dante smoldered and Lizzie slept.

"I can see it," Joe said finally. "I can see this working."

Alice was confused. When she'd said "want to do next" she'd meant as a subject for her own thesis. The ideas had started spinning inside her as she sat, ass numbing, on the floor of the stacks. There was so much to pick apart. She could do something on stories within stories, how they made people into paintings. And the way they captured love, as not just a thing but as a philosophy, as a particular way to order your life. She'd meant it for herself. But she saw his eyes lose focus as he drew deeper and deeper inside his own mind, as he always did when he was about to get obsessed, and she saw it was already too late to take it all back.

I don't own the past, she coached herself to dismiss her irritation. *No one gets to own the past.*

Perhaps the second sign she should have seen was a week later in bed when he asked her if she'd ever considered changing her name.

"You mean if I get married, would I take my husband's name?" She dabbed the sweat from her forehead with the corner of his top sheet. "Yes. Definitely. I don't want to stay Miller."

"I'm thinking of a smaller change."

"Like what?" She craned her neck to look at him. He'd been somewhere else all day. All through walks between classes. Through shooting her in front of the large windows of his apartment. Even when he was on top of her afterward in the typical finish to their work, he seemed only half present. Now, finally, he seemed ready to show her where he'd been all this time.

"What if you just changed the spelling of your last name. Just dropping one 'l.'"

Alice squinted in confusion.

"M-I-L-E-R? So My-Lur? Why would I do that?"

"It's more elegant."

"It barely changes it!" She laughed. "No. I'd want to take my husband's name, given the chance."

"To indicate a transfer or ownership?" he said, goading her.

"If I don't have my husband's name, I'll be stuck with my father's, and I don't want that legacy," she said, mirroring his distant stare up to the ceiling.

"I won't be stuck with my father's," she said.

"I won't be stuck with mine, either," Joe muttered more to himself than to her. Alice looked over in surprise, but when he didn't make to say anything else she let her attention drop away. Alice leaned over to nestle her temple against the point of his shoulder, as she liked to do, and after a moment Joe leaned his head against hers.

Two weeks after, she knew for sure. It was the first time they fought about their work. There'd been fights before. Days and nights when some switch inside would finally flip and he'd turn into something else. He'd scream in her face, call her names, long uninterrupted obscenity-filled soliloquies. Throw things at the walls, at her. Break furniture. Once he even punched the wall in his apartment so hard he broke clean through the drywall, and he had to hire someone to fix it. She'd do her part. She'd cry and cower. Sometimes she'd just sit stock-still in the middle of the room and wait for a slap or punch that never came. And then when it was all over, they'd move on as if nothing at all had happened. But this time was the first time Alice had argued back. Joe was staging portraits and Alice wanted, just this once, to be Jane Morris in *Proserpine* instead of always having to be Lizzie Siddal.

"I just have so much more in common with Jane than I do with Lizzie," she explained. "She was a textile designer and an embroiderer, and I've done that work—"

"You are Lizzie," Joe cut her off. "You look like her. You are her. The hair, the skin, the eyes. It's all there. You can't just decide to be Jane."

"But I—"

"I'm not taking notes from you on this. You are Lizzie. You are not Jane. You will *never be* Jane. That's that. Now drop it."

Alice opened her mouth to speak again but he rounded on her suddenly and her mouth snapped shut.

"Good girl," he said, then turned and walked back to his work.

Alice was sure they'd made their girl in January of 1995, the evening after the disastrous shoot that began as *Woman of the River* and ended as *Ophelia*.

It was the first time they'd attempted an outdoor shoot in winter. At Alice's urging, Joe had conscripted twice the number of help for the day. The labor of his whole life was eased by this skill for inspiring envy in strangers. He had an unstudied, unearned beauty in him that made people want to hang on. Most didn't actually care about being his friend, they just wanted to be seen as his friend. The usual students from the art department were there, now joined by extra technical support in the form of theater kids, and extra muscle in the form of basketball players no one knew. One of the new additions, Simon, doubly useful for his summers spent as a lifeguard and his work-study hours in the theater's scene shop doing basic construction, had jumped feetfirst into the project. He'd been happy to teach

Alice everything he knew. In the margins of Joe's most ambitious shoot yet, Alice began learning how to use power tools, how to measure and cut, how to make her own wood frames.

Alice and Simon stood shoulder to shoulder at the summit of the single bridge crossing the river. It was day two of a false spring. Snow and ice melted into the river, raising the water, making it rush and tumble, turning the banks slick and steep. They watched a dead branch crack and fall off a tree upriver, then land with a splash in the water. Their eyes followed as the wood was pulled under and buoyed back up, toppling over itself end to end, hitting hidden rocks on the riverbed. They stepped forward, leaned over the rail, heads craning in unison as the branch was finally pulled under as it rushed beneath their feet.

"Three Mississippis," Simon said. "Just three seconds. You sure this is the day for it?"

Alice shivered in response. She'd have better luck asking the river to stop running than asking Joe to delay another day. Everything was set up, and she didn't want to risk setting him off right before she got in the boat.

"Let's start," she said.

Joe had decided on a cotton Gunne Sax prairie dress she'd found for him in a thrift store. Originally a lovely tan-and-cream color, he had insisted she bleach it. He'd wanted her to look virginal, to wear white as a modern bride might on her wedding day despite the colorful dress *The Lady of Shalott* wore in the original painting he was referencing. Bleaching the dress had been painful for Alice. Joe had no sense, no care, for the history he was erasing in the vintage garment, the pattern and color she'd been forced to ruin. She'd warned him bleaching would wreck the dress and weaken the fabric but if he'd heard her warnings, he'd given no sign. As she walked to the boat, Alice shed her winter coat and stepped out of her rain boots. The frigid air whipped right through her thin dress and once again she started to turn into herself, where she always went when her fear rose up, to the place where physical things did not matter.

"Are you sure?" Simon asked.

"I'm sure," Alice said.

The basketball players—Alice wasn't sure of their names—helped her into the wooden boat and waded knee deep into the river to push her in. They'd decided, with the current, to attach ropes to both ends to keep it from slamming up against the riverbank. Two more players from the opposite bank stood next to Joe and pulled the boat out and a team behind her gave them the slack to move. The physics of it all seemed wrong but no one objected. When the boat took to the water it suddenly rocked hard to the side. She was knocked forward with the river, then back when the ropes snapped taut, and her arms flew out to grip the sides of the boat. She heard everyone else gasp, but she just gripped and ground her teeth.

Someone new had decorated the boat to Joe's specifications. Big red and pink quilts lined the sides with a stained sofa cushion in the middle for her to sit on. The boat rocked, water rushed, debris knocked against the underside of the boat. One quilt was a series of triangles patterned to look like stars, and the other was a series of overlapping circles. A baby's blanket and a wedding quilt. They were both stained, and the padding inside had gone flat. Alice imagined a baby spitting up on the stars, and a mother knocking over a glass of red wine while she and her husband fumbled on the floor.

The sides of this boat are too low, her mind warned with every swell of the river. But in the original you could see the Lady's lap, so, she reminded herself, this is how it had to be. She tried to turn to look at the boys behind her, but even that small shift in weight upset the balance of the boat. Her head snapped forward, and she stayed as still as she could. The shuttering brought her back to the task at hand. Joe was crouched on the opposite riverbank, and she could just hear the sounds of his camera's eye capturing her over the rush of the river. The longer she stayed on the water the more soothing the rush became, consuming and constant, like listening to a storm from the comfort of her room. Joe was finding the angles, sometimes taking long strides, sometimes little creeping steps, always one foot in front of the other, in and out, up and down. The only time she saw his face was when he lowered it to shout directions at the team. The air was washed clean, and the direct sunlight blanched the shot. He wanted the boat to go this way, he wanted the framing branches to be held at a gentler angle. When he finally turned his attention to her, he left words behind and started to mime his wants.

He circled his face and pointed at her. Time to pose. Joe settled into his range of angles and Alice struggled to find hers. She studied his stance and reverse traced where her lines needed to land. Alice tilted her head like she'd practiced in front of the mirror at home. Her hands were supposed to be gentle and relaxed but every time the boat pitched, she instinctively clutched the sides of the vessel. Her stomach ached from trying to hold on to her center of balance. She was getting nauseous and dizzy.

Joe lowered his camera and shook his head. No good.

Alice's stomach wound tighter. Joe crouched and tried miming something, but she didn't get it. She squinted and shook her head. He handed the camera to his assistant and got on his hands and knees. He crawled forward, then pointed at her. She tried to stay upright in the boat, the knuckles of her red, cold hands turning white with the intensity of her grip. He had to be kidding. She couldn't move.

She saw him snap his fingers at her, but the sound was drowned out by the rushing water. Alice looked at the assorted strangers on the shore watching her, hoping one of them would step forward and explain to him that she could barely turn her head without threat of capsizing, let alone crawl forward to the front of the boat. But they all just stood and stared and waited for her to obey. Joe mouthed the word *Come* and beckoned her forward like an owner might command a dog.

Alice sucked in burning breath after breath, hissing out steam as an exhale. She slid her hands forward on the sides inch by inch, teetering off-balance then readjusting in each incremental advance. Joe stood and took back his camera, the large black eye of his lens ready and waiting to capture her. She rolled onto her knees, brought her hips forward, and finally looked up. The wind picked up, and she tried to spit her hair out of her mouth. She tossed her head, but the wind was strong on the water. The black eye waited. Alice pried her left hand away from the boat side to push her hair away from her face and in the moment her hand left the side the river swelled up beneath her. The players on both sides of the bank pulled their ropes taut in unison to keep control, lifting the boat just high enough for the water to tip it over.

Alice felt herself suddenly lifted and only had time to gasp before being poured, face-first and mouth open, into the river.

She somersaulted, head down, feet up, curled around herself underwater. She tasted dirt. She was submerged in icy water. As she finally had thought enough to kick out and swing toward the surface, her head was knocked sideways by something hard, the world went black, and the river pulled her further in.

As she came around, she dreamt she was coughing hard. No, she was coughing hard. Choking on water, turning her face to spit out the mud. She twitched her arms and legs to test if they were still there. The hard, wet thing at her back was the ground. The too bright thing blinding her was the sky. In the distance she heard sirens wail, growing louder, getting closer. In her head she heard a loud, constant ringing. Between the two sounds she dreamt she heard a camera lens shuttering. No, she did hear a camera lens shuttering. Joe stood over her, face replaced by his single black eye, capturing shot after shot of her as she coughed and struggled to breathe.

After Alice had remembered how to breathe, after she'd been checked out in the back of an ambulance and lectured about the absolute idiocy of their plans that day, after Joe had convinced the paramedics to leave without calling anyone's parents, even after the crew had begun to laugh to break the tension and someone had suggested they all find a warm place to consume large amounts of cheap liquor immediately, right at the point when Joe would usually step in and offer up his apartment for another all-night party, was when the conception was set in motion.

"You all go ahead," Joe said, handing them some twenties for a few bottles. "I need to take Alice home."

Alice sat up straight in alarm before realizing Joe meant his apartment, not her father's house.

The apartment was dark, dry, and warm when they arrived—the opposite of the shoot they'd just left. Alice was still wearing the muddied, ruined white dress and plastic rain boots from the shoot. She clung to the reflective heating blanket the EMT had wrapped around her. She paused at the door, unsure if she should undress where she stood to keep from tracking in mud or try to clean up in the small kitchenette a few feet from her. Joe took her hand in his and led her across the carpeted living room to the bathroom. Wordlessly he led. Wordlessly she followed.

First, he had her sit on the closed toilet while he pried off her muddy boots and dropped them in the tub. He ran a hand towel under the faucet until it was saturated with warm water, then he washed her feet. He took his time. Took care to hold each foot gently and wipe every inch like he was cleaning precious marble. He washed up her shins, her knees, and began washing her lower thighs when she first stiffened. He went to the sink, wrung out the towel, and wet it again.

Joe took away her heat blanket and gave her a dry towel to wrap around herself instead. It was only then that Alice realized her bodice had ripped at some point and her right breast was partially exposed, her pale pink nipple visible. How had she not noticed? The cold she guessed, had distracted her. The cold and the trying not to die.

Joe carefully folded the reflective blanket and laid it next to her boots. He gestured for her to stand, and she did. He brushed the towel off her shoulder and brought her arms up above her head. He knelt and peeled the hem of her dress up and off her like a second skin. Once free, she turned and grabbed her towel, wrapping it around her naked body, still shivering but gradually feeling the pins and needles shoot through her extremities as she warmed. Joe turned the mess of a dress right side out and draped it over the shower curtain rod. She froze as he reached up under her towel and peeled off her soaked underwear. He knelt in front of her again and she put a hand on his back to balance as she stepped out of it one foot at a time. He dropped those, too, on the curtain rod. Then he gestured for her to sit.

When he went to the sink again to wring out and rewet the towel was when she finally started to warm. He began again with her hands and washed up to her shoulders. Then her shoulders and her upper chest, squeezing the towel at her clavicle so the warm water ran in rivulets down her chest, between her breasts, and trailed ticklish to her stomach.

Here Alice decided to move herself. She turned on the seat, pulled her ratted hair to one side, and dropped her towel a bit so he could wash her back. She turned to face him and let the towel fall around her waist. He washed the dirty residue trails off her breasts, sternum, and stomach. She kept her head up, facing him, watching him the whole time he worked, but he never once raised his head or met her eyes.

She knocked the towel off to let him wash her hips and thighs. He went back to the sink and wrung out the cloth another time. Alice parted her knees and lifted herself up to let him wash her underneath. She waited for him to look at her. For his body, at least, to respond, but he managed to keep himself in check. When he was done he stood, cleaned the washcloth a final time, and then draped it over the curtain rod with the other relics.

Alice wrapped herself back up in the towel and wondered what would come next. Joe opened his cabinets and pulled out some combs and a drinking glass he filled with water. She turned on her seat and let the towel drape low so the mess of her hair fell against her skin. Joe was always touching her hair. In bed he liked to wrap it around his hand like a rope and grip her close to the scalp. On shoots he was always fussing with it. Teasing and spraying it to make it look bigger, wilder. But this was different. This was new.

Joe wet the comb and started detangling her hair from the bottom like he'd done before photo shoots to get her hair just the way he wanted it. He brushed up higher and higher, working out the tangles and knots, snipping away anything that was totally hopeless. When he reached her scalp, he titled her head back and started pouring the water along her hairline to wash out the hidden silt, dabbing at her back with the towel to keep her dry.

Alice held out her right hand and after a pause, Joe passed her the comb. She ran through her hair fast and rough. Then she started piecing out three strands to start a braid. Joe stood and watched her for a moment as she twisted section over section, side over side. When she reached the base of her neck, where her arms always started to feel weak, he took over for her and braided it down to the end. She passed him an elastic she'd left in the bathroom during some previous visit, and he tied her hair off with a small, satisfied noise.

Now he starts something, she thought. But when she turned around, he was back at the sink getting another cloth wet. She stood and faced him, leaving the towel behind, and opened her mouth to speak but Joe only brought the damp cloth to her face and started wiping the last of the dirt away. He dabbed at her lips and her burning eyes. He passed over her face again and again until she felt goose bumps rise on her skin, then he dropped the cloth back in the basin. He took her face in his hands, finally looked her in the eye and said:

"I love you."

She studied his face. No guilt, no anger. This did not seem to be an "I'm sorry" or even a "you should be sorry."

Alice didn't know of any acceptable answer besides the obvious one, so truthful or not, she responded.

"I love you, too."

They did things slower this time. He led her by the hand back to the bed and held the blanket up for her to crawl in, keeping her warm while he undressed. Kisses were long and deep while their bodies found place alongside each other. When he put his hand on her he kept it there, pressing in tandem with her hips until she came. They ate up the time. When she was on top, she worked up the tempo until he was close then brought it back down again. She enjoyed this part even more. Bringing him closer and closer, coaxing him to last longer, until he'd finally had enough and grabbed her thighs to keep her going. At the exact moment he should have pulled out Joe held on to her even tighter and cried out.

They went to the bathroom together after, Alice to pee and Joe to clean up. It was only then in the after-sex haze that they realized they'd made another major miscalculation that day. Joe had forgotten protection, and Alice had forgotten to make sure he had it before they'd started.

Unbelievable as it seemed to Alice months later, pregnant in the basement of the art building, they had laughed it off. Alice figured this was when it happened. Not because it was the only time they forgot, or even the only time Joe insisted on staying when he should have left, but because it was the time Alice remembered best. And so, she assumed, the time she remembered must have been the time worth remembering.

By February, Joe stopped taking pictures and spent all his time reading books—anything and everything he could get his hands on that might relate in one way or another to Dante Gabriel Rossetti. Alice watched him crash into the library, her special place, and drag away every reference she might have used for the Pre-Raphaelites like a rough wave. She knew he had never been the best student in his general requirement courses but that was disinterest, not stupidity. When he was on fire like this, he became unmanageable, unstoppable. A spark that grew larger once fed with solitude and focus. Alice found her own thesis material, a meditation on the Baroque female form and the golden ratio. She let herself get lost in her own mind, in her own imagined world. She didn't notice when he stopped showing up for his classes. She wasn't aware when he stopped returning the department's many concerned emails. When the odd art student asked if she knew where he was, she could honestly say she had no idea.

In March, Alice dismissed her vomiting as anxiety, her bloated stomach as constipation, and her sore breasts as proof her period was going to appear any day now. Then Joe sent out a deeply worrying email to his entire contacts list. The subject line read: "my name is Might-have-been; I am also call'd No More, Too Late, Farewell" but the body was empty. Attached was a twenty-page single-spaced letter addressed to "All People of the Earth Past and Future." Alice could barely get past the second page. The sentences made no grammatical sense; the text was riddled with typos and jumped from subject to subject with no clear bridge. The only clear message she was able to glean was that he would be changing his name. Joseph Turner was dead, and Gabriel Grant had taken his place.

All his talk of death, metaphorical or not, triggered an automatic investigation. Art school faculty interviewed each student to retrace Joe/Gabriel's last known actions on campus. Alice was made to go through the event of the river shooting again and again. She was lectured, condescended to, and by Joe's advisor outright blamed for failing to take care of him after what was clearly a traumatic experience. She tried to defend herself, but she was mostly forced to sit and listen while an adult she barely knew, who barely knew her, interrogated her every thought and action since the shoot and picked what they liked to prove she'd been neglectful. Was she aware no one had seen or heard from him in a month? That he'd cleared out of his apartment some time ago and never told his landlord? That even his parents didn't know where he was?

It was this last point that brought her up short. Joe had never needed, and most likely would never need, to work. From the few times he'd shared some hint of his family life Alice knew his father was some judge working in Annapolis, that his mother was heir to a mayonnaise fortune or a relish empire or something like that, and that he'd had a brother he referred to in the past tense. A single heir to a great deal of money. He was cheap the way rich people often were, stiffing waiters of tips for the smallest perceived slight, demanding refunds for any possible reason, asking for discounts any- and everywhere.

This was her one comforting thought: Sooner or later he would run out of money, and it wouldn't even occur to him to make his own. Then he would have to reach out to his parents. Then he would have to reemerge.

When the truth finally burrowed deep enough to reach her, Alice tried to find the calm place inside her, but it was gone. She wanted to have someone to call. Someone who'd make everything alright. Make everything bearable again. She wanted her mother. She told herself she'd cry for an hour and then she would have to pull herself off the floor. In an hour she'd start figuring out what to do.

But then the hour was up, and the stick was still blue, and she couldn't stop crying. So she called Arthur Snyder.

The Present Past
2011

Alice Snyder
American, 1974–2017

Painted archway

Debuting at the Suki Gallery in Old Town Alexandria, Virginia, before being added to the permanent collection of the American Visionary Art Museum in 2012, this piece represents a major leap forward in Snyder's development as a sculptor and experiential artist.

This slim arch is the first of Snyder's major works to interact directly with the viewers' experience of it in a museum or gallery setting. While the suggested 3D viewing stations for *Red/Blue* introduce the concept of the viewer as an active part of art making, *The Present Past* relies on a viewer's awareness of their physical interaction with the piece to create its meaning. A mere six inches across at its face, nine feet at its apex, and nine feet wide at its base, this sculpture is too large to take in with a single glance and so thin it requires close, concentrated attention. The sculpture's height, width, and general shape also make it impossible for the viewer to take in the whole of the image all at once. Your vision is always limited.

For many years it was believed that the night sky design wrapping the arch was merely a representation of space or a reference to Van Gogh's *The Starry Night*. It wasn't until we began assembling this retrospective that we discovered Snyder's design notes for the piece which revealed that each section of night sky pictured on this arch illustrates a different phase of a star's life, known as stellar evolution. In this single delicate structure, you will see billions of years of history.

In May of 1995 Arthur Snyder left his office hours thirty minutes early, posting a small notecard on the front of the shared space to warn any late-coming students he'd had a family emergency. And that's what it was to him. Even then, before children and attraction and love, when they were each just the only true friend the other had in the world, he considered her family.

He walked quickly between the brutalist mathematics building and the nursing school, cut through the first floor of the law center, and wound up in the student center. He'd broken into a sweat by the time he got through the throng of students churning in the lobby between the cafeteria and the coffee stand. He'd heard a single "Hey, Professor Snyder!" behind him as he went through the front door, but he did not turn. He had never gotten used to the incline of Kenning University's campus. Not when he was adjunct, or full time, or tenured, or chair of the physics department had he ever stopped feeling winded when he made this hike from the science side of campus to the art building, at the top of a hill on the opposite end of the map.

At twenty-eight he was still the affable young adjunct teaching intro courses to undergrads while he worked on his postdoc research with a team at Goddard. Arthur had started immersing himself in spectroscopy, using shifts in the electromagnetic spectrum to track the paths and compositions of distant celestial bodies. This was the simplest description of his job, the one he would take out when he chatted with the other dads at pickup. It was specific enough people knew it was complicated, but general enough they could partway understand.

As Arthur pulled himself over the last rise of the campus, he finally caught sight of Alice and let himself slow down. He hadn't realized how scared he'd been until he saw she was safe. Physically at least. She wasn't bleeding or crying or throwing up. Just sitting and staring out into the middle distance like she only barely existed.

"Allie?" he asked gently as he got closer, trying not to startle her.

She blinked and shook off her stare, then turned to him. She looked him down and up then tilted her head. He tried to cover how hard he was breathing.

"Are you okay?" he asked.

"I don't know," she said, her voice caught. She cleared her throat and sat up a bit straighter.

"I don't know what to do," she said. "I don't know where to go."

From what he could tell the only people she had in her life were himself, Joe, and her father. Since Arthur had been called, he could be reasonably sure it wasn't anything he'd done. The father, from the extremely redacted versions of her past she'd allowed him to see, was mostly absent. Joe was the most likely candidate. Alice had been less careful talking about Joe, especially when he overlapped with her work. Arthur knew there had been fights. If you could call it a fight when one person stayed silent and the other screamed his head off. And there had been one rainy night when she'd had to call Arthur to pick her up from outside Joe's apartment after he'd thrown her out. She'd stayed silent the whole ride back to her house, dripping in his passenger seat.

"Can you tell me what happened?"

She was sitting right in the middle of the bench with her bag to one side so there was no room for him to sit next to her. Arthur slowly bent down on one knee in front of her and took her hands in his own. That seemed to focus her even more.

"Allie, can you tell me what happened?" he asked again.

"Yes, but . . . it's not something I should say here. Can we . . . can we talk in your car?"

"Sure," he said eagerly. "If you'd feel more comfortable there. I can bring it around—"

"No, let's go there," she said, standing up. Arthur pushed himself up after her.

"I don't want to be here anymore," she said. Alice looked around, suddenly agitated, as if she'd woken up in the wrong place and she wanted to go before she was caught.

Every time Arthur had someone else in his car it aged and dirtied before his eyes in a time-lapse of neglect. The fabric on the ceiling was starting to bag. Receipts and fliers gathered at the corner of the footwell. In the back he had the same white trash bag of old clothes he'd been meaning to drop off at Goodwill for months and he knew his cassettes had spilled out all over the floor. It was the same '80s Corolla sedan he'd driven to Kenning University the first day he'd visited the campus. The day he met Alice.

They met in May of 1993. Arthur was driving to D.C. from Baltimore where he'd had a disappointing second interview for a postdoc position at the Space Telescope Science Institute. The traffic on 95 had been at a crawl all the way down and he'd only just made it to another interview at Kenning University on time. This one, the teaching position, was at least going better. It appeared his syllabi for Intro to Astronomy and Intro to Physics were worth a lot. None of the tenured faculty wanted to do it, so a fresh-out-of-grad-school adjunct was just what they needed.

He kept his navy blue blazer on, knowing his white shirt was completely sweated through. His pressed khakis and stiff collar had softened in the early summer humidity. The men interviewing him, Dr. Amram and Dr. Richards, wore versions of the same academic uniform. They moved on to a tour of campus after the formal Q and A, which Arthur took as a good sign. They toted him around in a physics department golf cart. They wound their way through the concrete and steel buildings referred to as "B.S. Corner": chemistry and biology, physics, mathematics, computer science, and nursing. They drove him past a relatively new dining hall, the entrance to the underground parking lot, and the main library. The last place Arthur had taught was a community college whose campus felt more like a high school. Here, though, were actual tree-lined walkways. Students walking shoulder to shoulder with books in their arms. University life felt good to him, like putting on an old familiar jacket he'd thought he'd lost.

As they passed the dining hall again, this time seeing it from behind so that Dr. Richards (driving) could prove to Dr. Amram (passenger seat) that the new coffee shop on the second floor was, in fact, still open if Arthur needed some caffeine before his drive back up 95 at rush hour. As the two professors devolved into a Statler and Waldorf scene about whether the school was currently in a summer schedule or a holiday schedule, Arthur's attention caught on a tall white building poking out above the treetops at the crest of the campus. Dr. Amram (Waldorf) was barking orders to Dr. Richards (Statler) about the best way to get back to the physics building and "No, he doesn't need to see the dorms" and "Yes, we should tell him about the gym." Arthur raised his voice above the labor of the cart engine.

"Excuse me, but what's that building there?" he asked, pointing to the tower on the hill. If that was the highest point on campus, as it appeared to be from the ground, it might be the best place for his personal viewing. The roof of the physics building was fine. Plenty of room to fit a class of students, high guardrails to prevent accidents, and the telescopes would be close by, but he didn't like how close it was to the school's Metro stop. Too much noise, too much light. Dr. Amram peered up from under the cover of the cart and followed Arthur's sight line.

"Oh that." He made a shooing motion. "That's up at the humanities side of campus. It's probably an art school. Not sure which one. Do you know, Dr. Richards?"

Statler and Waldorf dove back into another argument about which school had which buildings. Arthur tuned out. He tried to see more of the white building through the trees that surrounded it. It wasn't like the old stone Romanesque buildings in the center of campus. There was no ornamentation that he could see, just a simple rectangular tower with plain white plaster and recessed windows. As the cart took a final large U-turn and began to roll back down the hills to the science side of campus, Arthur kept turning back to look for the peak of white in the trees.

After the interview Arthur headed to the Visual Arts School at the top of the hill. He traded his blazer for the emergency telescope in the trunk of his car before hiking back up to find the white building. Excitement had brought him this far, but now, at the actual front door to the building, he considered the wisdom of this little adventure. The front door was propped open by some invisible force. But still. If he was found, did he really want to explain to Dr. Richards and Dr. Amram why their potential new lecturer had broken into a building on campus less than an hour after his interview?

He sighed and ran a hand over his face. It wasn't worth it. He turned to leave just as a female voice called out clear and loud from somewhere in the darkened building.

"What are you waiting for?" she said. "Come in. I'll be on the roof."

The sound of footsteps receding.

The woman couldn't have been expecting him, he knew that. But he still felt some tug in his gut pulling him forward. He stepped into the dark, cool room sideways to not bump his telescope, sliding one foot in front on the other and displacing the pebble Alice had wedged in the track of the door to keep it open.

He found himself in a kind of lobby that led directly back to a large, empty room undergoing some kind of construction. The lights were all off, but the afternoon light still poured in from some offstage windows. At the center of the first room, he found a circle of small ladders and step stools surrounding some metal and wood contraption hanging from the ceiling. He stepped over kneepads and toolboxes as he made his way farther back, scanning the walls for a stairwell, but there was none. The walls were all smooth plaster with hooks and nails scattered across their faces.

Then he heard music. He followed the sound back to the front room and around the corner to a set of wooden stairs he'd overlooked when he'd come in. He opened another propped open door, and the sound of strings and piano floated down to him. The stairs were loud under his weight but for once he didn't mind. He wanted whoever it was to know he was coming so she wouldn't be scared when she turned around expecting someone else and got him instead. It was a move Arthur had to pull a lot. He'd been a twig of a kid but then puberty hit, and he had started shooting up. As much as he'd hate to admit it, he'd come to closely resemble his father. Six-foot-one and built like a boxer. But with his mother's blond hair, green eyes, and gentle nature. He had to be careful when he walked home late at night or passed a strange woman in a hallway not to make eye contact or make any move in their direction. No matter how pure his intentions actually were, he knew he looked like a threat.

As he pushed open the door at the top of the stairs, he called out. "Hello?"

No response. He took a few steps out onto the roof. The guardrails were much lower here, and the corners were all littered with cigarette stubs, but he could tell already it would be a better place to stargaze. The light came from the sun and the noise from the crickets.

"Hello?" he called again.

"You're not what I was expecting," said a voice behind him.

He spun a bit faster than necessary and the young woman leaning against the door to the stairs snorted. The first thing he noticed was her height. Tall enough to stare him down. She was dressed in men's work clothes, a tank top under overalls and black boots, red hair pulled back. No one had ever looked at him the way this woman looked at him. He froze. He felt her take in his face, his hair, his clothes, even his shoes, then trail all the way back up. He heard her make some little assessing noise in the back of her throat before kicking herself off the door and walking around to the other side of the roof.

Well, what else could he do? He followed her.

She'd set up some lawn chairs, one for her, one for her books. Some overturned milk crates and cardboard boxes served as tables and footrests. The boom box playing the music he'd heard was propped up on an old green plastic crate. Everything was covered with paint splatters.

"Welcome to my office. I'm Alice Miller," she said as she eased herself down onto a lawn chair. "What can I help you with? You lost?"

"No, just new."

"An art student?" She was incredulous.

"An astronomer," he said.

She narrowed her eyes.

"Bullshit," she said.

He laughed in surprise.

"No really!" He put his telescope case down and fished his wallet out of his back pocket. He pulled out three cards and handed them over to her but stayed standing where he was. When appearing non-threatening it was best not to move around too much. She scanned each one.

"University of Maryland student ID card, driver's license for Arthur Snyder—hello, Arthur—and a membership card for the AstroTerps?"

"The amateur astronomers' group at UMD. I'm also a part of the Delmarva Stargazer Society, but they don't have cards."

"You drive to Delaware to look at stars?"

"And Pennsylvania, and Virginia. But mostly for bigger events, like meteor showers or something."

"Right, well." She nodded in deep understanding. "If it's for the big guys..."

"If I'm interrupting something I can go."

"Oh no. Not necessary." She took the pile of books off the chair next to her and gestured for him to sit down. He sat, surprised but pleased.

"So, Arthur, you're a grad student at UMD?"

"Recent graduate. I have a postdoc position up in Baltimore."

"You have your PhD already? Nerd."

Arthur let out a startled laugh.

"Well, yes, that's accurate."

"What brings you to my humble rooftop?" she asked, flipping through his ID cards again.

"I just finished interviewing for an adjunct position. I saw this building and thought I might be able to see better up here." He patted the telescope case at his feet.

"Did you get the job?"

"I did," he said, pleased with himself. Arthur felt something large and heavy in his chest begin to ease, like there was some great muscle that bound his whole body finally relaxing after carrying a heavy invisible weight. A kick of panic shot through him at the unfamiliar sensation.

"I can leave," he said suddenly. "I don't want to interrupt your evening. Or if you have plans—"

She didn't even turn to look at him as she waved a dismissive hand.

"You're not interrupting," she said. "I come up here to do my homework while my friend works down in the studio. I'm kind of on call in case he needs me."

"Oh." Arthur settled back in the lawn chair. "I was afraid the building was closed."

"Technically it is but—" She cut off and shot him a sideways glance.

"What?"

"You familiar with the phrase 'snitches get stitches,' Arthur?"

"Yes." He grinned. "Relax, you can trust me."

She considered him for a moment before going on.

"Well," she said. "My friend is very particular about his process. He hates working with an audience. Prefers if everyone sees only his finished pieces. So he comes in and works nights when we aren't *technically* supposed to be here."

"He has a key?"

"I have a key," she confessed. "I do my work-study hours in the office downstairs."

"And the teachers, the facilities staff, they don't know?"

"Of course they know. They just don't *know*."

"Plausible deniability?"

"Exactly." Alice bent over to search for something in her backpack and came up with a water bottle and a pack of electric green Snoballs. She opened the pack, hesitated, then passed one of the desserts to Arthur, who took it with a nod. They cheersed the small mounds and flakes of green coconut fluttered down onto the roof.

"When does your friend get here?" Arthur asked.

"Soon." Alice started taking apart her dessert, peeling back the layer of coconut-covered marshmallow, then breaking into the chocolate cake, laying each piece out on her lap as she worked toward the cream in the middle.

"He actually should be here already." she continued. "Maybe he's running late."

"Will he mind that I'm here?"

She grinned.

"Unlikely," she said lightly. "You know those people where, when they're working, the rest of the world just kind of stops existing?"

Arthur nodded.

"He's one of those. Even I exist only when he needs something from me."

"So, for all parties involved, us being up here—it's real and it's not real at the same time?"

"Kind of a mindfuck."

"Not really." Arthur began to relax again. "In fact, I kind of like it."

In 1995, Alice decided she'd waited long enough and finally told Arthur the truth.

"I'm pregnant."

Arthur nodded but said nothing.

"I fucked up," she says. "I fucked up, and I don't know what to do."

She stared out the front windshield at nothing. She saw nothing. Since the moment the stick turned blue, she'd stopped imagining what came next. A switch flipped and Alice felt panic bubble up in her chest and rise to her mouth, but instead of vomit it came out as laughter.

Arthur jumped and stared at her, more worried than she'd ever seen him.

"I'm fucked," she said through the giggles as she tried to calm herself down. "I'm so fucked."

"You're not fucked," Arthur said. But that only made her start laughing again.

"I am. I am. I am."

"Have you told your friend?"

Alice wiped her tears off her cheeks. A year of meeting up on the rooftop of the art building and Arthur still only ever referred to Joe as "her friend."

"He's gone. Disappeared."

"What?" Now Arthur started looking genuinely concerned.

"He dropped out!" she announced, like it was the punch line to the funniest joke in the world. "Packed up his apartment and left without a word. I haven't heard from him. No one's heard from him."

"Does the school know?"

"The school won't tell me anything. His friends from school don't know anything, either."

"His parents—"

"I've never met his parents. I don't even know their names. Just that . . . I think his dad is a judge? Or something like that. And they live in Annapolis. Oh my god, Arthur . . ." The laughter ebbed and behind it was her normal panic-induced nausea. She wrapped her arms around her waist and started rocking back and forth.

"Head between your knees," Arthur ordered. He reached into the cluttered backseat of his car, pulled out an old plastic shopping bag, and handed it to her with a shake.

"Just puke, if you need to."

"I'm pregnant," she said again quietly. "I'm pregnant . . . I'm pregnant . . . I'm pregnant."

"It's okay." He reached out to lay hand on her back. "You can do this."

"Do what?" she snapped at him. He jerked his hand back like she'd bit it. "What, am I supposed to have this thing? At twenty? This can't be happening. This can't be real. My life can't be over at twenty."

"Whoa, whoa, you are not there yet, okay?" Arthur laid his hand back on her upper back and rubbed between her shoulders. She tensed for a second at his touch, then began to relax under his slow, soothing circles. "Your life is *not* over. Now, you just found this out, so it's very fresh and—"

"Do *not* patronize me right now," she snapped, and he again took his hand back.

"Okay, you're right. You're right. I'm sorry."

She put her head in her hands. Arthur sat forward in his seat and waited.

"I don't have anywhere to go. My dad wants me out of the house by graduation, says he can't support me forever. I was supposed to move in with Joe but now he's . . ." Alice said quietly.

"I'm sure if you talk to your dad—"

"You don't know what he's like," Alice cut him off, anger melting into exhaustion. In their year of friendship, they'd both avoided bringing up the topic of parents. He only knew the basic facts, and those he'd had to pay for by offering his own personal history. He said his father died two years ago, she admitted to a dead mother. He complained about his neurotic, self-obsessed mother, she matched with her cold and absent father.

"Do you want to go to my house?" he asked.

Alice sat back in her seat, nausea ebbing. The house was another shadow. He'd told her he lived outside the city in some little suburb. That he owned the house, and that he'd been thinking of renting out the extra rooms to his friends though he hadn't gone through with it yet. But he'd never asked her over. And she'd never invited herself.

She buckled her seat belt.

"Let's go," she said.

Earlier than this scene, there was another: Arthur quizzing Alice on the names of his telescopes.

"Ah yes, the orange one." Alice tried to remember. The telescope was orange. Orange like ginger, like a redhead. Who's a famous redhead?

"Archie!" she shouted triumphantly, bouncing in her seat and sloshing her Slurpee. They'd been meeting up for months at this point. It was late summer, and they were celebrating the physics department's decision to hire him full time as junior faculty. When he told her, she made a joke about him arriving just as she was departing. She'd sent in the last of her Intent-To-Graduate paperwork that same morning. They were glad for their new beginnings and sore at the thought of a shared potential ending.

Arthur insisted they celebrate their accomplishments properly, so he drove them both to the nearest 7-Eleven, bought a white-and-blue cooler, and together they assembled a feast. Mini Utz potato chip bags, white powdered donuts, Lunchables, apple hand pies, and a Big Gulp Slurpee for each of them. Arthur even went next door and bought a bottle of cheap vodka to mix with the blue raspberry ice drinks. The salt and sugar and vodka did their job. Their tongues were blue and everything, for once in their lives, seemed painless.

"Yes!" Arthur gave her a high five. It was the first one she'd gotten right on the first try. "and Archie stands for . . ."

". . . Archibald Andrews?"

"Archimedes."

"Merlin's little owl friend."

"The ancient astronomer and mathematician."

Alice raised her eyebrows and signaled for him to go on.

". . . and Merlin's little owl buddy."

"Does your mother know how affected you were by all those Arthurian bedtime stories?"

"I'm sure she does, and I'm sure she's very proud of her handiwork." Arthur took another swig from his Slurpee and made a face. The vodka had sunk to the bottom so now every sip went down like a shot. "I lucked out, though, with the Arthur thing. My father wanted to name me Douglas."

"Doug?" Alice leaned back and looked him over. "You are *not* a Doug."

"Who picked out your name?" The question was out of his mouth before he realized what he'd done. Usually, a mention of her parents and Alice would snap shut like a clamshell and stay guarded the rest of the night. He froze and waited for her to close down, but she didn't. If anything, she looked a little further away than usual, but she stayed with him, and miraculously she kept talking.

"I know my father wanted Alice because it was his grandmother's name. Well . . ." She swirled her Slurpee like wine. "Really, he wanted a boy. He wanted Frederick Miller V, but he got me instead. But my mom . . . I'm not sure but I think she wanted to name me Daisy."

"Daisy," Arthur repeated, testing it out. "I like it."

"I like it to. She was Rose, and she was always gardening, so I think she liked the flower thing. But I'm Alice instead."

"I like Alice, too," Arthur tried reassuring her. "Alice is nice."

"*Alice in Wonderland. Alice Through the Looking-Glass.* You know, I've never even read those books? I think my mom read me bedtime stories, but I can't... I don't remember any of the actual stories."

"Not in school, either?"

"Nope." She shook her head. "Lots of Bible stories, not a lot of fantasy."

They both drank from their cups. Alice looked up at the fading evening light.

"What's your birthday again?" she asked. Arthur felt her trying to drive the conversation back to safer ground and he let her.

"October tenth."

"Mmm." She nodded. "So, you're a Libra."

"Don't. Start." He walked into the trap happily.

"A Libra, very interesting, very interesting. I'm an Aries, so that doesn't bode well for us generally..."

"The Zodiac is not real." Arthur turned to her, playing up his irritation, getting her to smile. "It is a made-up system of imaginary lines, and it *cannot* predict the future. You can't see the future up there. No future, just the past."

"Is that supposed to be deep?"

"No, literally, all light we experience here on Earth is old. Sunlight? Eight minutes old. The next closest star is Alpha Centauri and that light takes four years to reach us."

"So, if a star goes out it doesn't blink out of the sky right away."

"Correct, 'right away' isn't a thing. 'Gone' isn't a thing, either."

"Hold on." She turned to him. "'Right away' isn't a thing, that's fine. Space is big."

"Space *is* big," he agreed. A part of him thought it was time to stop drinking his sugar-vodka, but another, stupider, part of him didn't want to "waste" the money he'd spent so he took another sip. "So big."

"Right. But let's say the sun goes out, the light disappears—"

"It can't disappear, that's what I'm saying, it doesn't pop out of existence, it just changes form. The hydrogen becomes helium or energy. When the hydrogen burns up, the star becomes a red giant or a white dwarf. Sometimes a black hole. But even still a black hole is *something*, a mysterious something but still." He hiccupped and Alice stifled a snort of laughter at the sound. "The universe is frugal," he went on. "It reuses everything it can to make something else. Everything here"—he gestured out to the roof and the treetops and potentially the crickets—"everything here was once something else. These bodies you and I have hold carbon and oxygen that used to burn in the heart of some star four and a half billion years ago. We used to be other things, and . . ." He slumped back. "And when we're gone, we'll become something else."

"So, nothing dead is ever gone," Alice said.

Arthur nodded.

"And everything past is present."

"Elementally, yes."

"I like that fact," Alice said. She sounded dreamy to Arthur's ears. Or was that just the remembering that made her sound that way?

"That's a nice fact," she said.

"I'm not sure a fact can be good or bad. It just is."

"But it can make you feel a certain way, can't it?" She turned to him as she thought aloud. "We were nice stars. A fact that has beauty."

"But isn't that just more of humans drawing lines in the sky and pretending it means something? The universe exists with or without us to observe or understand it. It can be known or unknown, useful or not useful, but its reality isn't determined by our experience of it. What you or I find beautiful, someone else could find depressing or unnerving."

Alice nodded and passed him a little Lunchable. Dinnertime.

A crashing noise rang out from downstairs in the studio loud enough to reach them up on the roof and over the music. Alice and Arthur froze and listened. A second crash, wood and metal, muffled cursing. Arthur had learned this was a signal for Alice. The friend in the studio, Arthur called him her boyfriend once and she emphatically denied the title, would crash around louder and louder until Alice went down to scream it out with him, then there'd be an awful silence, then she'd come back. On any other night she would have gone. But tonight she stayed where she was.

Arthur's mind whirred. He'd never officially met the friend in the studio. Arthur knew he was a student the same year and age as Alice, that they slept together and worked together, and that the spell of destruction unfolding below them was a common occurrence. They'd never exchanged names, never spoken, but had made eye contact sometimes as Arthur made his way up to meet Alice on the roof. The friend never came up to them. Arthur never walked through the studio. Alice avoided talking about the friend to Arthur, and, he assumed, avoided talking about their meetings on the roof with him. If she'd asked, though, he would have been honest. He would have told her the friend reminded him of his father, and she would have known exactly what that meant.

A third crash, this time cascading. Maybe a table or a cart being overturned?

"What if something is true but not beautiful, not useful?" Arthur asked quietly, not daring to look at her. "If the fact doesn't do anyone any good, changes nothing practically and only causes pain, should we still admit it?"

"Don't make it sound simple when it isn't," Alice whispered back, pained.

"One day the sun will die and swallow the earth. We know this. It is a fact. But do we tell a child this when she asks? No, because the facts of existence are sometimes too large and too painful for people to hear. And if hearing them and knowing them doesn't actually change anything, then why say it? Why choose pain if you don't have to?"

Alice stayed wound tight, face unreadable for another few seconds, then eased back into her chair.

A yell from below. Frustration or pain.

Arthur turned up the music on the boom box and sucked at the insides of his cheeks to keep from smiling.

In 1995, Arthur pulled up to the brick split-level house at 4321 Artemesia Drive, praying that the neighborhood kids weren't there in case even the sight of children was enough to make Alice reject the possible future he was showing her. Three of them, the brothers from three houses down, walked past with a basketball as he parked. He watched Alice's face for any hint of a reaction, but she didn't even glance at them. He wanted to start talking just to fill the empty air. To explain why he had it, how he got it, why he picked it, what he wanted to do with it, how it could be improved, but instead he just got the door for her and led her up the walkway.

He let her in to the small foyer and then she took over the tour. She went downstairs first and walked into every room, flipping light switches, making small "hmms."

He waited at the door of every room as she inspected.

It's not done, he wanted to say. *I know it's just boxes and dust, but I haven't really unpacked and furniture is expensive.*

He said nothing and waited.

They went upstairs, wood stairs creaking loudly.

Real wood! he wanted to say.

He said nothing and followed.

The upper floors seemed much more to her liking. She spent a fair amount of time in the front room with the large bay window. She barely looked at the kitchen and bathrooms but took a clear interest in the two smaller bedrooms on the top floor across the hall from the master.

She poked her head into Arthur's setup in the largest bedroom. A mattress on the floor. A milk crate nightstand. A pile of wrinkled clean clothes on a metal foldout chair and a pile of wrinkled dirty clothes in the far corner.

"Really?" she asked him.

"I've been busy! And what's the point of a bed frame, really?"

"You own a house but no furniture?"

"Well, the bank owns the house, and I'm just buying it from them very, very slowly."

She walked back out to the living room.

Arthur followed.

Alice put her hands on her hips and looked around again, nodding.

"I can make this work," she said. "Now don't get ahead of yourself," she warned him as his face lit up. "I can't pay rent right away because I still need to find work, and I don't know what's going to happen with my... I don't think I can count on any financial support from my—well, from anyone actually—for my medical stuff, you know, for the..." She cleared her throat like she was angry at her own mouth for tripping over the words. "For the *birth*," she ground out. "But I think I can make this work."

At first, he was confused, trying to catch up with the speed of her. But as soon as the meaning of her words came into focus, he felt stupid for not seeing it before. Of course, Alice should stay with him. Her father was kicking her out, the friend was MIA. She needed a safe place to live while she figured things out, and he needed to know she was okay. And why the hell did he have this stupid place if he couldn't use it to give help when help was needed. It was not perfect, but so obviously right.

"Rent is whenever. I can afford this place on my own and—"

"That's the other thing—" Alice cut him off. "How do you even have this place? The short version, please."

Arthur nodded, mentally searching for the nearest route through the story.

"So, you know my dad died two years ago?"

She nodded and crossed her arms.

"Well, we were never . . . we weren't close. He wasn't an easy man to get along with, and he didn't care much about trying. So when he got sick all he wanted to talk about was the money. Who's getting what and how much and how exactly it should be handled after he was gone. My mom is . . . well I've mentioned before, she's not the most together person, so she wanted me to deal with all of it. So he's giving me all these detailed instructions about how he expects me to live and how to take care of my mother, which is pretty rich coming from him since he's been bullying her pretty much since the day they got married. One time, she told me about this time, when they were still newlyweds, he didn't like her tone of voice, so he threw a plate of spaghetti—"

"Arthur."

"Right." He waved away the side story. "So, he's dying and all he cares about is making sure the lawyers don't get his money. I mean, the man is facing death and that's seriously all he ever wanted to talk about. So he tells me, doesn't ask, just tells me that I'll be moving back home after grad school to take care of my mom and manage the house. It's not even a conversation, he just draws up this account with a manager and those two decide how it'll go. And then—um..." Arthur bit the inside of his cheek to keep his emotions in check.

"And then he died. It was really slow and then really sudden. And a little after that I was sitting at home with my mother, and it was the stupidest little thing—" Arthur ran a hand through his hair and kept his eyes on the ground. "We were just talking about what to have for dinner and I suggested ordering a pizza because we were both exhausted, but my mother says, 'Your father says pizza isn't dinner' and my next thought was 'Fine I'll make some pasta' and a second later I thought 'Who cares what he thinks, he's dead.' And after that thought I just went through everything and tried to think of it all without him. Because he was dead. Gone. And I don't have to listen to a ghost. So I took the money he left me, and I bought this place."

Arthur looked around at the empty rooms and, though he couldn't yet think of them as "home," he at least thought of them as "mine."

"No one thought it was a good idea," he admitted. "My mom thought I was having a breakdown. None of my friends get it, they think I just shot myself in the foot committing to a mortgage. That no one wants to date a guy who is already set up at a house, but I just needed it. I needed permanent."

He'd never had to explain himself like this before, and the more he talked the less clear it was to him. Alice, however, recognized it and named it for him.

"You wanted a safe place," she said. "And when you couldn't find it, and no one would give you one, you decided to make one for yourself."

"Yes." Arthur half laughed, surprised and a little pained for the shame of being seen. "Yes, I think you got it there. Well done."

Alice stared at the floor now, as well, building up to something. Arthur waited, relieved his time to talk was over.

"Do you mind," she started, "I mean, can I live here ... with you? Would that be alright?"

"Yes." Arthur smiled. "I think that would be great."

"And the baby, you know, *obviously*."

"I figured that might be a part of the deal when I suggested you check the place out."

"Did you?" Alice huffed, getting exasperated. "I mean, really, have you *really* thought about this? You want a single mother and her newborn baby staying here. You want to be in for the trip to the hospital, the night feedings, the shit that I imagine will be everywhere, all over every surface of your house?"

"I want you to be okay," he said. "I want your baby to have a safe place to cry at night, and to throw up everywhere, and the shit everywhere. And honestly, you know, no! I don't know everything for sure!" He laughed and threw his hands up. "I've never done this before, *you've* never done this before, and we're probably going to fuck a lot of this up, but you're going to do this. Then, as your friend, I'm going to do what I can to help. And besides, I was always going to use this house to rent out to friends."

"This is a lot more than just—" she started.

"I can do this. I can help," he reassured her. "So let me help."

A week before Alice's graduation from Kenning, Arthur drove to the Miller residence in D.C. for the first and only time. She was waiting for him on the stoop, bags packed, boxes taped and labeled, and not a hint of sadness. The sight of her stunned him. The way she bounced her knees while she waited, the way she clutched the plastic bag in her lap like it was a life preserver or a teddy bear. He'd never seen her look so young.

They packed the car up quickly. Miraculously everything fit. Alice said that was a good sign. Her father never showed, and Arthur didn't ask. She kept the plastic bag in her lap all through the drive and it was the first thing she brought into the house when they started unpacking. Alice never explained what it was or why it was so precious, and Arthur never asked.

A month after they'd moved in together, Arthur in the master and Alice in the next biggest bedroom, Arthur finally asked how, exactly, she was planning to afford her pregnancy and birth. She was showing. She should be going to the doctor more often, should have prenatal vitamins.

"I don't have the money," she said. She'd been picking up all the work she could doing alterations and tailoring for costume shops and bridal boutiques, but people didn't know her well enough yet to give her more. Without insurance, she'd have to start this new life under the weight of massive hospital debt. She needed more time to find a real job, she said, but the time would not appear.

He brought her to the couch, sat her down, told her to let him talk all the way through without interruption, and then he got down on his knee and took her hands in his.

"I want you to marry me," he said. "You can get on my insurance, you can make this place your home. You can take my last name, or don't, either is fine. But, Alice, *I need you to be okay*. And right now? You are scaring the shit out of me. I can't—" he sputtered as he released his frustration. "I can't sleep sometimes because I can't stop thinking about everything that could go wrong. What if you go into labor and you can't get to the hospital yourself? What if you need a C-section? You could die and—" Alice sank back further into the couch, like she was trying to pull away from his words.

"I'm not going to die," she said, squeezing his hands hard in her own.

"You can't," he said weakly. "I don't think I could live with myself if I didn't do everything possible to make sure you are okay. I don't have family, not like other people do, and I know you don't, either . . ." He trailed off as he tried to bring his point home. Finally he let out a heavy sigh, straightened his back, and look her straight in the eye. "I'm not asking you to be my wife. I'm asking you to be my family. And I am asking that you let me be your family, too. We can go to the courthouse and do the paperwork and get you to a doctor, but really, I'm telling you that I want to be in this *with you* for the long haul. So, what do you think?"

"I think you should get up here and sit down before your knee seizes up." She patted the sofa next to her. Arthur managed not to groan while he stood up and took his place at her side. He tried to limit how much he stared at her, but he was desperate for some kind of reaction. But there was none. She looked calm. Calmer than he'd maybe ever seen her. She was staring at the opposite wall sort of dreamily like she was imagining paint colors or deciding what decoration to hang there.

"You did a good job," she said politely.

"Yeah?" Arthur turned to her. "I had a whole other thing planned but then I just—whoosh—forgot it all and just went with what I was trying to say."

"No, it was good." She smoothed her shirt over the curve of her growing stomach. "Not just a wife. Family."

"Family."

"I have no idea what I'm doing," she warned.

"Neither do I," he said. "But I'd rather figure out big problems with you than face even small problems without you."

Alice seemed to take that in. She started slowly nodding.

"I'm not as afraid of things when I know you'll be there," she said.

"I think that's a good start."

"I do, too."

"So . . . ?" Arthur prodded.

"Yes," Alice said. She looked light, not happy, not squealing or crying with joy like he'd seen with TV proposals, but settled, confident, sure. He collapsed back on the couch in exhaustion.

She held out her hand to him, and he held it in his own.

A week later they established the ground rules of how their marriage would go. That Arthur would raise the child, that he would be the father in place of the father who wasn't there. That they would keep their separate bedrooms. That they would be partners in this. That they would talk even when it seemed impossible, and that neither, no matter how bad it got, would suddenly disappear. They were not, either of them, alone anymore or for the rest of their lives. They agreed to these vows, as some might call them. They agreed to this new life with their eyes open, pleasantly surprised at how sure each of them was that the other told the truth. Letting everyone assume it was his child seemed a rather small detail in the grand scheme of it there at the beginning. It was mostly for the benefit of Arthur's mother, retired and rich as she was, to allow the possibility of financial support. They were in this together and every lie was jointly told.

On a Thursday in July, when sudden and violent rainstorms overpowered the overbright summer sun, Arthur and Alice got married at the courthouse and every stranger assumed what the pair had intended. Older male, young, pregnant female, no witnesses. They celebrated with a picnic on the floor of the living room back at home, with a wedding feast of pizza for dinner and Snoballs for their wedding cake.

In the beginning of autumn, Arthur secretly hoped the baby would be born in October, as he had been, so they would be marked this additional way as a pair. He took Alice to see the new visiting exhibition at the National Gallery of Art. The friend had said he would take her when it had been announced, so once more Arthur stepped into the space where the friend was not.

They walked shoulder to shoulder past the entrance sign.

Pre-Raphaelites: Art and Design, 1848–1900

"Fifty-two years?" Arthur whispered. "That's nothing. Hubble Space Telescope took pictures of galaxies thirteen billion years old. That's old. You can't get anything done in fifty-two years."

Alice swatted him lightly and walked over to the opposite wall. He'd noticed she liked to look at things out of order, always starting somewhere in the middle or close to the end before jumping back to the actual beginning. Arthur fell into his own rotation, letting the crowd pull him along in the intended order.

He found Alice again an hour later, sitting hunched in one of the back rooms staring up at a large painting of a woman. There was so much happening in the single frame he had to take a step back to take it all in. The woman was tangled in a mess of fine thread, her skirt puckered and bunched in odd places, her hands twisted out as she tried to pry herself free. Her brown hair was fanned out above her like a cirrus cloud, waved and wispy. The figure was standing inside a large circular frame on the floor. Everything was colorful and intricate from the ceiling to the floor. Directly behind her was a mirror, and reflected there was a tree line, a knight on horseback. Then Arthur saw that the room was half covered in shadow.

He sat down next to Alice on the bench.

"This is my favorite one," she said.

"Why?" he asked. She shrugged. She always shrugged when the answer was personal.

"It's the Lady of Shalott," she explained. "It's from a Tennyson poem."

"'There she weaves by night and day,'" Arthur recited.

"A magic web with colours gay.

She has heard a whisper say,

A curse is on her if she stay,

To look down to Camelot.'"

Alice watched him speak with shock plain on her face.

"Excuse me?" she said. "Where the hell did that come from?"

He laughed.

"They made me memorize it in school," he admitted. "I guess it stuck."

"I'd say so, yeah."

"She was trapped in the tower and she was weaving a picture of the world using that mirror but if she ever looked straight out at the world she died, right?"

"Basically. She hears Lancelot singing and she can't help but to go look at him directly even though she knows she'll die."

"What is she standing in?" Arthur asked.

"A giant loom. See there?" Alice leaned into him and pointed at something in the frame. She smelled like soap and roses.

"Wasn't she based on Elaine of Astolat?" He scrambled for any other half-remembered details. "Elaine was in love with Lancelot, who was in love with Guinevere. There was a tapestry in the last room with the knights of the round table, did you see it? I think it was made by Morris?"

"Designed," she corrected him.

"Hm?"

"He didn't make it, he *designed* it. They never list who actually wove it, but I assume they were women. Men are designers and women are fabricators. I doubt history would remember it if it was *women's work*," she sneered in a clear impersonation of someone. Arthur raised his eyebrows.

"Touchy subject," she explained.

"Good to know." He took in the rest of the room again. "I can see why you like this era so much."

Alice rolled her eyes.

"You mean 'cause I look like the Pre-Raphaelite girls?" she said.

"No, I meant . . ." That was what he meant, but he scrambled for another reason.

"It's fine." She waved away whatever he was going to come up with. "I've heard it a lot. I can't help who I look like. Her name was Elizabeth Siddal." Alice pointed to a tall painting over on their left of an angel poking a towering redhead with a stick. "She was one of their most used models. Especially with Rossetti. He used her all the time. Even married her at one point."

"Didn't last long?"

"She died. Wasted away. He never really wanted to marry her anyway; he just wanted to have her around."

"How do you know all this?" Arthur asked.

"I read the letters he wrote to his friends. Primary sources. First-hand accounts."

"Did you write a paper on them?"

"Gabriel was obsessed with them." The shock of hearing his name stunned Arthur into a temporary silence. He was so used to "the friend" or even just "him." Alice had even let him read the email where he'd renamed himself. Where he'd left Joe Turner and Alice Miller behind. With a pang Arthur realized both names were gone. Alice Miller was Alice Snyder now. She asked to take his name, and he gave it gladly. It was Gabriel Grant, Alice Snyder, and plain, reliable Arthur Snyder to round out the three.

Arthur stood up, suddenly needing to be anywhere but near a Rossetti.

"Well, I've seen your favorite. Do you want to see mine?" he asked.

"You have a favorite?" Alice raised an eyebrow.

"Hey, I can like art. I surprised you with that poem, didn't I?"

"You did," she admitted. He took her hands and counterbalanced her weight to pull her up. She followed him back to the connecting room. On the interior wall, just past the entrance, was a small, shadowy painting. A woman was placed center under an ivy-covered arch. Her right arm was crossed over her body, and she looked down and away, conflicted and intense. Alice recognized it on sight.

"*April Love*. Hughes, I think."

"You could be a tour guide."

"Maybe when I'm retired," she said. "Why is it your favorite?"

"Because it is. I came back to it three times. Didn't do that with the other paintings."

"But *why* did you keep coming back?"

"Because," he said slowly. "I like the story in it. She's conflicted. She's running away. She's doing something. A lot of these are pictures of ladies doing . . . not a lot. Brushing their hair, sleeping. I mean they're very pretty, but there's not a lot going on."

"But you like the one with the secret love affair?"

"What?" Arthur leaned in to look closer, but he didn't see it. "What love affair? There's a girl, there's ivy, there's a pretty purple skirt. I see no affair."

Alice pointed to the shadows on the girl's left.

"There. That's a guy. It's called *April Love*. It's about love in April."

Arthur tried seeing it again but failed.

"I don't see it. And I like my version better."

"How can you not see it?" she said, laughing. "It's right there."

"I'm not so sure it is," he countered.

"Fine!" She gave in. "You see what you see, and I'll know what I know."

"Was this model the same redhead as before?" he asked.

"No, they had a few. This one's name was Tryphena."

"Terrible name!" Arthur rocked back on his heels. "What kind of parents name their daughter Tryphena?"

"I'm sure it was appropriate for the time." Alice stepped in closer to the painting. "You know, I think I'm beginning to see what you're saying about the lover."

"You see? Purple was always one of my favorite colors. That and yellow."

Alice looked over at him in disgust.

"Mardi Gras colors, really?"

"Are you telling me *that* is not a good color?" He pointed to the girl's skirt. "Or *that*?" He pointed to the gilded frame.

"Well, first of all, Dr. Snyder, *that* is not yellow," she said of the frame. "*That* is gold. And that skirt isn't purple, it's violet."

"Violet," he said with sudden inspiration. "Violet is a much better name for a girl."

Alice cocked her head as she studied the painting. Then she reached out a hand and Arthur took it.

"I agree," she said. "Violet is a good name for a girl."

Thresholds (little failures)
2012

Alice Snyder
American, 1974–2017

Fabric doorways

Enjoying its premiere here at the National Museum of Women in the Arts, Snyder's *Thresholds (little failures)* is a fascinating contribution to the artist's body of work. While the title suggests that the artist herself was unhappy with the end result in some way, she nevertheless passed it on to her agent for consideration where it stayed in limbo for years. Upon rediscovery of these pieces, Snyder's agent, Dee Ng, worked with Snyder's daughter and assistant, Marigold Snyder, to help with the reconstruction.

    This piece also marks the end of Snyder's body of work created solely by her own hand. As her pieces grew larger and more ambitious, she began renting larger studio spaces in warehouses and business parks, hiring local art students as assistants to bring her visions to life. While production of her pieces may have outgrown the house on Artemesia Drive, Snyder maintained her home studio as her artistic safe space, jokingly referring to ideas that were quickening at home but not yet ready for fabrication and that needed more time as "in the incubator."

    These spectral doorways are made from sewn, stiff gauze and show the embroidered outline of a female figure as she walks through her home. As you walk through this series of three doorways, try to track the path of the embroidered outline and identify which minor action she is meant to be taking in each scene. *Thresholds (little failures)*, showcases Snyder's lightest embroidery work, often only using single pieces of thread to capture whole images. Notice that she's left the end of each strand loose and hanging from the gauze where the intention lines end without tying off. The only other time we see this technique repeated was in *Veiled Seascape* earlier in this room.

In 1996, Alice sat on a pile of pillows on the floor of the dining room and watched Arthur bounce a six-month-old Violet in the backyard.

I am grateful. Alice mouthed the words and waited for gratitude to come.

Nothing. She tried again.

I am grateful. She sat back on her pillows and sighed.

Motherless, girlfriendless Alice had not been warned of what would happen to her in birth. She knew the facts, as given by her doctor, but she had been in no way properly prepared for the tearing she would live with, not just in her body, but in her mind and soul as well. That she would willingly rip herself. That she would need so long to heal from that tear. At least, one of the nurses had commented, at least you're a natural nurser. And it was true. That may have been her favorite part. Not the pain and pressure in her breasts that equally scared and fascinated her, but the blissful moments of silence she was given while Violet's mouth was too busy to cry.

She would hesitate to admit it to anyone but her husband, but the worst part was actually her hair. Always it had been waist-length and barely shaped. Always, it had marked her. First as her mother's daughter, then as a rare beauty, and later, in the Gabriel years, as his perfect muse. Alice didn't think she'd had a special connection with her looks outside of their usefulness in Gabriel's pictures. But then came the time after birth. The time when she could barely clean herself regularly. When the hormones made her mane twice as thick, which made it twice as hard to keep clean. She was constantly picking out lint and crumbs, wiping away sprays of milk or urine. It got tangled constantly and bred ratty nests at the back of her head. Arthur tried his best to brush and wash it for her when he coaxed her into the bath, but it was beyond him. They didn't have the money for a hairdresser, but when she asked him for it, he found a way to get it. And one Saturday afternoon the three of them went to a salon in a strip mall and a beauty student cut off the rat's nest length of her hair into a look she'd later call "the mom-bob."

She thought of cowboys breaking mustangs. She thought of farmers branding cows.

She forced herself to think, *I am grateful.*

Alice let go a bit at that moment and started assuming the change was permanent. That in order to pull a new life out of you, some part of her must have died. She assumed this must just be the price of it.

She watched from a distance as she turned in on herself, and Arthur turned out like a leaf to the sunlight. As she slowed, he quickened to counter. He got them on his insurance as soon as he could. Got the university to cut him some slack on his work hours so he could take her and Violet to the doctors. And when the diagnoses came back, colic and postpartum depression, he tracked down the help they needed. He told the same lie over and over to his employers, to his mother, about how he knocked her up and now he had to take responsibility, and couldn't they all just find it in themselves to help just a little bit. And they did. The old ladies that worked in HR felt for him and pushed paperwork through. His mother, a woman Alice knew for a fact hated her, managed to lend them a small monthly allowance for supplies and food. If Arthur was ashamed of all this, he didn't show it to her. Alice saw no trace of resentment, just his open friendly face making allies where there were only strangers.

Alice's new doctor was waiting before trying pills. He wanted to see if he could get her better with just words. So now, in addition to the feeding and shitting and the reorganization of her body on a cellular level, she also had to do homework. This lesson was about gratitude. About appreciating the things she had to help get over the things she'd lost. So, every day when Arthur came home from work he pulled on a baby vomit-stained shirt, fed Violet outside, and let her scream into the open air for a while so Alice could practice being grateful by herself. She watched them through the glass of the back patio door, swaying and bouncing in the shaded part of the yard.

Alice watched Violet scrunch up her little face and hike up her legs as Arthur bounced her. Arthur jerked his head around to look at Violet in surprise, then he switched his hold and held out the arm that had been supporting her butt. A trickle of liquid baby shit trailed down the inside of his arm. Arthur looked stunned, and a faraway part of Alice braced for his reaction. For the anger she'd been silently expecting since the first day she moved in and accidentally spilled water on one of his articles, but he did now as he had done before. He laughed. He looked disgusted, yes, but still he laughed.

Her eyes followed him as he walked to the spigot at the bottom back corner of the house where the hose was. She waited to hear him, at the very least, say something to Violet about blowing out her diaper on his arm, but he merely hiked the baby up higher on his other arm, and held the offending limb out to his side as he walked. She was confused, even disappointed. Not that she wanted Arthur to finally break, but she wished he would, at least once, have a reaction she could clearly recognize.

I am grateful, she mouthed, mind slipping like a raw egg from one thought to the next.

I am grateful.

By the end of April, Arthur was in the same place, repeating the same soothing sway, now dressed like a reject Big Lebowski. He was at the absolute end of his non-stinky laundry options and so bounced Violet around the backyard after work in swim trunks, plastic work boots, and a bright yellow T-shirt he'd forgotten he owned. On it was a brown illustration of Woodstock, the bird from Peanuts, with a speech bubble over his head filled with exclamation points. Violet gave a wet cough and Arthur pulled back to see if she'd spit up. He found a small dark spot on the dish towel he had draped over his shoulder. He hiked the rag up further so she wouldn't have to put her cheek against the wet part and wiped at the side of his neck with the back of his hand. Violet cooed once, a little loudly, rubbed her face into his shoulder, and quieted back down.

He already had so much more than he'd thought was possible for himself. His old life, the one he'd kept purposely small to avoid the risk of any real loss, had been blown up by the arrival of Alice and Violet in his life. Now he felt he had real purpose. Not just a job or a way to spend his time, but an all-encompassing, all-consuming vocation that imbued even his smallest decisions with importance. He had to save money to pay for Violet's doctor visits. He couldn't pull an all-nighter at work because he had to go home to relieve Alice from baby duty. He a reason to do things now. A reason he'd chosen. Like some kind of modern monk dedicating himself to a higher calling, to a life of service outside himself. He never had to think of himself these days, and that was a relief.

Baths and naps. These were Arthur's true calling in life, he'd discovered. Now that the worst of the colic was behind them, Violet seemed ready to pass out on Arthur's chest any time of the day or night. And the baths. Alice was concerned her arms weren't big enough to properly hold a squirming, soap-slick baby, so Arthur was in charge of bathing Violet in the kitchen sink in the evenings. The last time he'd talked to his mother on the phone, after explaining once more that he couldn't drag his newborn and depressed wife to Northern Virginia for a visit, she'd said his baby skills came from his large, warm chest and strong heartbeat. The heartbeat reminded the little thing of being in the womb, she said. His mother never actually used his daughter's proper name and had even tried convincing him to name the child something more "normal" after Alice had given birth. Violet was never Violet, but the baby, the little thing, my granddaughter, and occasionally, bizarrely, Emily. Alice was never Alice, either. But that was less of a name issue and more of a you-trapped-my-son-with-a-baby issue. Alice was always your friend, or your special houseguest, and once, with sarcasm, your loving wife.

Each barb was a little gold star of success. It meant she believed him. It meant she bought the lie. The doctor had finally agreed to let Alice take some medicine and she'd begun showering regularly again. Arthur stayed by her side, asking little follow-up questions about her pump schedule, her sleep schedule, her food intake. Now he was the one that fell asleep first, often on the couch. Now she was the one who made him get up, brush his teeth, and go to bed properly. They still had separate bedrooms at this point—Alice and Violet in the smaller room and Arthur in his large one—but the lines had been blurring since Arthur first accompanied her to a sonogram and cried when he heard the baby's heartbeat. Arthur would bottle-feed Violet in their room. Alice would sneak a nap on Arthur's more comfortable bed when she got the chance. It was all of them, together, all the time, and next to that the sleeping arrangements just didn't seem that important.

They were not the ghosts they had been, but they weren't quite human yet, either. Alice was still healing, surrounding her body with pillows before sitting, and stuck to a uniform of pajamas, overlarge exercise wear, and Arthur's shirts. Arthur stopped speeding home after every errand out of fear something had happened to Alice or the baby during the thirty minutes he wasn't keeping an eye on them.

It was so nice out that day. Arthur knew he should bring Violet in and put her down in her crib for her afternoon nap, but the sun felt too good on his skin. There was a slight breeze. Comet Hale-Bopp would be passing soon. He had planned to go see it but the motivation he'd had to seek out those passing marvels had dimmed considerably. It had started before the birth, before the marriage even. Probably it had been that day he went to get Alice in the basement of the art building. The day he realized he wasn't the only one in their little kinship who didn't have anyone else, either.

The phone rang inside the house. Everyone he was willing to talk to right now was here. Everyone else could wait. He heard Alice pick up and speak to whoever was on the line. Eventually life's needs called back to him louder and he returned with Violet to the house. Laundry, dishes, shopping, cooking, cleaning, unpacking. All of it pressing, but only one could be done at a time. The shower in the master bathroom started and a tightly wound spring in Arthur's chest relaxed a bit. Alice was showering. Her second that week. Without having to be reminded.

Finally, he thought, *she's starting to come back.*

He put Violet down in her room and crept from room to room gathering all the dirty clothes he could find, which was to say all the clothes he could find. He sorted the laundry downstairs, mixed ownership but separated by color, and at the last minute peeled his Woodstock T-shirt off and draped it on top of the brights. He stretched and heard a series of little pops deep inside his body in his lower back. He scratched his bare stomach, a bit rounder than usual. He couldn't remember the last time he'd gone for a run. What a luxury that seemed now, to take a whole hour out of the day to loop his neighborhood. Arthur stood in the laundry room, listening to the rush of water through the pipes in the exposed ceiling above him, and waited until he heard the shower shut off before starting the washer.

Upstairs the pantry door was off its hinges and leaned against the far wall of the kitchen. Another thing he needed to take care of eventually, but one that was so far down the list it might as well not exist. The adult food was down to a quarter gallon of milk, cereal, boxed rice, canned tuna, cheese slices, and beef jerky. The baby food, at least, was well stocked thanks to his mother. He was starting to jot down what they needed with a Sharpie and a paper napkin when he heard Alice leave the bedroom.

"Do you need anything from the grocery store?" he asked as he pulled a moldy bag of bread out from a drawer and tossed it in the trash. "I think I can get to the store tomorrow if you can watch Vi for a few hours," he rambled on. "Or I can stay, and you can shop if you want. Oh, and there's laundry going so if you suddenly have nothing to wear it's because everything in this house smells like pureed carrots and spit up."

Arthur looked up and froze. The Alice hesitating in the doorway of the kitchen was an Alice he hadn't seen for a very long time. It wasn't just the clean, damp hair or the dress he didn't recognize. It was the faint scent of her rosewater perfume, something he hadn't smelled since the rooftop days. He'd gotten so used to the sight of her unadorned that he caught now the subtle makeup she wore. Brown liner around her eyes, colored-in eyebrows, a little pink on her cheeks and lips. A flare of anger went up inside him, a bit with Alice but mostly with himself. She hadn't told him things were changing. That it was time to look good again, be a person again. Anger that she looked like that and that he was still wearing his swim trunks and rubber boots. He'd missed some obvious sign. Anger he hadn't kept up on the groceries and the laundry. That he wasn't keeping up his end of their agreement. He was angry, especially and in spite of himself, that he'd stopped running. *What did I miss?* He scrambled in his mind to find the source. There was only that phone call she'd taken while he was outside. And there was only one person he knew of with a hold on her strong enough to overpower the stasis they'd both been caught in.

"Going out?" he asked.

Even though he guessed who it was for, though he hoped he was wrong, he was happy to see her looking like herself. A seedling of fear had taken root when he'd taken her to get her hair cut—that he'd forced her to do something unforgivable—but here she was again. He could feel her being there in the room, being scared. Of him? No, never of him. Of the invisible third person in the room they lived with and tried to ignore.

"He says he finally wants to meet." She kept her eyes on his face, reading his expression. He made sure to breathe and unclench his jaw, but his body was slow to perform when it was tired.

"She's sleeping," Arthur said. Waking Violet up now and taking her out of the house would throw off her eating and sleeping schedules for the day. Which would in turn throw off her schedule for tomorrow, and presumably on and on until she was an old gray woman in a rocker bemoaning the fact her parents had ruined her eating and sleeping schedule so early in life, never to be reconciled. Alice hadn't gone out alone with the baby yet. If they went somewhere they went all together. And Violet's onesies, he remembered. He'd just put all her presentable onesies in the wash, and she shouldn't meet her maker in nothing but a diaper.

"I could try to get her ready, but the laundry—" he began.

"No, no, he wants to meet with me finally. Just me."

Arthur had a wild flailing thought: *Is this really as long as we get?*

He knew what a paternity test would reveal no matter what lies he'd told. Marriages could be annulled. Homes could be unmade and families disassembled. And the tug on a piece of string that undid the holding knot could be a surprise phone call from a man he'd never met on an unexceptional April afternoon. But what could he do? The only thing that would really make him Violet's father in place of that other man was time. And his time might now be up.

Arthur got up from his crouched position in front of the bottom drawer and went back to reinspect the empty pantry to give him something to look at besides Alice.

"He might not even know about the baby," she said suddenly. She crossed into the kitchen to keep their line of sight. Arthur couldn't help a little snort.

"No, really," she said, her voice edging into a plea. Pleading to whom? To him? To herself? "He probably doesn't. I assumed someone from the art department must have told him because they all love to gossip so much, but I never got any real proof they did. I know we did everything we could to try and get a hold of him, and we left him messages, but what if he never got them? There wasn't any response, so he could have not gotten anything. Or maybe he understands there's a baby, but he doesn't really get it yet. He's like that sometimes. He has to see something, interact with it, before he totally accepts that it's real."

Arthur imagined a stranger holding a screaming, writhing Violet. Violet calming down, drifting off into sleep, curling up to this unreal chest of her real father. Arthur started pulling out cans. The first one he set down hard and loud, sending a little shock through his own chest, so he forced himself to set down the second can over-gently.

"I don't know." Alice's voice crashed against his ears. "Maybe I'm being an idiot. I know I should be mad at him, that I should hate him, but he's just so . . . unattached . . . to everything and everyone. It's like he's visiting from somewhere else, and he just woke up one day to find himself in this body and this life he has no attachment to. When he's here, he's really here. But most of the time he's off in Joeland. Or I guess it's Gabrieland now. I don't know, Arthur. I don't know."

"Do you want to go see him?" he asked.

"Yes." The word was small, quiet, but undeniably there. "I want to go see him."

"Then go see him." Arthur stood and turned to face her, knees popping and back aching. The chorus of his insecurities started chattering at him again. With every major development Arthur expected the low thrumming fear that he could lose everything would dissipate, or at least quiet, but it only got louder. The day Alice moved in, the day he went to hear the sonogram, the day Violet was born. The chorus repeated ever louder, *They can always leave you.* Their family, his friendship, their little house, and their stable life. One decision and he'd be alone again. The louder the chorus got, the more helpless he felt. Because what could he do? He couldn't force her to stay; he had to be chosen. All he had to do was wait, he coached himself. Let her leave and then wait for her come back.

"Go see what he has to say. Tell him about Violet. Tell him about how you've been doing." He cleared his throat. "Tell him the truth about us. And maybe you're right." He finally forced himself to meet her gaze. She looked scared. Her eyes were wet, and her face was flushed. It eased his own fear to see hers. She didn't seem to know what was going to happen next, either. "Maybe he never knew about Violet. If he's really the way you say he is . . . maybe he's been in denial." He felt his voice threaten to break but he muscled out his normal tone. "Maybe this means things can get better?"

"I knew you'd understand." Alice smiled and tears escaped. She wiped them away impatiently. Arthur fought the urge to bridge their distance and hug her. Touch was difficult for her. It had been before the baby, and it was even worse after. Even the slightest brush against her and she might flinch or shrink away from him like she'd put her palm too close to an open flame. But since she'd started to see the doctor, since the meds, she'd been getting better. There was the day they stood shoulder to shoulder over Violet's crib and watched her little chest rise and fall in sleep. When Alice had caught him saying "DA-DA" over and over to Violet as he held her, she smacked him across his upper arm in play and accused him of trying to get their daughter to pick sides. And just last week there'd been an early Saturday night where Alice had leaned her head on his shoulder as they watched TV after dinner and tried to fight off sleep.

She took a shaky breath. Then, putting her head down, she crossed the room and hugged him. It wasn't like any hug he'd ever had before. And even some of the sex he'd had hadn't felt this intimate. Him shirtless, her in her dress. If she minded his chest hair or his extra weight she made no show of it. She was stronger than she looked, and she held on to him like it was easy, like they'd done this every day of their lives. He wrapped his arms around her shoulders and upper back. Enough to be there, but not so much she might feel trapped.

"I'm scared," she confessed.

He pulled away and she stepped back, but he left one hand on her arm to keep the scene going as long as he could.

"Just remember," he said, "no matter what happens, if it gets bad you can always come home."

Alice nodded once, then headed for the door. Arthur heard her stop at the top of the stairs, then head back. He was about to ask if she'd forgotten something when she suddenly appeared from around the corner again, walked straight up to him, and gave him a peck on his cheek. Just a brush of her lips against his stubbled cheek.

"I'll find a way to call you if this goes long," she said. Then she disappeared again. Arthur stood there, frozen in place, for longer than he'd ever admit before the alarm went off on the washing machine and it was time to move things along.

As Alice passed under the courtyard archway of the National Gallery of Art where they'd agreed to meet, she thought, *I am grateful*. The weighted net that held her down when she was hypnotized by the unending needs of her infant had begun lifting somewhere on the Metro ride into the city. Back into the city. She was closer to being Alice again than she'd been in months. There were endings again. Clear lines of separation that limited her to the body she was in instead of slipping her all over everywhere like some gelatinous creature brought up from the deep sea, unable to hold her form without constant pressure all around her. Here she was someone again. Herself again. She tasted the metallic, recirculated air, smelled the dull iron of the water fountain and thought, again, *I am grateful*. She searched back through her memories for the last time she'd been there with Joe—no, not Joe, Gabriel now—but the only memory that heeded her call was the day she'd gone there with Arthur and they'd found the baby's name.

She remembered being alone in the museum. Taking notes, doing figure studies. Serious, studious. And it was only logical Gabriel must have been there, too. She wouldn't have gone without him. Or more accurately, he would not have liked her going without him and so she doubted she ever would have. But no image appeared at her calling of them walking together, drawing together, sharing time. They had worked together all over the place, they had developed ideas and edited photos and developed film together in the school darkroom, they had slept together in his bed. Yet in the museum it was a series of her pictured alone with the art and ending with one bright moment with Arthur.

She walked with confidence off to the left-hand galleries. She knew she'd find him in his favorite starting spot, *The Voyage of Life* room. As she crossed, she scanned the small, rotating crowd for his familiar shape and on recognizing his back, she exhaled. Her relief reached muscles she hadn't known were tense. So she had missed him after all, she realized. She hadn't meant to get attached. She'd coached herself, for all the times they slept together, on how disinterested he was in staying in one place with one person, but still when the stick turned blue some part of her must have hoped, and that same part of her woke up at the sight of the back of his head.

More details registered as she got closer. His coat was new, the fabric still taut and even at the shoulders where she knew his messenger bag would eventually wear it down. He wore his hair longer now, wet from a shower and combed back. And as she stepped into the room, she realized with some surprise he was her same height. Even in the year they'd spent apart her memory of him had apparently begun to edit itself without her permission. She remembered him standing over her, towering, his figure stretching in her mind like a shadow in the setting sun, but perhaps that had been a trick of perspective. He did have a tendency to photograph her sitting or reclined, often climbing ladders and stools to find his upper angles.

"Gabriel?" Her hand rose to touch his shoulder, but she pulled back before they made contact. He turned and his eyes widened in surprise. There were purple-tinted bags under his eyes and a new splatter of freckles across his nose and forehead, but under that his face was exactly the same.

"Oh no." His face fell as he took in more and more of her details. "What happened to you?"

Alice reflexively reached up to tug at the ends of her shorn hair.

"It got to be too much upkeep," she explained.

"God, that's upsetting to look at," he said with wonder, scanning around her face like she was a puzzle he was trying to solve. "You're just not you without your hair."

She thought that same thing but never said it. Hearing it come out of his mouth, though, was the first time she prickled at the claim.

"It's just hair," she said with a tight laugh.

"But it was your best feature." He raised his right hand like he was going to run his fingers through her hair, the way he'd done a hundred times before, but then he jerked his hand back at the last moment in a motion Alice could only interpret as regret with an edge of disgust.

"It'll grow, Joe," she said. An older man to their right threw her an affronted look. She must have been a step too loud. "Let's walk." She turned and headed into the next gallery before he could respond.

"You were right the first time," he said as he caught up to her and they fell into a plodding pace. "It's Gabriel now. I know a lot of people thought I'd gone off the deep end when I sent that email last semester, but I hadn't. I was, am, totally sane."

"So, it's Gabriel Grant? Joe Turner is no more?"

"Gabriel Grant." He nodded. "Had it changed legally and everything."

"And your parents are fine with that?"

"Of course not." He smirked. "But there's not much they can do about it now, can they?"

Alice turned this over for a moment before realizing what he meant.

"You're twenty-one," she said. "Your trust fund kicked. Wait, when did—"

"In April," he cut her off, excited.

"I thought you had to graduate—"

"I had to *attend* a four-year university, they never specifically stated I had to graduate. The lawyer I hired to deal with it was pretty good. And I think my mom got my dad to back down. She didn't want to risk pissing me off. I always had the option of just cutting contact completely, and what are they going to do then?" He looked away like he was suddenly caught up by a large landscape they were passing, but Alice saw through it. She thought what he'd left unsaid. *I'm their only living child. She's not going to risk losing me, too.* What a place of power that was, to have someone love you more than you love them.

"So, you still talk?"

Gabriel shrugged. "I call every once in a while. Have dinner if I'm nearby, but work has kept me pretty busy in L.A. these days."

"I know," Alice said.

Alice had seen the magazine spread when she was at the grocery store a month earlier with Arthur stretching his mother's recent check as far as it could go. She had grabbed a copy from the checkout lane when Arthur wasn't looking and flipped through it in the sanitary napkin aisle. Gabriel's breakout shoot was a beautiful spread and the cover of the cast of a new movie everyone kept calling "award bait." A retelling of *Doctor Faustus* set in modern-day New York City wherein the doctor was a heroin-addicted PhD student with terminal brain cancer and Mephistopheles was gender-flipped, now a barely legal sex kitten in red leather and lace.

"It's been a hit, that shoot," Gabriel said, smiling. "I'm all booked up now. Appointments with magazines, here and in Europe. I had to get a passport! And then I'm getting some commissions for private commissions. And the *money*!" He turned and grabbed her arm for emphasis. His hands were smaller than she remembered. "The money is crazy, Lizzie."

Alice blanked for a moment before her brain finally caught up to what he was saying. *Right, Lizzie*, she thought. *That's supposed to be me.*

"I just need to keep up with this work for maybe a year, year and a half, and then I can finance my own work fully." He charged on. "My real work. Not the pretty, pretty photos of the pretty, pretty people." Alice started to ask a question, but Gabriel spoke over her, "And I have this apartment I'm renting that's right in the city with huge windows. All the light I want, all day long."

As he spoke Alice tried to slip back into the skin of the girl she had been a year ago. The girl who'd let him talk to his heart's content, whose only pleasure was to listen and enjoy the sound of his excited voice. But some new part of her refused to devolve and she—still silently but no longer passively—listened and mentally notated as he spoke.

"Compared to my place in L.A., my place in D.C. was a hovel." *You had a one bedroom to yourself, and your parents paid for your cleaning lady.* "I don't know how I managed to light the place properly." *You didn't light the place. I did.* "I have assistants on these shoots who do all that for me now. I just tell them what I want, and they make it happen. No questions asked." *Sounds familiar.* "Long way from my starving artist days." *You were never starving.* "And I guess there's a different pressure when you have success, when you're suddenly so rich." *Your father is a judge. You grew up sailing.* "And everyone thinks it's *so* gauche to talk about money, but if we don't talk about it then no one will ever know, right?" *Rich people love talking about* money. *It's all you ever talk about.* "So, I try to be very open about how difficult it can be to be so successful, so fast. Pisses people off sometimes. Apparently, I sound 'ungrateful,' but my success wasn't, like, *bestowed* upon me by a higher power. I made it happen for myself. It gets lonely sometimes, but I try to remind myself it was all me." *And me. I was there. Your portfolio that landed you that job was all me. All my body. All my face. All my time and energy and vision and no credit and no name—*

"Lizzie."

Gabriel stepped in front of her so suddenly she almost walked into him. She pulled up short in alarm and froze under the intensity of his stare. He didn't touch her—she could see his hands were balled into fists in his pockets with the strain of it—but he had that same old look. Like he was beginning to lose it. Like if he could just look at her sharp enough, he could pierce her butterfly wings and pin her to the spreading board, examine her, preserve this exact moment of her, pull her out and study her whenever he wanted. Alice remembered what it used to feel like under his eye. The rhapsodic surrender, the faithful feeling. But again some new, hateful part of her would not give way. Anger and resentment, at herself and at him. They had started something together and they never got a chance to finish. Wasn't that why she had come here? To feel like herself, to feel like she had the last time she was sure of her role in the world?

"Lizzie," he said again. "Can we—I want to talk but not here—I need . . ." He shifted his weight. Whatever he was saying seemed to cause him actual physical pain. "I need to be able to speak at full volume." He half laughed. "And I need a cigarette. Outside, okay?"

She nodded. He turned and led her to the nearest exit. They walked close, but never touching, out of the building, and pulled up to a low wall next to the stairs to the museum. She wanted to sit out in the sun to keep warm, but Gabriel didn't want to stand too close to some other small groups congregating on the other side, so they wound up shivering in the shade of a large tree by themselves.

Maybe it was a trick, the old part of her thought. Maybe he just wants an excuse to sit closer.

But the moment they got to the low wall and sat Gabriel bounced right back up, rocking on the balls of his feet, and took out a cigarette. He lit up, then held out the pack to her, half joking. She smiled and shook her head. He'd always smoked and offered her one and she'd always said no. Gabriel liked to say he preferred his girls to be "clean." Not too much drinking, no drugs, no smoking, no spitting, no swearing, and no sleeping around. Alice had no problem being that girl. She'd sworn off all the addictive habits at the wizened age of thirteen thanks to her father. She'd never been around many boys, so she never learned how to swear or spit. And even by the time she figured out she had sexual options she was already with Gabriel, and it never, not even for a moment, occurred to her to pursue them. Why go searching for someone new when she already had the person everyone else wanted? It may have made her unpopular with the other art students, but it mattered to the one person whose opinion she actually cared about, so she'd kept completely clean.

"So . . ." He blew out smoke with a sigh.

"So?" she asked.

"I'm glad you came." He let a bit of the L.A. act drop. "I wasn't sure you would, given how everything . . . ended."

She nodded.

"I'm doing a lot better now," he continued. "Not just the work and everything, but me, I'm doing better. I know I freaked some people out at the end there."

"You did."

"I'm not crazy," he said with sudden force. Alice flinched. He caught himself, pulled back, started again. "I know that's what people were saying about me. That I went crazy and that's why I sent that email, but they're full of shit. You know the school went to my parents?"

She shook her head.

"They sent them my email and my incomplete record and suggested I might need 'professional help.' And it wasn't just some academic dean doing his job, it was my fucking advisor who snitched! Probably covering their asses legally in case I killed myself or something. Fucking bullshit—not like they actually cared. They already had my money, no need to—"

He stopped and shivered.

"Never mind, that isn't what I wanted to talk about." He cleared his throat and shifted his weight between his feet. Alice pulled her thin jacket tighter around her. She'd gotten a bit big for it since the baby, no longer able to button it closed over her swollen breasts and soft belly, but at least it kept her arms warm.

"I'm doing a lot better now," he started again. "And I'm sorry if you were hurt by the way we ended things when I left."

"Well," Alice puzzled that out. "We didn't really end things so much as things just stopped. I mean, you were here one day and gone the next."

"Yeah, well, things happened fast for me," he said quickly. "I had one of those moments one night where I realized how fake everything here was—not you, or us—but everything else, like school and other people and even my work. I mean what were we doing, like, really? Fucking assignments. Like children. They told us to make something, and we made it. They told us to do something, and we did it. These people that haven't made any relevant work in years telling us, people trying something new and real, that it wasn't up to some made-up idea they had in their minds about what art is supposed to look like. And then they give us fucking grades on it? And that wasn't the worst part, the worst part was I fucking cared about the grades! I tried taking their notes, trusting them, doing what they wanted me to do, and you want to know what happened? I got worse! My work got worse. I barely used any of my stuff from class for my portfolio when I got to L.A. It was all the stuff I did independently, with you, that actually landed me my agent."

He ended by looking over at her, focused, like he was trying to place the words he wanted to hear out of her in her mind telepathically. Unsure of what to do, Alice stared back and said, "Okay."

"Okay . . . so . . . I go, I leave, I make the big move, and I land the agent, then the jobs, and then The Job. My photos are in print, they're everywhere, I'm finally the person I knew I was supposed to be and it's all almost perfect except, I dunno, except it felt like you should have been there. And it was weird that you weren't. It was all exactly as it should be, except for you not being there."

Heat rose in Alice's face. Her eyes filled but she blinked away the reaction. She looked away, up, over, anywhere that wasn't his face finally telling her honestly all the things she wished he'd say. *Say it,* she willed him. *Say you want to come back. That we'll start over. That you want to meet your daughter.*

"Just say what you need to say," she said, voice thick. He caught her eye, held it, and said:

"I want you to come to L.A. with me."

The flush ebbed as shock took its place.

"I—" she started, before he cut her off.

"Wait. Don't say anything just yet, let me just . . . I know there are issues. I know you have a whole little life set up here with a house and everything, but I want you with me. You belong with me in L.A., working together. And I know there will be issues and a lot to figure out, but it's not too late for you to come out West—"

"Really?" Alice cut him off. "I mean, that's really what you want? Because you could have had that already." Alice hated the gummy sound of her voice while she tried to power through the emotions gripping her body. But she knew he wouldn't give her a second chance at this. One wrong move and he'd split again. "That's what we could have been doing this whole time, but you disappeared."

"Kenning wasn't the right place for me, okay? It was too small, too much the same people with the same ideas. I was dying there."

"Dying when you were with me."

"No." His voice raised as he defended himself. "We were having a bad time. You can't blame it all on me. Maybe I was taking my frustration out on you, but you pulled away. You can't say you didn't."

Alice thought of the first night she stayed on the roof with Arthur when she knew Gabriel had needed her downstairs with him. She thought about all the hours she spent at the library getting lost in her own research. A weak pang of guilt rang out when she remembered the moment she found out he was gone, a whole week after he had left. He was right. She had taken her eyes off him.

"Things are different now," she threatened. "I have things, people, in my life that don't just go away because you suddenly want me somewhere."

"You mean your husband?" Gabriel smirked.

"And our daughter? Remember her?"

"She can come!"

"Jesus fucking Christ." Alice shook her head. "You haven't thought this through at all. You don't know what you're saying."

"Yes, I do." Gabriel stepped in with surety and caught her gaze in his own. He placed his hands on the wall on either side of her hips like his body was a claw gently pinching her own. "I know I need you in L.A. with me. I know it won't be simple and I'm sure we'll have plenty of fights about it in the future, but I know that I need you and I love you. And I asked you here to see if you still need me and love me, too. It's a yes or no."

Alice looked down at her limp hands and Gabriel pressed his forehead against hers. Hard bone and thin skin. Just that touch was enough. Alice felt herself sink down into guilt. She thought about Arthur, holding her hand while she was in labor, changing diapers, lying to his mother, all for her and Violet. She thought about their perfect quiet when they watched the stars together. She would lose all of that when she left. She needed them both. But beyond need, who did she love?

"Yes," she said, as soft and sure as she'd said her wedding vows.

Gabriel pulled her off the wall and pressed the whole length of her body against his and kissed her. The first second was awkward, but then their bodies recognized the feel of each other and they relaxed right back into the people they had been a year earlier. It didn't matter that the building pain in her breasts meant it was time to pump, or that her hair wasn't the way he liked it. Her arms encircled his waist, and they kissed again and again. Longer and deeper, little pecks in between, only stopping for Gabriel to whisper "Yes?" and for her to affirm "Yes." Over and over again. For this moment they were them again, like they had been before, like they would have been before everything got so dark and complicated. Someone across the steps let out a wolf howl at their public display and they broke apart laughing. Gabriel offered his arm like a gentleman, she took it, and he waved like royalty to the wolf-howler as he led her toward the sculpture garden. They walked arm in arm and Alice finally fell back into who she had been, her "Yes" and the kiss overpowering that stubborn, evolved part of her. She asked more about his new place. He talked more about his work but talked around the women. She supposed he was trying to spare her feelings, but she didn't really have any. He'd always had other women, when they were together and apart. But he hadn't flown across the country for them, had he? He hadn't taken them when their bodies were still swollen and scarred, inside and out, when they were tired, when their hair was wrong and their lives were complicated. He took those others when they were around. But Alice was the one he had come back for.

After they'd looped the path twice, ignoring the art and invested in each other, Gabriel turned to her practically jumping with excitement and took her hand in his.

"So," he said. "My hotel is just a car ride away." He pulled her into his arms. "I figure we have dinner in bed, then more talking in bed, and then other enjoyable bed-related activities."

She giggled but didn't pull away.

"What?" he asked. It took a moment before she realized he was genuine.

"Gabriel." She tried to sound light and almost succeeded. "Come on, you know I can't."

His eyes narrowed.

"I had a baby seven months ago." She said it like that was the end of it. When he didn't seem any less confused, she continued, "It was a rough birth. My body isn't—I'm not ready for any of that."

"You're honestly telling me you haven't had sex in seven months?" he asked.

"No." Alice pulled away and crossed her arms. Gabriel jammed his fists in his pockets again. "I'm saying I haven't had sex in way more than seven months. Since the last time we did."

"Oh, come on, Lizzie," Gabriel tried to keep a smile on his face, but it was souring into a smirk. "You seriously want me to believe you and your *husband*, the guy you were seeing behind my back for a year—"

"It's not like that," she interrupted. "You know it's not like that. Arthur and I are friends, it's not a *marriage* marriage."

"Stop!" he barked at her. "You're starting to piss me off and I really don't want to be pissed off right now. Not by you and not about this."

"I'm not lying," she insisted.

"Listen, I get that you have a kid, and that's not going anywhere. And we can figure out a way to make it work. Once you're set up at my place maybe he can bring her over for a visit or something."

"A visit? She's coming with us. Our daughter is coming with us, Joe."

He changed so suddenly Alice only realized how angry he was when she felt his spit land on her cheek. He grabbed the lapels of her coat and pulled her in close so all she could see was his face and all she could hear was his voice. Her arms went limp at her sides, like they always did. She knew what this was. She knew how to surrender.

"My name isn't fucking Joe, it's fucking Gabriel Grant and maybe if you'd managed to be a little less of a slut and stayed clean like I told you, those glaring daddy issues of yours wouldn't have gotten you to whore yourself for a little bit of comfort to the first old man with a little money who tried to get between your legs, and you wouldn't be in front of me now, fat and used up and stretched out like a sagging old leather couch, and you wouldn't have a whole miserable life of housework in front of you where you're just going to get uglier, and fatter, and less interesting so you can clean up after your piece of shit husband that I know for a fact you don't love and probably never will, at least not like you love me, and you'll get wine drunk every night and tell an empty room all about how you used to be an artist and if you'd just kept your panties on long enough you could have actually made something of yourself with me instead of being a little piece of comfort for him and *his* kid that you push out of you that'll suck all the life and thought and energy out of you until you're even more *nothing* than you are right now." He leaned in so his lips grazed her cheek. She closed her eyes and held her breath. "And if you *ever* try to tell anyone I had anything to do with that kid—if you come after my money—I will set. Your life. On fire."

Alice felt his fists shake against her chest with the effort of holding on to her so tight for so long. She waited and willed it to end. And then it did. Just as suddenly as he was in her face, he was on his knees in front of her, right there in the middle of a public garden, arms around her legs and face pressed against her stomach moaning, "I'm sorry, I didn't mean it, I'm terrible. I'm sorry."

The sky was beautiful. Alice kept her gaze there. The wind was high and moving fast, pushing the white clouds across the expanse, but the air down on Earth was dry and still. The kind of cold that chapped her cheeks and nose just from being outside for longer than a few minutes. Her fingertips would go white and numb, her feet would be filled with pins and needles. *I should get a better winter coat*, she thought. *I should get gloves.*

She was supposed to pull him off the ground in front of her, that's how it normally went. She would pull him up and tell him all the ways it was okay, or she'd sink down on the floor next to him and dive into her own apology routine about how she was wrong, being a bitch, and then she'd never make him feel that way again. Either way they'd usually have sex after. If they were alone and not in a public garden in the middle of April. Before, in his apartment, or sometimes even in the studio, she'd kiss him once and he'd take over, go through his motions and get what he needed and her lying there and letting him would be the seal that ended whatever fight they'd had. She just had to give him what he wanted and it would all be fine again. It would fix the wrong of the day, and the next time they saw each other they would start all over. But she wasn't lying before, about any of it. She didn't want to, she wasn't ready, and standing there looking up at the sky to keep herself from following down the same old path the two of them had always taken, Alice wasn't sure if she'd ever wanted to, if she'd ever been ready, or if she'd just never said no.

"Gabriel," she said, voice cracking, just above a whisper. He kept clinging to her. It felt like he was crying.

"Gabriel," she said again. She took hold of his shoulder and pried him off her far enough for her to lower herself onto the ground next to him. The moment she sat on the cold stone a shiver ran up her whole body. She was so cold.

"Gabriel," she said as she took his pinched, miserable face in her hands. "I am not coming to L.A." He jerked his face away and opened his mouth to say something, but she pressed two fingers against his lips to silence him. "You're right, okay?" she continued. "I'm not the same as I was before, and I'm probably not ever going to be that person again. And that's the person you want. Not this one." She pressed the back of her hand against his clammy forehead and smoothed out his frizzing hair. She'd been wrong before, his hair wasn't wet from a shower, it was slicked back with hair gel, now dried and breaking up into white flakes. "And you were right about the baby," she said. "You're not her father. Arthur is her father. She belongs at home with him. And I belong at home with them."

"What?" Gabriel reached for her again, but he didn't have the strength he had before. This sometimes happened after he exploded. Sometimes he didn't even have it in him to finish afterward. All his energy would rush out like a receding tide, and he'd have to take a nap just to get some of it back. This seemed to be one of those times.

"You're punishing me for what I said," he complained. "I said I'm sorry, I don't know what else I can say."

"No." Alice pulled his hands off her gently and laid them in his lap. "I'm not punishing you. I'm not mad. I want you to go back to L.A. I want you to have everything you want there. I'm tired and I'm cold and I want to leave."

She leaned in and he touched his forehead to her.

"Goodbye, Gabriel." She kissed him one last time, just a quick peck on his lips, before she detangled herself, stood, and walked away toward the train.

It was dusk by the time Alice got back to Artemesia Drive. She was all cried out from the very public sobbing session she'd had on the Metro on the way back from the city. She felt hollowed out but peaceful, like the serenity reached after a fever had finally burned out. The outdoor lights were on, pushing shadows away from her front door. Through the thin white top sheet they'd hung in front of the bay window as a temporary curtain, she could see Arthur's figure walking back and forth.

The front door was left unlocked for her. As she stepped into the foyer the smell of Chinese food wafted down to her and her stomach kicked with hunger.

"Arthur?" she called out.

"Nursery!" he called out. "You're just in time, dinner's on the table."

Alice saw the large brown bag of delivery on the card table they'd been eating at. She went to the kitchen to wash some plates, but the sink was empty for the first time in weeks, a pile of clean dishes resting on a towel on the counter. She dried off two plates and some cutlery and carried them back to the card table, appreciating how her shoes no longer stuck to the tile as she walked.

He bustled in and collapsed with a sigh as she was divvied up the food. Extra beef and broccoli for her, and both egg rolls for him. She could feel him studying her, but she didn't mind. It wasn't the intense, probing attention she'd felt with Gabriel. This was pure observation. She'd been going over the conversation with Gabriel over and over again on the train ride home. She'd cried, gotten angry, cried again. She'd practiced how she'd tell Arthur what happened. What tone she wanted to use to keep him from seeing exactly how close she came to leaving. It wouldn't do any good for him to know. He didn't deserve that pain, she decided, and she could keep it to herself with a few turns of phrase and a convincing performance.

"How'd it go?" Arthur asked. He sat back in his chair, hands on his lap. He eyed his plate like it might be a trap.

"Eat," Alice commanded and pushed his plate toward him. He hesitated, took one more assessing glance at her, then obliged. She took a few bites before answering. The loud crunch of the broccoli helped her refocus on the present moment. She'd decided on being hurt, but superior. Like Gabriel was nothing to them. A nuisance. Distracting but ultimately small when standing next to the life they'd started to build together. When she put her fork down to speak, so did Arthur.

"I'm fine," she said.

"You've been crying."

"On the train. He didn't—I'm not hurt."

Arthur gave her a look.

"I'm not *physically* hurt," she clarified. "I don't even know where to begin. He's an asshole," she said simply. "And I don't know what's wrong with me for expecting . . . anything, I guess. Expecting him to be different? To feel better after talking with him? He refuses to believe that Violet is his. He's convinced she's yours. I mean, biologically, in addition to actually."

"But you two were together way before—" Arthur said slowly.

"Oh yeah, apparently a cheating whore as well." She'd come up with that on the train. "And you and I were sleeping together behind his back for months before he went AWOL."

"Really?" Arthur leaned in. "Wow. I'm glad he told you or we might never have known about it."

Alice laughed. She picked up her fork to eat again but dropped it back with a clatter.

"Oh, and get this." She started buzzing as the thrill of reframing the meeting fueled her. "Apparently, not only am I going to live a life of absolute misery and failure, if I ever ask him for support or try to acknowledge that Violet is his in public, he's going to ruin my life. Which is also now your life. So I figured I should let you in on it."

"He threatened you?" Arthur turned serious. Alice waved him off as she took up her fork again. She was suddenly ravenous.

"He's said shit like that before." She shoved some fried rice in her mouth and kept talking. "It's always, 'I'm gunna kill you if you don't leave. I'm gunna kill myself if you do leave.' He means it until he calms down and then he completely forgets he's said anything at all."

"Is he— I mean, do you need to get a restraining order or something?"

"No." She tapped Arthur's plate to remind him to eat, and he started up again, though the worried creases on his forehead stayed in place.

"Doing anything official would just get him more agitated. Best not to engage. Starve him for attention and eventually he'll go off and find it somewhere else."

"So I should not worry about it?"

"Don't even think about it. I doubt Gabriel Grant is going to want to talk with me again for a long, long time." Alice kept the sadness from her voice when she said it, but she felt it lurking in her chest. Things were never going to be like they were ever again. She was never going to be young and fresh and new. There would be no Gabriel and Alice versus the world, no more years as his muse, no more thrill cycle of his moods. She wasn't the damaged but talented student everyone overlooked. She was rapidly changing every day into someone else, into a new future she hadn't imagined. There wouldn't be a singular moment when a teacher or mentor descended from the clouds and pointed her out as special. She'd have to get there some other way. She couldn't rely on being chosen anymore. Alice reached behind her and untied her dress to make more room for her stomach. She could be comfortable now that she was home.

The Two Faces of Janus

2015

Alice Snyder
American, 1974–2017

Painted and embroidered quilt

This piece was commissioned by the Fabric Arts Center for their 25th Anniversary Celebration and is on loan from their permanent collection. The theme for the Center's Celebration that year was "changes" and so Snyder looked to the ancient Roman god Janus, ruler of beginnings, frames, and transitions, for inspiration. This dual-paneled quilt depicts the artist as Janus, her mirrored image framed by different landscapes, both twins and opposites. This beginning depicted here is primarily seasonal, the transition from winter to spring, but as you look closer you will notice iconography repeated from her earlier work. She returns again to the fig and the pomegranate, to filled and spilled wine goblets. Notice how the highlights and shadows on her two faces change based on the color composition of each panel. The left's bluish-white turns her shadows purple while the right's luminous yellows give her highlights a brassy finish. The closer one looks at this piece, the more variations, obvious and subtle, one can see.

    We thank the Fabric Arts Center for their support.

Winter 2006

Sitting in the Garden Café of the National Gallery of Art with Gabriel, eating food she could never afford and letting him pay for it, Alice felt like a different woman than the one who lived with a husband and children at Artemesia Drive. After Gabriel had called and insisted that they needed to talk, demanding they let him meet Violet, threatening to show up at the house unannounced if she didn't meet with him to set it up, she pulled up her memories of the disastrous meeting here ten years earlier, and she could only look back at the people they'd been and wonder at their energy. She wondered at her own actions back then. She saw her younger self as a raw nerve, electrified with pain and careening into anything that looked like relief. But now, after ten years of routine, stability, ten years of finding ways to keep making art, she felt she was ready to handle whatever Gabriel threw at her feet. She knew where her barriers were and where they needed to stay. Absolutely no meeting her family, no coming to her house, and no working together. It calmed her to know those things in her life were safe from him. And if she managed to prove how wrong he'd been about her, then that would be an added bonus for the day.

They could take all the time they needed in the café. There were no picky eaters that needed their meat cut, no bedtimes or deadlines to meet, just her taking a whole hour to eat this glorious piece of fish while the man paying grinned at her. She took another bite of her blackened salmon, still tasting a bit of the sea it swam in. The potatoes had real cream whipped into them that made them so rich they were almost sweet, and each carrot was bright, sun fed, and harvested fresh. It was all so different from the routine of canned vegetables, instant mashed potatoes, or boxes of stuffing, and easy recipes she could make in less than an hour.

"How is your food?" Gabriel asked.

"It's fine." Alice shrugged.

"Mine is pretty good, you want some?"

She nodded. Gabriel stabbed up bits of lemongrass chicken and risotto and leaned across the table to feed her, biting air just as her mouth closed around the fork. Alice swallowed, nodded, and put down her cutlery.

"I take it that means you're ready to start now?" he asked.

"Ready *now*? No, I said what I needed to say on the phone last week when you called, but you said let's talk over lunch, then let's talk once we've ordered, then let's discuss once we're finished."

"Then let's discuss after dessert," he joked, managing to wheedle a reluctant smile out of her. She raised her eyebrows.

"Okay, you win, let's discuss now," he said. He put down his knife and fork, mirroring her.

"You're not going to meet her," she said.

"How's Arthur?"

"Arthur is fine. I am fine. Arthur and I are fine. You are not going to meet her."

"Fine, not good?" he countered.

"We're good." Alice rose to the bait.

"Good, not great?" he countered again.

"Look—"

A woman at the table next to them flinched at the volume of Alice's demand. Gabriel smirked. Alice considered stabbing him in the hand with her dinner knife, but they were in public, and she really needed to stay out of jail.

"Look," she said again, calmly, "you got me here. You've taken up all this time. Now tell me what you wanted to say to me that couldn't be said over the phone, or I'll go home to my kids."

"That's right, I heard you had another." His eyes dropped down her seated figure then back up to her face. "Looking pretty good for two kids in two years, Allie."

"*Body Electric* airs on PBS." Alice picked up her glass to give her hands something to do. "Why are you here, Gabriel? You already have your answer."

"You and the old man are still going strong? Still married?"

"Obviously."

"No, I don't think it's obvious at all." Gabriel sat up in his chair, elbows on the table, leaning forward. "I mean, last time we were here you said it wasn't a *marriage* marriage? He was just a friend? Seems like a pretty good friend."

"It started that way, but things changed." The smarter part of her wanted to tell him it was none of his business, but there was a stronger, still angry part of her that needed him to know she'd been in the right. He was the one who ended them. She just did what she had to do to survive.

"We were friends," she said, "and then when Violet was born everything got turned up to a hundred. We did everything together; our lives were completely enmeshed. We were real partners, like I've seen other people be. After that, falling in love just kind of happened. I can't even say when exactly. One day I looked up, and it was . . . there."

Gabriel nodded. "And you heard about me?" he asked.

"Yes." She'd followed his exploits with his more-famous model-turned-actress wife via the cheap magazines in the supermarket checkout aisle when she went grocery shopping with the girls. It was all a hot flash in an oiled pan last summer. Their meeting on set in Malibu, their marriage in Vegas one month later, insane parties and paparazzi stalkers, then calls to the police for domestic disturbances, leaked stories from concerned friends about drug use, infidelity, a psychotic break. One last issue about her private heartache when the divorce was announced and the husband in question, the man sitting across from Alice now, announced he'd be checking himself into a yearlong in-patient program for addiction. But that last copy was only from a few months ago.

"So, you checked yourself out of... wherever it was."

"I'm not an addict, Allie," he said, "I had to do that for the divorce."

"You're not here as a born-again AA Christian, trying to make amends for your wicked ways?"

"No, not reborn. Just slightly improved. And I want to stay that way. I want to be better."

"Okay," she said slowly. "That sounds good."

"And being better means meeting Violet."

"No," she said immediately. "Absolutely not."

"She's my daughter." He leaned across the table. "You can't just—"

"Is she your daughter?" she demanded. "Is she finally your daughter, Gabriel? Now? Now that we're past the diapers and the screaming and the never sleeping through the night. Now that Arthur has tenure, so we have enough to get by on. And now that I'm finally back to working, back to making art. Now that she has a whole family where she's safe and loved. Now, suddenly, she *is* your daughter?"

"Okay, you're right." He put his hands in the air in surrender. "All of that is right. I skipped all the hard stuff. And you and the professor seem to be doing good. I'm not here to mess any of that up. I just want to meet her." He smiled at Alice and she felt the wild urge to cry. "I know I said, and did, some really bad things last time I was here. And I know I'm not the easiest person to share a kid with, but that doesn't stop me from being her father. Does . . ." He hesitated. "Does your husband know you're meeting with me?"

"Does he know?" Alice pushed her chair out in agitation but managed not to walk off. "Of course he does. You think I lied to Arthur about where I was going? Affairs are for people with time and money, Gabriel. He had to move some meetings around, so he could watch the kids, so that I was *able* to meet you."

"Good, I'm glad he knows," Gabriel said. "Because I think he'll agree with me."

"How do you figure that?"

"He's a father, too."

"Yes, he's *her* father." She put her hands up to stop him from interrupting. "Her genes may be your genes, but Arthur Snyder is the only father she has ever known. He helps her with her science projects, stays up hot-gluing fake flowers to a headband for her Halloween costume, he's the one who carried her to her bed when she fell asleep in the car as a little kid. That's her dad. She doesn't know you and it would hurt her to tell her the truth now." She looked into his eyes. "Please tell me you understand that."

"I do," he admitted. "But I also know you can't keep it a secret forever."

"We won't." Alice sighed. "We agreed to tell her when she graduates from college."

"Why so late?" Gabriel objected. "Why not eighteen?"

"She gets free tuition to Kenning now that Arthur is tenured there and she'll need to live at home, because we can't afford room and board, so we thought—"

"Better to keep the peace?"

"Basically, yes. And besides, eighteen is too young. It sounds old, but it really isn't."

"We met when we were eighteen." He half smiled at her.

"Proving my point." Alice half smiled back.

"So, college graduation, she'll be twenty-two?"

"Twenty-three," Alice corrected him. "She has a late birthday, October, so she'll be twenty-three."

"And she's twe—no—eleven now. So I should just wait around for twelve years?"

Alice sighed and looked away. Her eye caught on a marble statue of a woman in the center of the café. They sat behind her so all Alice could see was the figure's back. There was her hairline curved to meet her neck, the muscles in her shoulders, the hem of her tunic caught on the back of her sandal as she took a step forward. Alice wished she could work with marble, but there was no way. What she'd said to Gabriel earlier about affairs was true for art, too. There just wasn't enough time or money. But those were two things Gabriel had always had. Time and money.

"Maybe," she began, still not looking at him, "maybe we can introduce you as a family friend, or a work colleague. Something neutral. Then you can meet her, but she doesn't have to know."

"Do you think Arthur would go for that?" Gabriel asked.

"I'll talk to him," Alice was already coming up with a strategy for it. If she started with something much bigger, then walked him down to this, it might work. No, she was sure it would work.

"I suppose he'll want to meet me officially."

"No." She cut him off. He looked surprised. "It would be best if you just deal with me for now."

"Alright." His surprise melted into a smile. "I can work with that."

That same evening Alice stood next to Arthur at the stovetop. She as still wearing the clothes she'd seen Gabriel in, but now the sleeves were rolled up and the top button of her pants was undone. They'd sent the girls to their room down the hall so they could have a "grown-ups" talk in the kitchen, but they kept their voices low just in case.

"I just want to know when we're supposed to get her ready," Arthur said as he dipped down to the simmering pan of tomato sauce to blow on his wooden spoon. He tasted the sauce then held it out to Alice. She took a taste; it was still too bland.

"More salt," she said. "No, do garlic powder, and . . ."

"Black pepper," he supplied.

"That's it." She nodded. "It's not like he wants to meet her tomorrow or anything. Just a casual run-in, or maybe he comes over."

"No," Arthur said suddenly. "I don't want him here. In the house. If it's going to be a casual thing, it can be in a public place."

"What are you afraid is going to happen?" Alice asked. "Listen, I've known this person a long time, I know him better than anyone, and he wouldn't hurt Violet."

"So, you trust him?"

"I know him. I know who he is and what he'll do. Trust me, honey," Alice stepped in and put an arm around Arthur's waist. "He's a jerk, but he's *consistently* the same jerk, all of the time. There's nothing he does that I can't anticipate."

A creak in the hallway. Arthur and Alice glanced over to the hallway.

"We can hear you," Arthur announced at full volume. Marigold's frizzy head peeked around the corner.

"Can we come out now?" she asked. Alice sighed.

"We said stay in your room until dinner, so that means you stay in your room until dinner," Arthur said, firm but patient. Alice could never get her tone to hit that balance, though she'd tried a lot. Hers always came out with just a bit too much edge and sounded angry, or too much whine, which made her sound like she was about to start crying when really she just wanted them to follow orders.

"But I need a glass of water," Marigold said. Alice said, "Mm-hmm," but still took down an old jam jar they used for kids' glasses and filled it from the tap.

"Now scoot," she said as she handed her daughter the glass. "Stay in the room with Lettie until we come get you, okay?"

Alice kissed her daughter on the top of her head, the fuzz from her tangles tickling her nose.

"Baby, when did we last brush your hair?"

"Um, I don't know," Marigold said slowly, trying to gauge if she'd just gotten herself in trouble.

"Tell your sister to brush it out," Alice said. "Tell her it needs to be done before dinner."

Marigold looked uneasy.

"But," she drew out her words again, "I think that maybe she might be reading her book right now? And she doesn't like it when I ask her things when she's reading."

"I can brush it after dinner," Arthur said to Alice.

"And Violet can brush it now," she snapped at him. This was one thing she could not stand about Arthur. He was forever letting the girls off the hook, letting her be the bad guy while he got to be sweet and fun. Even this little thing, this tiny job to brush her sister's hair before dinner, he wanted to take on himself. He tried to cover for the girls' every little mess and mistake, snuck them cheap snacks between meals, shot them looks behind her back when she was forced to hold them responsible for their actions. He wanted to keep them from ever seeing the ugliness of the world, but she was more practical. The ugliness would come for them eventually, so she'd rather have strong daughters than weak ones. He never defied her or contradicted her outright, but he always undermined her in these tiny hacks to chip her away in front of her kids. When she looked at her children, she saw all the softness she'd worked hard to give them, comfort they never appreciated. The same refrain came back to her over and over: *You have so much more than I did, and you don't even know.*

"Get your brush from the bathroom," she told Marigold. "Have her use your water for the bad tangles." Alice pushed her daughter gently toward the hall. Alice and Arthur waited until they heard the closing of the girls' bedroom door before turning back to each other.

"I think it's a risk," Arthur said. "I mean, I don't know this person. I've never met him. What if he blurts it out? What if he, I don't know, snatches her and runs off. I don't trust him."

"You don't have to trust him," Alice said flatly, suddenly over this conversation. "You have to trust me. And you either do, or you don't. Do you trust me to do what's best for Violet?"

"Of course," he said at once.

"And to keep her safe?"

"Yes."

"Alright then. End of conversation." She nodded to the pot of pasta. "Is it done?"

Arthur spooned out a single bowtie pasta and ran it under the tap to cool it. They'd made this exact dinner together hundreds of times and could do the whole dinner half asleep if they needed to. Next, Arthur would bite off one half, teeth cutting right through the pinch, and hold the other half out for his wife. She would open her mouth upward like a baby bird so that he would have to toss in the little bit of pasta. When the pasta was done Alice would drop the colander in the sink while Arthur turned off the burners and dumped the pasta. They'd both turn away from the plume of steam heat that rolled up and out of the sink.

"Then I guess it looks like I'm meeting him," Arthur said, resigned.

"Absolutely not," Alice said.

"If he's going to meet Violet, I need to meet this guy in real life."

"But that's the thing, he's not meeting Violet. At least he's not meeting her as himself." She explained, "It'll be quick, casual. She'll never know what's going on."

"I still need to—"

"No. Trust me, Arthur." She stepped toward him to make her point clear. "I can handle this. I can handle him. If you step in now . . ." *You'll make this all about you two.* But she couldn't say that. She tried to find the right angle to get straight at what she wanted.

"You know you're Violet's favorite person in the world, right?" she asked him.

He was startled with the sudden topic change.

She continued, "She definitely likes you more than me."

"That's not—" he started.

"Before you lie and say, 'That's not true,' don't bother. It's painfully obvious. She'd sleep in the corner of your office like the family dog if I let her. And I'm not saying she and I don't have a thing, we do. But we both know she's yours the way Goldie is mine."

Arthur leaned against the stovetop and crossed his arms to match her. He smiled and shook his head but didn't disagree.

"If you meet him, what's the likelihood it'll get bad fast?"

"I can behave myself, Alice," he said.

"Yes, I know you can. And I know he can't. Not if he's around you. If you come it'll become a big territorial thing, and Violet will know something is up."

"She is pretty smart," Arthur admitted.

"She's scary smart. You know she corrected how much tip I gave the lady at the diner last time we went?" Arthur snorted, and Alice relaxed. He'd already decided to let her go without him; she just needed him to say it. "I hadn't even known she was paying attention to the bill until we were in the car and she asked why I tipped twelve percent instead of fifteen. Thought she had telepathy or something."

She waited for him to agree to the plan, but he stayed silent. Alice slid over to him and knocked her elbow against his arm until he gave in and pulled her to his chest. This was one thing she loved about Arthur. This combination of his size, his warmth, and the sense that life's pain was incrementally weakened, crossing over from unbearable to bearable.

"I'm scared of losing her to him," he confessed. "I'm scared of losing you to him, too."

"That's not going to happen," Alice said. "We're staying right here."

Winter 2007

Their second one-on-one meeting at the Garden Café was a slight variation on the first. Again, Gabriel called Alice and asked to meet in person. This time instead of threats there were thank-yous: Thank you for letting me meet Violet last year, how is she doing? Thank you for taking my call, has she asked about me? Alice felt like he was pretending to care but instead of challenging him, she let it slide. Again she resisted his invitation to meet, and again he convinced her. But this time the resisting was weaker and the convincing much more quickly achieved. Alice did manage to refuse eating another meal with him but negotiated down to coffee and dessert as they, according to Gabriel, "were things she would have eaten eventually anyway, so why not here and now?" The surrounding tables were half-filled with the other sorts of people who had the time to go to cafés at noon on a Wednesday. Retired couples, mothers and nannies with young children, and college students. Even though Arthur knew where she was, and who she was with, and even with "permission," though she hated that word and all it implied, she struggled internally with whether or not she had anything to be ashamed of. Eating chocolate cake while her daughters were at school and her husband was at work. But they were out living their lives, she reasoned, so why shouldn't she be here living hers?

"What is it this time?" she asked Gabriel when the idle chatter about his work and her life was over.

"Got to get back home?" Gabriel asked.

"You're cutting into my painting time," she said.

"Oh shit," he said. "Well, I'll be quick then."

Alice listened for a hint of mockery but found none. He was serious. A warm wave rolled up from her belly and crashed over her neck and chest. He was taking her, her work, seriously. She considered mentioning what she was working on. About her embroidery experiments and the way her mother's sewing box seemed to be haunting her studio time. She'd tried to talk to Arthur about it, but he was out of his depth in her art world.

"I've been offered a job," he said.

"That's good."

"Well . . . it's at the Corcoran School. Here. In D.C."

"Oh." Alice sat back in her chair and followed as the implications unfolded between them. The Corcoran School of the Arts & Design at GW was right in the center of the city, just across the street from President's Park, while Kenning University was tucked away in a corner of the northeast. Gabriel and Arthur would have no reason to run to each other socially, their lives were entirely separate, their worlds were light-years apart. But in reality what this job meant was that Gabriel would be less than a twenty-minute drive away from Arthur at any time. Less than twenty minutes to get to Violet or Marigold when they eventually attended Kenning University. It meant he was really staying. He would be here, in her city, for a long while.

"That's great," she said. "I'm glad."

"You are?" he asked. "You are," he said, answering his own question.

"Well good," he continued. "I asked them for some time to consider. I wanted to run it by you first."

"You did?"

"Of course, I did." He leaned in toward her. "I wouldn't stay if you didn't want me here."

"Well then." Alice picked up her coffee and hoped the cup would cover the rush of blood to her face. "You can call them back and tell them yes."

"That's great! I'm glad." He rocked back in his chair, visibly relieved. The happiness she'd caused with her consent reflected on Alice in his fallen shoulders and easy grin, reaffirming that she needn't have run it past Arthur. That she could decide for all of them.

"So, do you have to run back?" he asked. "Or can I ask another question?"

Alice made a show of looking at her watch, a present from Arthur for their five-year anniversary. Arthur probably meant to say *My love for you transcends time*, but all she heard was *Maybe now you'll finally be on time to something*.

"One more question," Alice assented.

"What are you working on these days?" he asked.

Alice picked up her coffee again.

Alice and Arthur were in bed the following Sunday morning arguing. Voices low so the girls couldn't hear through their shared wall, fresh coffee half drunk in their mugs, sitting up in their bed both staring ahead at the unsold work of Alice's hanging above their dresser called *The Astronomer*. Alice had never liked the painting, but it was the only one she'd ever asked Arthur to sit for, so she let him keep it. If she'd known he'd hang it in their room, she would have burned the damn thing and told him it was damaged accidentally in the studio. When they fought in their room she would fantasize about ripping *The Astronomer* off the wall, dousing it with turpentine and setting it on fire.

"I'm going to say this one more time," Alice said, frustration making her voice artificially high and tight. "He's taking the job. There's nothing we can do to stop him."

Arthur shook his head.

"What was I supposed to do?" She turned to confront him. The fact that Gabriel had asked her, had seemed to give her a choice, was not something she was going to bring up now. Not when she was this pissed at being held responsible for something he was always going to do anyway.

"What the fuck was I supposed to do?" she continued. "He told me about the job as a courtesy. To be polite."

"And you can't talk him out of it?"

"This is so fucked up," Alice flopped back against her pillows, coffee sloshing in her cup. "I can't believe you're blaming me for this."

"I'm not blaming you," Arthur countered. "I'm angry at him. I'm angry he's staying. I'm angry—"

"That he's Violet's real father," she threw at him. Arthur made a small sound like a gasp, like she'd hit him right in the center of his chest and he couldn't take a full breath in.

"That's not what this is about," he said quietly.

Arthur was big, but he was also weak. He was weak when it mattered. Weak when they argued, when she hurt him and he refused to hurt her back. Weak and so, so easy to wound. Alice had learned a long time ago she could win any argument, end any "discussion," by acting out the same series of verbal assaults, in the same pattern, every time. It went like this:

"You're angry because he's her father but you had to raise her and pay for everything."

"That's not true."

"And I gave you Marigold to try and make up for it, but it wasn't enough."

"I never asked you to do that." Arthur got out of bed suddenly, left his coffee on his nightstand, and went to the door. Alice thought for a second he might be storming out, which he'd never done, but instead he poked his head out to listen for any signs the girls might be awake before he closed it quietly, locking it, and began pacing at the foot of their bed.

"I never forced you to do anything," he said, voice thickening with feeling. This was another thing she hated about Arthur. When they fought, he always cried, and she always went cold and hard inside. Alice thought it was unnatural, a violation of their gender and roles.

"I never asked you to get pregnant again."

"But you had no problem fucking me," she said. It felt good, being this cold. She didn't even really feel human. She felt better than human. She felt divine, delivering punishments without care or guilt.

"You wanted to have sex," he said.

"But I didn't want to host a tiny alien inside me for nine more months just to rip my body open to push another one out. I *had* to give you one to make up for the first one."

"That's not what happened."

"You just keep telling yourself that." She took a sip of her coffee. It needed to be warmed up in the microwave.

"You can just admit it, Arthur," she said easily. "I trapped you with a baby you didn't want, and you trapped me with a baby I didn't need, and now we're stuck here." She gestured around to their room. "This is all we have. This is it. Forever. Until we die. And it's not enough, is it?"

Arthur sat on the edge of the bed with his back to her. Now that he was in his sulking phase, her part was done. She sighed in relief as the fight ended.

"It's enough for me," Arthur said, eyes on the floor. "It's enough for me. It's more than enough. And I know you're angry at life, and that it's easy to take it out on me because I'm your husband and that's what I'm here for, but I know it's not real. I know that's not how it happened."

Alice sighed and got out of bed. She pulled on a set of pajama pants, slipped on her slippers, and picked up her mug to go warm up her coffee. As she unlocked the door to their bedroom and left, she heard him say softly behind her:

"That's not how it happened."

Spring 2007

It just happened to work out that their third one-on-one meeting was at Gabriel's new apartment in Adams Morgan. He had bought a two-bedroom in a newer building. Alice could see his influence on the walls—all of his major shows and success represented in micro by the gallery-style spreads he had on every wall. But the furniture was odd. Alien. Chrome, dark wood and matte black, a leather couch that looked soft but barely gave when Alice sat. Everything was new and expensive and inhuman. This apartment was for a character of the man she knew, not the man himself.

Gabriel came back with two glasses of red wine, despite her request for water. He read the look on her face, glanced over the room, and laughed.

"What?" she asked.

"You look like you stepped in dog shit," he said, still grinning.

"Who the hell decorated this place?"

"You don't like it?"

"I hate it." She shifted against the stiff leather but even her bony hip couldn't soften the skin. She felt like she was sitting on a tire.

"My mother hired a decorator," he explained. "She was so happy to have me back in D.C., I think she would have bought me a whole house if I'd asked for it."

Alice brought the wineglass up to her nose, pretending to smell to cover her reaction. Of course, his parents had bought him this place. She'd never met them, but she knew the shape of them from the negative space they left around their son. They were the kind of people who made money from owning things they'd inherited from their own parents, and who would one day pass that along to their son. People who held jobs as a way to instill meaning to their lives and order in their days, who knew how to support their son only by the writing of blank checks, silence, and space.

"How is the judge and the little missus?" she asked, using the code names he'd used for them in college.

"The judge is still working. I think they'll have to cart him out directly from the courthouse when he does finally keel over. The little missus runs the DAR like the Kremlin. I think they're just happy I'm gainfully employed and close enough to be controlled. Those Hollywood years were rough for them."

"Really?" Alice asked genuinely surprised. Gabriel had always made it seem like his parents were as uninterested in him as he was in them.

"Not like that," he corrected her thought. She felt suddenly caught out to have been understood twice. She took another sip of wine.

"I was embarrassing them," he continued. "The gossip is bad enough but in L.A. you've got a small army of paparazzi stalking anyone who's even tangentially related to a story. During my little foray into matrimony"—he grinned at her—"they managed to get my address and then it leaked to the public, and then once the assistant started selling her story my dear wife's adoring fans took turns leaving flaming bags of dog shit on my doorstep."

Alice went to take another sip but was surprised to find the glass empty. Gabriel's was suddenly empty as well.

"A top up?" he asked. She nodded. He took her glass, the edge of his hand brushing against the tops of her fingers. She felt the blood rush up to her face, so she stood and pretended to be invested in his selection of coffee table books. With him gone and her on her feet, Alice finally registered the beginning effects of the wine. She and Arthur didn't drink. They also didn't *not* drink. Sometimes there was a glass of wine at a reception or a fancy dinner, but they never kept alcohol in the house. And they never drank in front of the girls. They never drank in front of their children because their own parents had always drunk in front of their children. Becoming parents themselves hadn't stopped her and Arthur from thinking about their own childhoods and their own parents. If anything, it had made it much worse. Even small decisions, what to eat for dinner, how often to wash their clothes, always seemed to wind back up in an instance in the past. Arthur couldn't bear the sound of glass breaking, so most of their dishes were plastic. Rough, painful hair brushing was the only kind Alice had known as a child, so she let her own daughters' hair be a mess from her own avoidance. No matter how old she got, she still managed to feel like that same silent girl with a newly dead mother she'd tried leaving behind.

Alice began wandering through the apartment, the wine in her blood making her bold enough to be nosy. She felt like a new version of herself here. She wouldn't admit it aloud but being with Gabriel made her feel grown up. Like life was still something she could mold to her liking. It had felt that way when she'd first gotten married, when those exact same qualities in Arthur that she'd fallen in love with, his sweetness and stability, were the ones that irritated her most now. Even the age difference that had made her feel safe at twenty-one was the one she'd begun chafing against at thirty-three. Arthur never meant to condescend to her, but sometimes it seemed he couldn't help it. When he tried recounting his day or explaining his work, he would talk to her like she was one of his students instead of his wife, explaining terms she already knew or simplifying things she didn't need simplified. But right after she went down that mental path the loyal part of her began to wind around her heart and constrict. As if just thinking ungrateful thoughts was as bad as acting on them. Gabriel would have blamed her Catholic school education, and he'd have been right.

She walked down the hall, past the bathroom, and paused outside the smaller second bedroom. The door was ajar, and she could see the outline of an unmade bed and papers on the floor.

"You can go in if you want," Gabriel said from just behind her and she jumped. He grinned but managed not to tease her. He handed over her wineglass, but she stayed put.

"Why don't you sleep in the master bedroom?" she asked.

"I needed a place to work," he said. "And it had the best ventilation."

Alice looked back at the door to the master and saw the black insulation puffing out around the doorframe.

"You built a darkroom in here?" she asked. "Is that even legal?"

Gabriel shrugged. He probably hadn't even thought about whether it was legal or not. He'd just needed it, so he'd done it.

"Can I see what you're working on?" she asked.

Gabriel's face lit up. He led her to the door at the end of the hall and opened it to reveal a small black antechamber created by thick black curtains. She stepped inside and he took his place beside her as he shut the door. Even though the curtain was heavy enough to settle at once and they knew the moment the door closed behind them there was no chance of light creeping through, they still waited. Side by side, close enough to feel each other's warmth but not enough to touch. They paused there, in that unnoted moment, and listened to each other breathe.

The glass in Alice's hand was sweating.

Gabriel pulled back the curtain and let her in.

The bedroom windows had been blacked out so the only light came from the red bulbs strung throughout the room. There was a long table with tubs of developing solution on the left side, clipped photos hanging from the drying line, and on the right was a large cutting table with proofs, strips, and loupe magnifiers. Everything was neat and top-of-the-line. This place, unlike the furniture outside, she recognized as completely him. Even back in school he could have food rotting in his kitchen for weeks, but his work area was always immaculate.

Alice walked up to one line of finished photos drying on a line over the developing tubs, the familiar chemical smell wafting up to mix with the scent of the wine. Portraits. He always went back to portraits. He was in a black-and-white phase now. And he was using long exposures to capture movement as well. Some of them were of himself staring straight into the camera with carefully ruffled hair and intentionally distressed black clothes. All of the others used the same model, a platinum-blonde doe-eyed woman who could be anywhere from her late teens to her early twenties. This girl was running around the frames in a selection of gauzy white see-through dresses and satin slips, her thin limbs in an awkward approximation of grace as she flung herself through the air.

One part of Alice appreciated the photos. The girl looked like more than a girl. Her angles, the pretty-ugly face, and the static that charged her crispy hair and lifted it, ghostlike, in the close-ups were pleasing enough for a cursory look. But there was also a second reaction, one of recognition chanced by some hollow emotion Alice couldn't name. She couldn't stop herself from knowing the girl must have been cold. She remembered that cold. Sitting half-dressed for hours, outside in winter or in a studio with the AC on full blast, freezing because even in the summer Gabriel hated to have sweaty hands when shooting. Alice stepped back and saw how many versions of this girl there were. With different clothes, in different locations, with different lengths of hair. Two pieces of information slid into place in Alice's mind: The girl in the photos and the unfamiliar handwriting on the side of the tubs.

"You have an assistant?" she asked.

"My students help out here occasionally," he said.

"Is she here full time?" Alice kept her eyes on the photos in front of her.

"Are you jealous?" he asked, only half-teasing.

"She's good," Alice said coolly. "I might like to hire her myself. If she's available."

"Oh, come on, Allie, you know the rules."

Alice turned around. "You've got to be kidding me," she said.

"I don't share," he said flatly.

"How are you still keeping that up, though?" Alice asked. Yes, when they'd been in school Gabriel had a strict rule that his favorite models couldn't pose for any of the other photography students. Alice had even turned down small paying gigs at that time out of respect for his rule. But that was different. That was them. They had been partners whereas these girls were just bodies in space.

"I'm always very clear, from the beginning, what the rules are," he said. "They can take it or leave it. Like you did."

She wasn't sure if he was referring to her taking it or her leaving it, but either way the mood in the room had soured.

"Have you ever thought about modeling again?" he asked. She knew he meant modeling *for him*. His ownership was implied.

"Never again," she said, gently and firmly. "Not ever again."

Spring 2007

At nine sharp on a Thursday morning when the sun had moved onto spring, but the wind and the ground were deep asleep in winter, Alice was informed of her father's death. She was surprised, at first, since she'd assumed he'd died during their thirteen-year silence, only to realize he'd been haunting the same house she'd grown up in all this time. It was thirty minutes away. He'd been thirty minutes away and he had never, not once, reached out.

His lawyer had all the details. Her father had been sick and had time to make sure his estate was all in order. Alice stood perfectly still in the kitchen as the stranger on the line explained everything. She would get nothing; her children, whom her father had never acknowledged, would get nothing. The soles and heels of her feet felt bony, like she knew the exact spot where each joint met the floor. The lawyer rambled on. She imagined him wearing one of those awful off-the-rack men's suits. Cheap, slick suiting cut large so no matter the shape of the man wearing it, the pants and jacket always billowed out from his frame. Those suits that creased like hell and breathed like rubber. She'd never let Arthur wear something like that.

"Wait," she interrupted the lawyer. "Say that again."

"I said, he'll be buried alongside your mother at—"

And all at once Alice was flooded by images of her mother. The same red hair on her own head but swept up into a French twist. A tailored navy blue skirt, black silk stockings. A pregnant woman sitting with an embroidery loop by a window aglow in the gold of an afternoon. The smell of roses, the stained glass Rose Window at her school, a perfect velvet bud opening into a perfect red bloom.

Alice hung up on the man mid-sentence. She walked to her bedroom, stared at the bed, sat on the bed, sprung off the bed, drank a glass of lukewarm water, and went to the bathroom to throw up the water. Then she picked up the phone to call Gabriel. She had never been the one to reach out—always it was his call, always she was the receiving one. But she'd found her mother. Years and years of not knowing, of living with the pain that she might never know what happened to the woman who was at the center of her life one moment and gone the next. She looked down at the stack of unopened mail on the counter beneath the phone. Written on the corner of one of the envelopes, in her hand though she didn't remember writing it, the address of a cemetery in D.C. and the location of the burial plot. She wanted Gabriel, but that wasn't who she needed at that moment.

Three rings. Then Arthur's voice on the other end.

"Hello? Allie?"

Alice jerked away from the phone in surprise.

"Arthur?"

"Yes, dear, Arthur." She heard a smile in his voice. There was a small echo, scattered laughter. She looked at the time on the microwave. He was in the middle of class. She'd called, and he'd answered his phone right there in the middle of teaching.

"I know where my mom is buried," she said.

"What?" A rustle over the microphone. He was saying something to his class. More rustling. Then louder and clearer he asked.

"Honey, what's happened? Is everything—"

"My father died, and his lawyer called. He told me where my mom is buried. We have to go see her."

"Oh God, are you okay?"

In frustration Alice's voice grew louder, sharper.

"We need to go see her now," she said. "And you have the car. So, you need to come home— No, go get the girls from school, then come and get me, then we go find her. I want the girls there. The girls should be there."

"Well maybe we can go this weekend—"

"No. We go now. He'll be buried this weekend, and I don't want to see him there. I need to see her. The girls need to see her."

"Allie, take a breath," Arthur said, so gently she wanted to scream.

"I'll call Gabriel if I need to. He'll pay for a cab—"

"No, you don't need to do that," he rushed to say. "I'm coming, okay? I'm on my way. Just stay where you are and don't— Just stay where you are."

She hung up, satisfied with the panic she'd sparked in his voice. He really would be on his way now. She went back to her office and loaded up her camera. It was going to be a reunion. She wanted to document the occasion.

"Take a left up here," Alice said. Arthur navigated the car over to the next lane and took the left.

"Right at that tree," she ordered. He obeyed. As they turned into a neighborhood, Arthur recognized where they were going, and he started anticipating her directions. As her childhood home came into view Alice unbuckled her seat belt, and as Arthur pulled up to the curb she opened her door and jumped out of the car before he'd even come to a complete stop.

Arthur and the girls watched as she bent and rustled through the bushes next to the front door. She struggled with the lock. Then the door was open, and she disappeared inside. The car *ding-ding-ding*ed, but Arthur left the passenger door open. Hadn't it been just like this thirteen years ago when he'd come to bring her home? Him waiting in the car, her fighting her way through that house to get to him. Fighting to escape.

"Dad?" Marigold's voice was only just louder than the door alert.

"Hmm?" He tilted his head her way, but kept his eyes on the dark hallway just inside the front door, watching for signs of movement.

"Where are we?" she asked.

"This is where Mom grew up," he explained.

"Really?" Violet unbuckled her seat belt and went over to her sister's side of the car to look up at the house.

"Hunh," Violet said. "It just looks normal." She sounded disappointed.

"What did you think it would look like?" Arthur asked.

"I dunno." She shrugged. "I didn't think she grew up in a normal house, I guess."

Marigold nodded. The girls seemed to understand each other. Arthur did not. He saw movement at the top of the stairs just past the doorframe.

"Seat belts," he ordered as the girls got back into position. Alice emerged from the house carrying an old suitcase. She kicked the front of the house closed, left the spare key in the lock in the hope someone would break in and burn the place down, and went back to her family. She slid into the passenger seat, slammed the door shut so hard the girls jumped in their seats, and told Arthur:

"We can go home now."

"Seat belts, Mom," Marigold chirped from the backseat. As she clicked in, the sleeve of her coat brushed against the top of the suitcase to reveal a cherry-red color underneath the thick coat of dust and grime, *RM* scrolled in cursive across its front.

Portrait of the Artist in Four Parts
2015

Alice Snyder
American, 1974–2017

Quadriptych

Embroidery and paint on linen with custom frames

First shown at the Suki Gallery before being bought and placed in the Virginia Visionary Museum's permanent collection, *Portrait of the Artist in Four Parts* is one of Snyder's most popular pieces to date, rising in renown after its inclusion in Bianchi's 2019 book *Women Without Mirrors: Women's Self-Portraits*. Here we see the artist's figure as a giant, barely contained by the multiple canvases that attempt and fail to capture her entire image. The material limits force her to be broken up into pieces, with each panel containing its own contained element of tension.

The construction of this piece is another area of interest. Included with this piece are strict instructions from the artist about how it is to be hung. Of tantamount importance was the direction that these four technically separate images always be hung together to form a quadriptych, or a multi-paneled piece meant to be seen together. From left to right the panels are labeled as such:

BACKSTITCH

> Child's Hands—a pair of small, fat hands enter from off frame to grab at the artist's skirt
> Needle—left hand out, wrist to the sky, as she draws her thread through its fabric
> Loop—right hand clutching her embroidery loop
> Face—the artist in middle age, looking up as if irritated by the interruption

PANEL ONE: CHILD'S HANDS

In December of 1983, Mr. Miller walked a young woman room to room in the dark house and pointed at everything she was meant to take away, while she took notes. Yellow stickers meant the item would be donated; orange meant it would be thrown away. There were orange stickers everywhere: on all the lace doilies under the vases, on every valence and curtain tie. It was like this sometimes when people were grieving. Some widowers tried to purge everything after a loved one had died, every piece of furniture they'd ever sat on, every curtain they might have peeked through, only to realize once they saw the stripped spaces that they did want to remember after all. Mr. Miller was not one of those widowers. Everything he got rid of would stay gone. The young woman could feel it.

After walking her through the major rooms downstairs, they went over the final handover checklist and he gave her the keys to the backdoor to lock when it was time for her to leave. She'd wanted him to go through the bedrooms and bathroom upstairs with her as well, but he insisted he couldn't. He said he had a meeting he had to get to. At noon on a Friday. His hands were beginning to shake.

He closed the front door with a bang as he left. The young woman shook off his bad mood. She pulled out her Walkman and got to work. As she collected items from the living and dining rooms, she decided to make some small edits to Mr. Miller's lists. The doilies, curtains, and quilts all commuted from the trash pile to the donate pile. She'd tried, at first, to just let them go but they'd been handmade just like the ones at her own grandmother's house, and she couldn't bring herself to throw them away. What he didn't know, she thought, couldn't hurt him.

A dead husband was easier to clean up after than a dead wife. A husband didn't make an impression on a kitchen or bathroom. A dead husband had only his sleeping area and maybe a den or an office to influence. But a dead wife? Evidence of them was everywhere. In the bathroom alone, the young woman had to pull and sort bottles of exfoliant, lotion, deodorant, perfume vials, makeup remover, lipsticks, powder boxes, eye shadow palettes, mascara tubes, shampoo, conditioner, the blow dryer, the straightener, the curler, hair spray, a variety of brushes each with its own job, hot curlers, rag curlers, elastic hair ties, bobby pins, clips, barrettes, decorative combs, functional combs, wax kits, and a set of razors. Not even a complete list of everything a woman needed.

The young woman had made a few trips up and down the stairs from the bathroom to the pile of donations she kept on the family's dining room table before she realized things were going missing. The young woman paused. She waited. She went into the living room across the hall and pretended to move things around in there for a minute. Then she rushed back to the dining room just in time to catch sight of the edge of a skirt as someone ran to hide in the kitchen.

"I see you!" the young woman called out. "You don't have to hide, okay? Just come out slowly and say hello."

The toe of a child's shoe slid out into view, then the edge of a kilt, then out stepped a little girl no more than eight years old. The woman lady knew on sight who she was. The little copy of the redheaded woman whose pictures she'd just been gathering from every frame on the house. This must be the daughter. The child was still in her school uniform: black-and-white saddle shoes, knee-high white socks, stiff khaki skirt, white blouse with a navy cravat layered under her navy blue cardigan with the school insignia sewn onto the front. Sewn, not just ironed on. Her long, tangled hair was raked back into a tight ponytail with a matching navy scrunchie around it.

"Hello there," the young lady said. "I didn't realize there was anyone else here."

"Your daddy didn't tell me you were here," the young lady said.

"He forgot." The girl didn't seem bothered.

"I'm sure he's been going through a lot these days." The young woman gestured wide to the house. "Is there anyone else here? Or maybe someone who's supposed to be here? Like a nanny or a baby-sitter?"

The girl went over to a pile of quilts that had already been saved from the trash pile and began flipping through the edges as if she was inspecting the young woman's work.

"I had a nanny, I think," the little girl said. "But I'm pretty sure she was fired."

"Oh," the young woman said. Even in the little time she'd spent with the father, he hadn't struck her as the forgiving type. "Well, I think your daddy will be—"

"I'm not supposed to call him that. He says only babies say 'Daddy.'"

"What do you call him then?" the young woman asked.

"I don't call him anything really." The little girl shrugged. "Most people call him sir. I don't know what you're supposed to call him. Maybe Mr. Miller. That's what the other guests call him."

"I'm not really a guest. Your— Mr. Miller hired me to help clean up your house. Did he talk to you at all about that?"

The little girl went from the quilts to one of the boxes of doilies.

There were matching sets for every season, and she flipped through the edges of the stack like they were the pages in a book, and she was searching for the place she'd left off.

"I don't know about things before they happen," she said. "I only know when they're happening."

"Well, I'm kind of like a maid. A special maid. I come in and help people clean up when they're having a hard time doing it for themselves."

"My father doesn't need help," the little girl said sharply. "And everything was already clean. You're just here to take her things away."

The young woman opened her mouth to reassure the child that wasn't true but snapped it shut again before she could lie. A child mourning could embody all the extreme emotions of an adult without the self-control. They could shut down, lash out, or seem completely normal, all within the course of a single day. The only constant the young woman had found with children like these was a hatred of being coddled and a greater-than-average need for grace. It was a hard balance to find.

"That's right," the young woman admitted. "I am not here to clean. I am here to take all these things away. But it's not everything."

The little girl gave her a pitying look. Pity, from a child.

"What's your name?" the young woman asked.

"Alice Miller," she responded. "My mother wanted to name me Daisy, but my father wouldn't let her, so my name is Alice."

"It's nice to meet you, Alice," the young woman said. "I know this is probably a hard time for you, but most people do feel better after I'm done cleaning for them."

Alice dug her fingers into the piles of doilies and nodded in response. "Are you going to clean my room, too?"

"I might need to, if Mr. Miller put any stickers in there."

Alice nodded again, then left the quilts to go stand at the foot of the stairs. She paused at the doorframe and looked back at the young woman, who only then realized she was meant to follow. The little girl led her up the stairs, down a small hallway on the right, and left the door to her bedroom open behind her as she went in. The young woman peeked inside. There were orange stickers everywhere, from the girl's small bed to her porcelain dolls to her closet, and on the other side of the room was something that hit the young woman like a metal prod straight to her heart. A brand-new blue bassinet and changing table with a rocking chair opposite. Orange all over everything.

The young woman turned back to the girl.

"I have a plan," she said. "I think it would be best if you stayed downstairs while I clean up your room the way Mr. Miller wants, and then after you can come up and look. Is that alright with you?"

"What should I do downstairs?" Alice asked.

"Why don't you . . . go through the piles I've made and make sure I've done a good job. And if there is anything that's super special you think I shouldn't throw away, make sure to put it in one of the 'sell' piles, okay? Do you know which is which?"

Alice nodded and went back downstairs. They both worked in silence, the young woman carrying box after box down the stairs, and Alice carefully unstacking then restacking each neat pile. The child's room was stripped bare by the time the young woman was done. Gone were the toys, the trinkets, the pretty dresses. Gone the pictures of mother and daughter, and left were the empty frames. Left was utility. School uniforms and drab, hand-me-down playclothes from some neighbor or cousin. Even the baby books the girl must have grown up reading were marked for removal and only the schoolbooks remained.

As the young woman put the last of the porcelain-faced dolls into a box, she heard a small gasp behind her. Alice's face was slack as she surveyed her new room. The child walked past her dresser, running a hand over the empty top. She passed her hand over the empty bedside table, then sat with a squeak on the edge of her bed. The young woman tried to read Alice's face but there was nothing there, and that nothing was worse than any of the emotions she could imagine. The young woman left the girl alone to get used to her new room and retreated downstairs.

Once the rooms had been stripped, the items sorted and packed, the young woman called her work to request the movers arrive with the company van to pick everything up. The young woman oversaw the process, directing the young men which boxes should go first into the truck, and which ones held fragile things that had to go last. She walked with them through the first floor, all while keeping an eye on the stairs in case Alice was ready to come back down. When the boxes were all packed and the van was running in the tight back alley behind the house, the young woman walked through the house one final time, ending her loop at the door of the child's room. She knocked. Alice opened the door.

"Are you done?" Alice asked.

"Almost, I just have one more thing for you downstairs and then I'll be done-done."

The young woman led Alice down to the dining room. On the table was the mother's red suitcase with its mouth open, packed tightly with everything Alice had saved from the piles while they'd cleaning. There were single crocheted scarves and knitted blankets, doilies in a deep purple-y red they used only at Christmastime, hair ribbons her mother had let her pick herself, a roll filled with hooks, needles, and pins, some embroidered pieces, and pressed between tissue paper was a single saved photograph of Alice as an infant sleeping in her mother's arms. Alice went up to the table and looked through the layers.

"Can you keep a secret?" the young woman asked Alice.

The child nodded.

"Now I saved all this for you, and *only* for you, okay? If Mr. Miller finds out I put all this aside I think he'd be very unhappy. And we don't want that, do we?"

"No," Alice said in a small voice.

"Good." The young woman closed the suitcase with a click. "Now I've been over every inch of this house, but I bet you know it even better than me. Is there someplace for you to hide this? Someplace he doesn't know about?"

Alice's face bloomed into a smile. She led the young woman back up to her room, went to the far side of the bed, and pulled the nightstand away from the wall to reveal a small door. She undid the latch and stepped back to let the young woman inspect. It was a small crawl space, most likely left over from before the house had central air and heat. On her hands and knees the young lady looked for signs of moths and patted the floor to check for dampness. It was a bit dusty, but nothing that could get into the suitcase. She gave the child a single curt nod and slid the suitcase in place. Alice closed the secret door, dragged her nightstand back into place, and studied her work.

"Do you think it's safe?" she asked the young woman.

"Safe as houses," the young woman responded.

The pair went back downstairs slowly, the young woman trying to delay her exit for as long as possible. Standing with her bag and keys at the back door, she hesitated.

"Are you sure there isn't anyone I can call to come look after you?" she asked Alice. "There has to be a neighbor or a family friend."

"I don't need a babysitter," Alice reassured her. "He leaves me home alone all the time."

"But . . . I can't just . . ." The woman struggled to find the right words to explain. It felt wrong to leave the girl there all alone. Like the violation of some solemn bond between women. A law that held the young lady, the child, and her ghost of a mother together in a nest of inherited maternal responsibility. The young woman doubted the movers waiting for her in the van had ever felt this: the sense that all women must substitute each other as caregivers if the responsible woman is absent.

"You don't need to worry," Alice said. "I won't tell him anything. And even if he finds it, I'll just tell him I stole it when you weren't looking. You won't get in trouble. I promise."

Alice opened the back door for her like she was a tiny hostess excusing a guest at the end of party. The young woman reached out her right hand for a handshake out of instinct, but Alice took it in her left and swung it between them like they were friends walking together on a playground. The young woman smiled, and Alice smiled back. The young woman gave her hand one tight squeeze, then left.

PANEL TWO: NEEDLE

As a teenager, Alice would wait until she heard her father leave for the bar in the evening, then an hour after that just in case he'd forgotten his wallet, and only then would she go for the suitcase in the crawl space. Now she picked up the bedside table instead of dragging it to prevent marks on the floor that might give the secret away. She popped the latch and pulled the suitcase out at an angle to keep from destroying the cobwebs formed along the door's hinges that would betray her weekly activities.

It hadn't started as the great secret life it now was to her. She'd only started this out of boredom. Despite the Catholic Academy for Girls' claims of providing academic stimulation to rival the best school in the district, Alice often found herself bored after just a few hours of homework. Each new semester promised to be the one that would finally provide her with a worthy challenge, and it did, for about a month. But then the hours she spent studying would finally add up and the small thrill she felt when she was in pursuit of a skill just out of her reach would ease as her mastery grew, and eventually she always outpaced it. In these lulls, when she waited for the rest of her class to catch up to her, Alice could get her homework done in half the time and use those empty nights for her own, autodidactic education.

Alice lay the suitcase on her bed and began unpacking her laboratory, as she called it, setting each item with the delicacy of a surgeon handling a scalpel. The picture in tissue paper, the roll of knitting needles and crochet hooks, a pair of embroidered roses on linen still in its loop, doilies, scarves, a blanket, and quilt. She passed her hand over them, to the right, then to the left, then picked up the embroidered roses and took it to her desk. She tugged the standing magnifying glass forward, the one she told her father she needed to buy for her honors biology, and flicked on her reading lamp. She lifted open the top drawer of her desk and once again made a show of passing her hand back and forth before selecting the small box of sanitary napkins shoved in the back right corner. She pushed past the two decoys and pulled out the third pad, the thin plastic barely rustling as she unfolded the two sides.

The pad was punctured by a line of sewing needles running down its middle. The thickest ones were up top, the ones she used to mend denim, and they grew thinner by fractions down the line. Some of the needles with finer points had the pink thread she'd been working with still running through the eye so she could pull her selection out with a single swift tug. She'd pricked her fingertips trying to wheedle them out of the dense cotton for a week before she thought of leaving them with a tail. Alice chose her embroidery needle, the one with the largest eye and the sharpest tip, and placed the roses under her microscope, rotating it from there right, then to the left, as she tried to decide on her best incision point.

The others had been easier. She'd started with one of the crocheted scarves. Simple shape, rectangle, simple structure, ten singles by twenty-five chains. She'd just snipped the end knot and followed the pattern backward, learned how each loop fed into the next by watching them slowly unravel. Feeling a thrill as the tension in each line gave way between her fingers. Halfway down that first chain she'd taken one of the hooks that seemed to fit and had tried reassembling the end line. By the end of the week, she could unravel the whole first line and redo it, cast off and all. A week after that she unraveled even more and taught herself the stacking technique that built the scarf long and thin.

The knitting was more difficult. She'd had failure after failure trying to teach herself how to work the two needles but eventually, she was forced to admit a need for a real teacher. Her home economics teacher was the only real answer. All Alice had to do was infer the existence of a dead mother and the woman naturally stepped in with coos and kind eyes to help her learn. It only took a month before Alice could unravel a whole foot of the blanket and reknit it again. She'd gone to the same woman again when she needed help with the doilies, and again the home ec teacher gladly set aside lunchtime to help the poor girl with her little projects.

All the projects until then had a similar sense about them. They were all sequences of the same actions repeated over and over again with slight variation in order to produce design. Embroidery was a different story. She'd studied the two roses her mother had left her from every angle and couldn't find a way to undo a stitch without risking the tension of everything else. She had even tried tugging the final pitch loose with the point of her finest needle but the hole it had made in the linen was permanent. There was no way to mend the weave once it had been pierced. So now, instead of reverse engineering what existed, sixteen-year-old Alice spent her nights trying to mirror what she saw in the frame just by looking at it. She'd finished her mother's second rose for her, with moderate success. The stitches were almost identical, but the old thread had clearly started to age in the crawl space. The new section was stronger and brighter than what was there before.

With that second rose done, the design was complete. Alice wasn't all the way happy with the product, but she couldn't deny the wholeness it now had. A wholeness she would ruin with more fussing. There was no other technique to master in the red suitcase, no other project to finish. So, this week Alice took out her secret work, threaded her needle, and waited to know what she was meant to do next.

A moment of silence, then sudden action. Alice unscrewed the hoop and pulled the linen out of its frame. Thin and malleable, but with a strong weave. Her mother's flowers had been beautiful and exact, but even as she'd mimicked them, she didn't feel that they'd captured the spirit of a rose. Its softness, the heavy elegance. As Alice made her first few marking lines for a new bouquet next to her mother's, she wondered how she could make it better this time.

PANEL THREE: LOOP

In 1995, a very pregnant Alice sat in the living room in her new house on Artemesia Drive and embroidered. She'd become so fond of sitting in the curtainless bay window, sections of her hair were beginning to lighten. Arthur sat with her every morning as he drank his coffee. In the hour after he left for work but before the demands on her bladder became too much, Alice worked. Needle diving in, rising out, again and again. Progress so slight she could only track it when she held the frame away from her and saw it at a new angle.

Her hands were strong but not yet worn—the hands of a woman who made things. All those mornings she sat in Arthur's mother's chair, wearing Arthur's mother's dress, using her own mother's skills, thinking of her daughter. She was making her. Just below the frame and fabric, underneath the loose dress and the layers of warm skin and muscle, there was a baby that would become Violet Snyder. The new name felt like magic to her. With a simple switch of family words she could transform Gabriel's child into Arthur's. She could end the Miller line. The baby could come out looking like a little carbon copy of her biological father and she'd still sign her name Violet Snyder every day, come home to the house, recount how she did on her English test to Arthur.

The house was still a stranger to Alice. There were boxes from her old room that had arrived unbidden to Arthur's office. Boxes from Arthur's parents' house filled with all their unwanted, duplicate, and hand-me-down things. This was all they had to build this new life they'd bet on together, the refuse of their parents. Alice groaned through the wave of ache in her body and she pick, pick, picked at the frame.

Clouds passed over the sun, dimming the day's luster. Alice stilled and examined what she was making. She'd begun stitching in the highlights, lining the existing burgundy with a gaudy orange. The combination was either brilliant or terrible. It had the seeds of both possibilities. The project had begun as a gift for Arthur, something to hang on the wall of his cramped office at the university, but it was something else now. Something for them both to see as she made his house their home.

The cloud passed and the sun shone brighter. Alice turned her face up to the window to feast on the light with her skin. Her forehead ringed with a beaded string of sweat; her hair, thanks to the hormones, was twice its normal thickness. She shook her head and the dust that had settled in it sprung up into the air.

She felt a tug in her scalp as she shook and discovered a ringlet of hair had been caught and held by the orange thread she was using for the piece. Alice tugged her head back in little jerks to check the strength of the hold. When it didn't budge, she slid her fabric shears from their plastic holster and snipped the cord that attached her to her work. Then she held the frame up to her face for closer inspection, trying to find the exact place where the piece had begun to blend with her, fiber by fiber. She held it out at arms' length. She pulled it in until it almost touched her nose. She turned it over, inspecting the back and front. She tilted it, angle to inverted angle, narrowing her eyes to make the pupils dilate, taking in more detail. She couldn't find the beginning or the end of it. The only difference—and she was sure she was imagining things—was that the most recent section of highlight might have an extra glimmer to it where her hair might be hiding in the weave. She went back to her work, brushing the curtain of her hair behind her shoulders, accepting that untied, it would eventually fall under her needle again.

Her hand stilled as she felt roiling pressure, movement inside of her. Violet kicked one, two, three times. Alice dropped her embroidery with a clatter onto the floor. She put one hand on her belly and tried to fight the panic that remained over her life like a gauzy curtain, diffusing light and blurring images. She was sure she'd live, and she was sure she'd die. She hadn't mentioned the second part to anyone else yet. If she told Arthur he would assume it was an effect of losing her mother to childbirth. And perhaps it had remained that way. But now it was its own living, breathing monster that stayed with her day and night, reminding her that with every week of growth, every doctors' visit and milestone met, she was drifting always closer to her death.

Alice balled her hands into fists and tried to ride the wave of panic that rose inside her, but it was refusing to ebb. Action was the only solution. She picked up her embroidery project and left it on the windowsill to pick up again later. She went to the boxes her new mother-in-law had sent over of their duplicate and hand-me-down housewares. The pieces she was supposed to make a home with. She unpacked box after box, sometimes only managing to move a pile of things inside of cardboard to a pile of things *outside* of cardboard.

It happened when she was unpacking the formal tablecloths Arthur's mother had sent, most too faded or stained to actually be used for their intended purpose. Suddenly the young woman who'd taken away all her mother's things after her death came roaring back to her with such force she had to steady herself against the dining room table. Then all at once she had a new mission. Somehow, someway, she had to get back into her father's house, into that crawl space, and steal back the small inheritance her mother had left her. She sent a silent prayer up to a god she'd been trained to believe in, *Please let me live long enough to steal it back.*

PANEL FOUR: FACE

At forty-one, the mother of two college students, Alice couldn't quite believe she was still here. Still on earth, forced to push herself through day after endless day to accumulate this thing called life.

It was the winter of 2015, and she was freezing because she'd changed into pajama pants after she'd gotten home and hadn't had time to change back before she'd stormed out after another fight with Arthur. It suited her mood. The fights weren't as fraught as they used to be, back when walking away was something both of them still thought she was capable of. Now they were more like pressing an old familiar bruise that never faded. It was a little pain and feeling it was, in its own way, a comfort. When she felt bad, they fought, and she went to hide in the workspace Gabriel had rented for her in an industrial park just a short drive from the house.

Alice saw now that Gabriel had changed her marriage with Arthur, though not in the way they had expected. When he'd come back, when they'd started meeting, when Alice had started being able to afford her own supplies without talking to her husband first, it was like all three of them had been bracing for impact. As if Gabriel's return, and the money that followed, would necessarily ruin everything they'd built in his absence. But it hadn't. Alice and Arthur had been thrown off-balance for a time, but then they course corrected. No one had been ruined; they had just found a new rotation that included Gabriel.

Alice flipped the light switch to her new space. The fluorescent bulbs flickered on overhead and the sight of her current in-process work brought her back into the moment. She was working on a new kind of form. A portrait of her mother in parts. A series of partial images that should, she hoped, hold more of the truth of her than a single clear image could. She was working on her face now. She adjusted the small mirror she had clipped on her tool cart and started selecting what she'd need. The basket with her sewing supplies and the tackle box with her painting tools were always given pride of place on the top shelf of the cart. Alice closed her eyes and took her ponytail down. Head in her hands, she rubbed her scalp with her fingers in small circles, pushing further back past her hairline until they overlapped at the back of her skull. She completed the ritual once more, then studied her boxes again. The basket, covered in a pink floral-patterned fabric, tufted on top, pink ribbon winding around the handle, rounded and soft. The tackle box, made from the same plastic used for the soles of work boots, with half-peeled stickers from the fishing supply warehouse it'd come from, hard lines and sharp angles. Inside the cover of each one was an index card with the same question written on it.

Why does it have to be this way?

When she'd bought both boxes the cashier had asked if they were gifts. Alice went to her sewing basket first. She took out the top tray with all the smallest things and started pulling out her tools. Fabric shears, a series of measuring tapes and rulers, the thread she'd chosen for this section of the piece. She pushed aside all the things she wasn't doing: the motherly duties, the wifely concerns, the distracting promise of fresh projects.

Why was it this way?

What was here and nowhere else?

She scooped out loose notions and buttons like she was digging through sand. The box she wanted was at the bottom, a matte gold jewelry box. Inside: two sets of embroidered roses, hers on top and underneath, her mother's. She closed the basket and laid the roses on linen on the top like an altar cloth. Alice didn't bother with paper anymore. She picked up her pencils and drew right on the linen.

The Lives and Fates of the Dioscuri
2016

Alice Snyder
American, 1974–2017

Polyptych

The greatest surviving piece of Snyder's work is undoubtedly this series of embroidered paintings she created for the reception hall inside of Kenning University's unfulfilled Women's Sport's Center. Snyder's participation in this project initially struck many as a mismatch. While she did have strong ties with the university, Snyder's typical focus on the domestic and personal seemed at odds with the modern design and grand scale of the proposed facility. However, Snyder managed to find a subject that joined together her strengths and the university's interests: the Greek demigods, the Dioscuri.

The Dioscuri is the collective name for Castor and Pollux, the half-divine twins of Leda and two separate fathers, one mortal and one a god. The Dioscuri are most associated with horsemanship and saviors of those in great danger, but also claim sports, the home, and hospitality as areas of association.

A few areas of particular note: While the Dioscuri are traditionally male, Snyder portrays them here as female twins, once more reclaiming a male-dominated story for her own purposes. Instead of depicting moments usually chosen for artistic attention like *Leda and the Swan* or *The Rape of the Daughters of*

Leucippus, Snyder creates her own imagined moments in the lives of the twins. She makes use of their traditional iconography but shapes it to her own interests. The *dokana*, two parallel beams with two others placed across them, becomes one of Snyder's thresholds. The sisters each carry embossed shields, one glowing gold for the sun, the other silver for the moon. Again, she returns to an image of her obsession, the twins, both identical and opposite, held in constant tension of attraction and repulsion.

BACKSTITCH

Pollux Visits Her Sister, Castor, as She Trains Horses
2016

Alice Snyder
American, 1974–2017

In 2016, Violet had all but secured her position as her senior class's valedictorian, solidly placed at the very top of her physics program's ranking. With her 5.0 GPA and her tours of graduate schools on weekends, she had reached that point at the end of college where everything lay ahead and her surroundings seemed to shrink and fade from importance, even as they continued to ask things from her. Sign this form. Take this test. Name here, initials there. Don't skip past this, everyone warned her, it's all downhill from here. But she wanted to skip past all of this. After being plagued by a constant sense of dread, her mind infected since childhood by the idea that she had something important she had to get to, Violet now allowed herself some light optimism. An undergraduate accomplishes nothing. An undergraduate's greatest achievement is only that they now know how to learn, and Violet didn't want to learn, she wanted to already know. Her BS was always just a necessary step she'd had to take to get where she was meant to be: graduate school, her PhD, and then her work. She would finally be free of the plague of anticipation and would arrive at the thing her whole life had been building toward. The past wouldn't matter then. Her life would be so full of the present and future possibilities that the mire of secrets that cast her whole childhood in shade would have to receded into memory. She was glad she'd saved money by living at home through college, but now she needed out of this house with these parents. She needed her own life. She wasn't sure exactly what that life would look like, only that she would recognize it within herself on sight.

Just across campus her sister, Marigold, was navigating the trials of her junior year as a studio art student with a focus in the newest specialty—digital arts. She'd just begun the long process her teachers called "finding her voice" and she complained to Violet about it every chance she got. According to Marigold everything was a failure. Her grades were fine, but she didn't really care about that marker of success. Her real goal was to get through even a single project, from beginning to end, without suffering a massive crisis of confidence that reduced her to tears and near-puking hyperventilation on the floor of her studio. On a Thursday night, two weeks from presenting at the junior year critiques, Marigold reached out to her sister for help.

Violet wound her way around the side of the art building, under the low branches of a few oak trees, her eyes trained on the steaming lattes she held in each hand. She was loaded down with a large duffel over one shoulder, her own backpack on the other, and plastic bags of food weighing down her elbows. She rounded the corner and shuffled along the worn dirt path to the first in a series of four small concrete boxes that constituted the art school's student workshops. Each cube was lit up, windows and doors open for ventilation as frenzied students pulled long days and late nights to get their projects done at the last possible minute. These were the procrastinators. People possessed. Over-caffeinated, under-hydrated, probably malnourished and sleep deprived. All with their own tricks to force their minds and bodies into a state of delirium that let them push past their insecurities and simply act. Violet was not a procrastinator. She liked getting things done the moment they cropped up.

Approaching the first box, she could hear the whir of a sander through the door. Marigold wouldn't be able to hear through her earbuds and the grinding tool in her hand. Even if she texted, the chirping phone would go unnoticed. Violet lowered herself down and carefully, delicately, put one piece after another on the ground next to the door. First, the Venti Americano no cream, no sugar, then the 7-Eleven bag with a king-size pack of Reese's Peanut Butter Cups, then the bag with their dinner, two large Penne Rosas with Chicken and Extra Cheese, No Mushrooms with side salads no one would eat but were purchased to indicate some attempt at a healthy decision. She swung her father's knapsack around, borrowed to transport the assortment of hand tools, handsaws, electrical saws, books, candles, and rolled-up plans she had unearthed from her sister's room that Marigold had listed piece by piece as integral to her continued work.

The ease of movement regained, Violet turned the metal doorknob and peeked inside the studio. The years had not touched the way she entered creative spaces. Whether she was five, eleven, or twenty-one, Violet crept in silently, peering around corners and keeping her footfalls light.

She stepped in farther and took in the scene. Bits of foam and balsa wood were caught up in the air like glitter in a snow globe as Marigold perched on their mother's paint-splattered metal ladder in front of her creation, shaving and smoothing out the edges, uncovering the life inside. Her back was turned to the door, and her head was ducked down to watch the effect of her hands. All Violet saw was her figure blocking out the single pillar of light coming down from the ceiling, shoulders covered in sweat and sawdust, mechanics uniform on, pant legs tucked into her black boots. The arms moved up and down in unison, the same curve to begin with and then with each additional downward stroke the end of the line would suddenly spike up in a different direction. After some amount of grinding was found to have acceptable effects, but still lacking in certain other areas Marigold must have felt but could not, at the moment, see clearly, she straightened up and took her safety goggles off to assess the change in her creature.

Violet knocked on the inside of the door as she stepped in. Marigold turned at the noise, smiled, and pulled her earmuffs off and earbuds out.

"The cavalry approaches!" Marigold cheered, hanging her gear on the top of the ladder and hopping down. Violet swung the door open and started bringing in the bounty one bag at a time. Marigold swept off a corner of her worktable to make way for the provisions. She pulled out her industrial fans and set them up to blow away the glittering specks.

Violet set up the table for dinner, dusting off one of her sister's overturned stools to sit on. Marigold stood feet shoulder-width apart, arms akimbo, assessing her progress. She was lost in it.

"Goldie," Violet demanded, pounding one fist on the tabletop. Marigold started and swirled around, looking shocked at the spread, as if she hadn't asked for it specifically an hour ago. Like it had poured out of her head directly into reality without her knowing. She smiled and shuffled over to the table, grateful and worn but happy.

"Looking good." Violet nodded toward the figure in the middle of the room. The dust, having been blown from suspension, had lost its magic and was once again simply airborne filth. The work had come a long way from the last time Violet had been here; the base and skeleton had taken the longest to figure out and had eaten up the first two weeks of Marigold's studio time and now, having tested the base and joints for weaknesses, the ideas quickened into flesh in just a few days. Violet could see it coming through the remaining work. She saw where it would be drilled and skimmed away, she saw where the detail would go without knowing what that detail would look like. The art was shining through the cracks of the unfinished work. And once the form was finished her sister could incorporate her second element. She would bathe the figure in digital projections to complete the piece, but Violet wasn't sure exactly what that would entail.

"Really?" Marigold asked between bites of food. "You think it'll be enough?"

"It's more than enough. Especially when you're done with it."

Marigold grunted. Violet noticed her eyes were red.

"Are you okay?" she asked.

Marigold shook her head slowly.

"Work or Mom?" Violet asked. It was always one or the other.

"Did you know Gabriel Grant has been financing her?" Marigold asked, the question bursting out of her like an arrow let loose from its bow and sticking deep into Violet's breastbone.

"What?" Violet asked. Her mind spun, trying to catch up.

"He's been financing her. Giving her money. He even buys some of her work. Has been for years apparently, but she never mentioned, she never said he was one of her buyers to you, right?" The words started as calm, but the more Marigold spoke the faster they got. "I mean, do you think Dad knows? Because it's weird they never said anything, right? I mean, she's avoided him for years, right? Since that time he came to the house? Do you remember that, when we posed for the Pre-Raphaelite stuff?"

"I remember," Violet said evenly. The one time they were all together at the house. *All the parents and both of the consequences*, she thought. Memories from that day started flashing despite herself. The stiffness of her dress, the cold, the sting of yard weeds under her bare feet. *Go away, go away, go away,* she tried coaching herself as she pushed each image back under the surface of her attention. Really what Violet came back to over and over again was that she didn't want to hurt the people she loved and there was no way to say this awful thing out loud without causing more damage. It was like they carried around matching broken ribs that had been damaged years ago and never healed right. Now they might all have the same wound, the same aches when the weather changes, they might all trace their malformed parts on their bad days. But really the only way to change the situation was to re-break the bone. Not just hers, but her parents' and her sister's as well, and try to heal them better this time. In the face of that challenge, Violet cowered. She hated herself for it, but she preferred to keep aching with all the old familiar pains rather than risking something new and devastating.

"Or maybe she hasn't, because really who knows what she gets up to, she's so hard to schedule time with sometimes, and she says she's always working but I have no idea where she goes most days, do you? But then it turns out he's been giving her money all this time? I mean, what is that? Did you know?"

"No, I didn't know." Violet felt a rush of cold wash over her as her sister talked. She was freezing up. Her emotions, sensing pain was near, were shutting down. "Wait, how do you even know this?"

"A girl in my class was his . . . assistant for a while last summer." Marigold raised her eyebrows. Violet nodded in comprehension, and Marigold continued, "So when she was over at his apartment she saw all this stuff, Mom's art, and she asked *me* about it this morning after class and I tried to play it cool but I had no idea they were even talking let alone giving him—" She took a shaky breath and Violet saw tears begin to well in her sister's eyes. The sight only made her colder. "Am I an idiot?" Marigold asked. "Am I just this stupid kid to not see it?"

Violet's stomach turned over. This was it. The thing they didn't talk about. The supermassive black hole at the center of all their lives. The thing they spent years refusing to look at directly, and why? Because that was what their parents did. Because they were afraid if they ever said anything it would catch them in its hold and destroy them.

"You think Mom is having an affair with Gabriel Grant," Violet said plainly, quietly.

Marigold let her tears fall, just for a moment, then tried to gather herself again.

"That's what this is, right?"

"It could be," Violet said slowly. "Or it could be something else."

"What else could it be?"

"I don't know," Violet said. "You know her better than I do at this point. What do you think?"

"I think... I think that ever since we went to high school, she has spent a lot of time working. I think whenever she asks me to assist her it's always at the home studio, not her other one. I know that she was with him before she met Dad and..." Marigold tripped over her words. Violet wasn't sure if she wanted her to just admit the next part of that implication, or if hearing the term "half sister" from her sister's lips would hurt as much as she always thought it would. "And I think she never really tells us what's going on. Ever." Marigold took a shaky breath and stabbed at her noodles absently. "I'm not saying she is a liar. But she leaves things out."

"She leaves a lot of things out," Violet agreed.

"And she doesn't ever just explain things to us!" Marigold let loose. "She just picks fucking fights and then disappears, and when she comes back, we're not supposed to talk about it or bring it up again. We're all just supposed to forget, but we don't forget, or at least I don't."

"I don't forget, either."

"You don't?" Marigold leaned in, desperate. "Because *we* never talked about it, either."

"I know." Violet struggled to find the words to explain. "It just always seemed like, I don't know. Like, if I start talking about one thing it will lead to another thing and eventually I'll have to talk about . . . things I don't want to talk about."

Now it was Violet's turn to pull a face and hope Marigold understood what she was saying. It seemed like she did.

"I get that," Marigold said. "I can see how it would be especially hard for you."

"Hard for both of us," Violet said hurriedly. "Just in different ways. And I can't imagine what Dad feels."

"That's the other thing!" Marigold shot up from her stool and started pacing. "That's actually who I keep thinking about, you know? Because Mom is who she is. She's kind of always been like this. But what does Dad know, and why doesn't *he* ever say anything, and do you think maybe he's just as bad as she is because it's one thing to act like a dick to your family, and it's another to make excuses for the person acting like a dick, you know? Because he could get her to stop."

"Do you think he can?" Violet almost laughed imagining their father trying to control their mother like he'd seen her friends' fathers do. To yell or throw things, to "put her in her place." She honestly couldn't even picture it. Yelling and throwing things was exclusively their mother's signature. Their father was always the one nodding and apologizing, the one who tidied up the mess after Hurricane Alice had passed through.

"I mean, he got her to stop using us as models, right?" Marigold said.

"I guess," Violet said.

"And they've been married for what? Twenty-one years? That's not nothing. That's not just 'divorce is expensive.' They have to be staying together for some reason."

"For the kids?" Violet suggested weakly.

"What kids?" Marigold exclaimed. "We haven't been kids since middle school, maybe ever. Do you remember being kids? Because I remember posing and assisting and working in every spare moment we had. I don't remember being kids the way I hear my friends describing being kids. And I'm not saying we had some awful childhood," Marigold corrected. "But it wasn't usual. And I think if you raise people to be odd, you have to expect them to keep being that same kind of odd when they grow up."

"Goldie," Violet said, now barely following her sister's line of reasoning. "Please take another bite of food." Violet helpfully grabbed her sister's fork, speared some chicken and noodles and held it out to her. Marigold grabbed it and took the bite but kept talking as she chewed.

"They wanted us to be these little grown-ups, but only sometimes. Like, we had to be obedient like children, but responsible, like, adults all the time. And I just think, if you do that, you have to expect those kids to want a vote in family business."

"Okay, I'm lost," Violet admitted. "What business?"

"In the Gabriel Grant business." Marigold handed her fork back to her sister who took it, stabbed more food, then passed it back. "I think we should be able to put our foot down on this. Our feet. Put our feet down? That doesn't sound right. You know what I'm saying."

Violet gave some noncommittal noise while she tried to think of what to do. She'd known this was always a risk. If anyone was going to force them all to change it would have to be Marigold. Their parents seemed more than happy to spend the rest of their lives in the same comfortable dysfunction they always had. And Violet wasn't going to bring up anything, though with her genetics she probably had the best claim. Sure, she knew that meant she'd probably never heal, but she knew that what she had right now, she could handle. Marigold, apparently, wanted to risk it.

Marigold sat and started eating again, now with real vigor. All her worries moved from her shoulders to Violet's.

"I'll take care of it," Violet said quietly, putting her fork down. She felt sick.

"What?" Marigold asked through a mouthful of noodles.

"I'll talk to Mom," Violet said. "And I'll mention it to Dad. And I'll see what I can do to make it better."

"Really?" Marigold asked. "Are you sure? Because I can go with you—"

"No," Violet cut her off. That really would be too painful. "Just let me take care of it, okay?"

"Okay," Marigold agreed. She sighed and looked back at her sculpture, attention and energy now ready to be refocused on her work. Violet followed her gaze and studied the form.

"Can you see what's wrong with it?" Marigold asked.

Violet tilted her head.

"The stomach?" she guessed.

"Yes, specifically the female musculoskeletal shape. That's why I had you bring these." Marigold pulled a few laminated charts out of the duffel bag. They were the kind of medical charts you'd see in a doctor's office of bodies stripped of skin in layers to reveal their inner makeup. "Female bodies have these long, lean muscles at the bottom of their torso and this is the closest I can get to a guide without getting a real model."

"So, you know the fix?"

"I know it, it's just that doing it is going to be a lot harder. And I'll have to get it right on the first try because I don't have time to fuck around in clay. How do they expect me to make a whole person without giving me a live model?" Marigold waved at the figure. "Honestly, it's ridiculous. I'm not a magician."

"I can pose," Violet said, still looking at the figure. She offered herself up without thought, and the reality of what she'd offered only arrived in her mind as her little sister turned back to her in surprise.

"Really?" Marigold said, trying to keep her obvious interest in check. "That would be amazing. If you wanted to. But only if you want to, okay? I don't want to be Mom."

"Relax." Violet waved her concerns away, even though the same comparison had skittered across her own mind a moment earlier. "I won't let you become Mom. And I can spare twenty minutes. It's mostly the lower stomach you need, right?"

Marigold nodded, almost tripping over her feet in an effort to grab her camera for the reference photos. Violet took off her scarf and sweater in two swift movements. She rolled up her shirt's hem and tucked it under her bra's band as she took her place to the right of the sculpture. She placed one foot in front of the other and shifted her weight back and forth, arms out, head up, so that the muscles in her abdomen would take the needed shape.

Marigold came up to her side and started placing her. Gently, precisely, her sister shifted the angle of Violet's shoulders, placed her hands on her hips so she wouldn't have to keep them aloft, then just as Violet was sure they'd achieved the right image her younger sister stepped back and frowned.

"What?" Violet asked, voice tight from holding her strained position.

"Could you ... ?" Marigold gestured up. Violet rose shakily onto the balls of her feet, feeling her weight shift into her center as she struggled to stay up, finally pulling the hard-to-reach muscles at the very bottom of her torso that ran from her belly button to her pelvis.

"That's it!" Marigold grabbed her camera and began focusing. "Stay right there."

The camera's shuttering filled the room, glass eye blinking as it captured angle after angle. At least it wasn't taking all of her this time. *Just the stomach*, Violet reminded herself. But it was the exact center of her, so she had to hold all of her body just so. Marigold's pictures might take only one part, but the pose required all of her to focus to get that one part just the way she needed it. Violet took shallow breaths, sucking in through her teeth and out through her nose.

Marigold made a small, excited noise, ran back to her table, and exchanged her camera for a sketch pad and pencil.

"One more minute," she said. "Almost there."

Marigold flipped to an open page in her notebook and started capturing the angles again in a series of quick lines, shuffling around Violet like a little crab. Her boots parted the settled sawdust and foam bits beneath her in an open, scalloped edge. Marigold shuffled behind her, taking the opportunity to do quick studies of her spine and back musculature. Violet's eyes fluttered up to the filthy ceiling where years of dust and detritus caught on the sprayed cement. It was too easy, doing this again. Remembering how to hold herself, how to breathe, how to be pinned down in that exact moment instead of always buzzing with thoughts of the future or haunted by feelings of the past. Some people might even find the focus clarifying, meditative, but to Violet it still felt the way it did to stare up at the ceiling in her bunk bed after her mother had let them go back to bed, waiting to wake up for real.

"Done!" Marigold said from behind her. Violet let her pose drop and shook out her tight limbs. She should have stretched. Marigold was much more settled after that. Violet sat with her, sweater and scarf back on, and they chatted lightly about the other students' projects while they finished eating. Violet could see her sister was trying to be polite but there was a light in her eyes she recognized. Now that she had what she needed, the art could keep going. Marigold was only waiting for Violet to leave to get back to it.

So, she did.

Past the hugs and the divvying of food for the continued labors of the night, Violet slipped back through the door a little sadder than she had been before she arrived. Childishly she wished that when she took one final look inside the studio before leaving, her sister would look back to her, but she didn't.

BACKSTITCH

> ## Pollux Before Leda on Her Throne
> 2016
>
> Alice Snyder
> American, 1974–2017

Violet decided that if she was going to ruin a place forever with the memory of what she was sure would be an awful discussion with her mother, she would pick a setting she didn't mind never visiting again. This is why she chose her mother's other studio. The one in the industrial park. The one with Gabriel Grant's name on the lease.

It was only in the moment before she opened the metal door that Violet considered what might be waiting for her inside. In the five years that her mother had worked in the second studio, Violet had never actually stepped foot inside the building. She dropped Marigold off, or picked her up, when her younger sister was working as their mother's assistant. She'd driven past the park that housed it countless times on her way to and from her father's office. But she didn't really know what was inside, and when she did push into the darkness she was surprised. It was not anything like she thought it would be.

Alice's second studio was much more like a storage facility than anything else. There was a wall of boxed and crated pieces waiting to be collected, a set of open storage units on the far wall with neatly boxed supplies, some random stools and another percolator, twin to the one they had at home, sitting on the floor next to a tiny white dorm refrigerator. It was nothing like the mess in their home. No piles of torn blank paper, no half-finished pieces lined up on the wall waiting to be resolved, no haphazard stacks of printed out research. No life. There was no feeling of a life in the second studio, just the mechanical movement of a waystation, substance moving in and out. It was the pumping chamber of an anatomical heart, not the hearth fire of a soul.

Violet walked farther in and saw that what she'd thought was a drop cloth spread out on the floor was, in fact, a canvas. Painted on it was a series of scenes from the life of a woman she supposed was a version of her mother. That's how she always thought of her mother's self-portraits: Truth told in a dream. A scatter of scenes from various ages as a little redheaded figure wound her way alone through the world. Violet searched for a throughline, trying to trace the chronology, but could find no linear logic in her mother's approach. But even that made its own kind of sense. Violet had watched her mother work all her life. Sometimes it was like this—just a person jumping in at no specific point and seeing what they felt like capturing that day.

The front door to the room swung open and slammed against the wall with a bang as Violet's mother kicked it open, her hands full of empty frames.

"Oh good, you're here," her mother said without a bit of surprise. "I have more in the car."

Violet didn't think to be irritated at the command until she'd already gone out to collect the next batch of empty frames, and by then it felt too late. Back in the studio, Violet let the empty frames fall with a loud clatter on the concrete floor, hoping the sound would be enough to communicate her irritation. But when she turned, she caught her mother's telling back, undisturbed, going out again for more. Once load-in was done, Alice started pulling frames from the pile and laying them out over sections of the canvas. Some were small enough to capture a single image, some large enough to capture a series.

"I have to talk to you," Violet said once the silence was too much. Her mother just glanced over her, as if to check she was still there, then focused back on her work.

"I figured that," Alice said.

"Things are not good," Violet halted, unsure of how to say what she wanted. "Things have not been going well."

"At school? Problems in your classes?" Alice rotated a rectangular frame ninety degrees, then leaned back to study the change. "Have you talked to your father?"

Violet jerked back in surprise, but then realized her mother was referring to Arthur, her real father, and not the other one.

"It's not that," Violet said. "I mean, school is hard, but it's fine. It's more about Marigold, actually."

"Goldie? I just saw her yesterday, she was fine."

"No, I mean she's good. I'm saying she's not doing good."

"That doesn't make any sense, Lettie."

Violet took a deep breath and tried again to find the point.

"Goldie knows Gabriel Grant has been giving you money," she blurted out. Her mother's head snapped up.

"Excuse me?"

"Goldie found out Grant has been giving you money," Violet said again. "And it's not good."

"How, exactly, is this her business? Or your business?" The deliberate smoothness of her mother's voice made Violet want to turn and run and never speak again.

"It's making things difficult for her at school," Violet lied. It was easier to try and make the pressure look like it came from the outside rather than admitting the hurt was coming from inside the house.

"How?" It didn't sound like her mother was buying it.

"Apparently he had one of the Kenning art students assist him recently..."

Her mother scoffed and turned back to her work, but Violet charged on.

"And she saw some of your art in his apartment."

"People really must be desperate if they're gossiping about who buys my art." Her mother shook her head as she switched two frames.

"So, he bought them from you?" Violet's mind spun trying to hold on to what she'd come here to say. But what was that again?

She wanted her mother to "stop it" but standing there in that strange, uncomfortable studio, barely holding on to a quarter of her mother's attention, she was having trouble remembering what she was meant to stop. All she kept thinking was "stop it."

"He bought the art?" Violet asked. "You didn't give it to him?"

"I gave it to him . . . when he bought it." Her mother said slowly, deliberately, like she was talking to an idiot. "Was I supposed to get your permission on that?"

"No, I was just surprised when— Hold on." A flare of panic climbed up Violet's chest. "Does he have any of your early work?"

"Hmm?" Her mother nudged one on the frames over with the toe of her shoe.

"Does he have your early work?" Violet said in the same slow, insulting tone her mother just used. Her mother looked up.

"Watch it, little girl," her mother said.

Violet lightened her tone, but her voice was taut as a high wire.

"Did you sell Gabriel Grant a painting of us?" Violet felt real panic begin to set in, buzzing around her ears and tickling her cheeks. "Does he have my face in his house?"

"I don't know why you suddenly care about all this. It really isn't any of your business," Alice went to the door, jerked it open, and held it. It took a beat before Violet realized she was meant to bow out, but she stood her ground.

"Does Gabriel Grant have my face in his house?" she asked again. This was apparently all her mother needed to lose it. She left the door and charged up to her daughter until her face was just a few inches away. The last time their faces were this close her mother was doing her makeup for her senior year prom. Her breath smelled the same, acrid coffee and something like a sweet onion.

"It's not your face, it's my art."

"It is my face," Violet whispered. Then again, she said louder, "It *is* my face."

"So now you want to approve every time someone buys a piece of mine?" Her mother backed up and started pacing. How many times had Violet heard her parents fight like this over the years? And now finally here she was, seeing the real thing.

"Are you an art dealer now, Lettie?" her mother went on. "Or maybe it's not the buyer at all, maybe it's the fact that I made a little money and I had the *audacity* to spend it on myself instead of on you. Is that it?"

"It's my *face*."

"You never said no, not once," her mother reminded her. "You sat as much as you could. You and Goldie both, you *loved* sitting for me. So what, now that you're grown up you want to change your mind?"

"I liked being *useful*. I liked being good." Violet had liked how happy it made her mother, how proud she felt when she showed them off, how peaceful the house would become when everyone just did what they were told. "But I was just a little kid," Violet explained. "I didn't understand that they would get sold someday. I didn't know that one day Gabriel *fucking* Grant could just write a check and then own me forever."

"He doesn't own you," her mother scoffed. "So dramatic."

"But it's *him*. I don't give a shit about other buyers but he's—he's my—"

Alice rounded on her so suddenly Violet's shut her mouth with a snap.

"He's your *what*?" She held Violet's gaze with a terrifying forced calm. "Come on, Vi, you came here to make a stink. You want me to stop working and give you attention, you have it. You've already ruined my flow here. You clearly have something to say about Gabriel Grant, so why don't you say it?"

Violet tried to recall the strength she felt when she was talking with Marigold. She tried to dip into her protective instincts and to be strong for her sister, but in the moment, on the brink of standing up and changing things, she felt the small, scared little girl who wanted her mom to stop being angry start to take over.

She tried to summon the right words. She failed.

"It's my face," Violet repeated weakly.

"It's not your face!" Alice yelled. Violet winced, and despite the lecture she'd given herself on the car ride here, she felt herself melt back into childhood. She wanted to stick her finger in her ears and curl up in a ball to stop hearing the loud angry voices. There were even some horrible times, and this was one of them, when Violet wished her mother would hit her. At least that way it would be clear. She'd have a red mark or a bruise on her face she could point to and say: "This is where you hurt me." But instead, all she had were things like this. This nebulous, indistinct hurt that rolled over her and settled deep inside her body. Violet felt her feelings begin to flicker and shut off, and the part of her that was *her* began to pull away.

"It's not your face," her mother repeated, charging up to get within inches of it again. This time Violet looked down at her feet. "It's a painting of your face. It's something I made. Just like your actual face!" Her mother gave a humorless laugh. "Your *actual* face that I made. That I grew inside me for months and almost died bringing into this world. That I fed with my own body, and gave up my work for, and almost went insane for. I have built an entire world all for you and all you want to do is complain about how I built it?"

Violet was very far away now. There weren't even tears on her cheeks. She wasn't even flushed. Just calm and cool and dead all the way down.

"Oh, honey." Her mother wrapped her arms around Violet's shoulders and brought her in for a crushing hug. Violet let it happen, arms hanging at her sides.

"I know it can be hard to be the girl in the picture sometimes," her mother said into her hair, "but this is just how it works. No one gets to tell me what to do with my art, not you or Goldie or Dad. And no matter how big you get, or how much you piss me off, you'll always be my baby." Her mother kissed her hair. "I'm never going to let you go. Ever."

Violet didn't know what to say so she nodded and waited for her mother to dismiss her again. This time she'd just walk back out the door.

BACKSTITCH

> An Appeal to King Tyndareus of Sparta
>
> 2016
>
> Alice Snyder
>
> American, 1974–2017

Arthur found his eldest daughter sleeping on the large gray armchair he managed to squeeze into the corner of his office in the physics building. Despite being tenured, a senior member of several committees and boards, and serving as the advisor to every freshman class for five years, Dr. Arthur Snyder had still wound up with the smallest office in the entire department. He thought he'd made it when he finally transitioned from the shared cubicle in the building's damp basement he'd used as a lecturer to the small room he still used today because he finally had a window. Granted, it didn't actually open due to safety concerns, and it was tinted to reflect the sun, so the world he looked at outside his office was constantly cast in a dull shade of blue, but still, a window. Then the years kept passing, semester by semester, and there always seemed to be some pressing reason why he couldn't have one of the bigger offices. There was a shiny new faculty member they'd wooed from a different school. The graduate student union complained about the asthma risk in the damp basement, so now one of the bigger rooms was converted to a shared desk system. Dr. Winslow had a note from her doctor because she had claustrophobia. Again and again, Arthur sent requests. Again and again, they were met with sincere apologies citing unusual challenges and included overwhelming thanks for his continuing patience and stellar attitude.

Once Violet started as a freshman at Kenning, Arthur stopped sending the requests. There was something incredibly settling about having his daughter on campus. They had lunch together every Tuesday and Thursday after her morning Introduction to Anthropology class but before his Classical Mechanics course. They went to lectures together. Sometimes they just worked alongside each other, Violet doing her homework, Arthur doing his grading. One of them would get snacks from the vending machine in the faculty lounge.

Sometimes they listened to music. And she made her mark on the place, too. She insisted he get table lamps and floor lamps to avoid using the harsh overhead fluorescent bulbs that flickered when the class above it was dismissed. She stole one of his drawers to store some emergency supplies: granola bars, pads, and an extra change of clothes. The old gray armchair he used for student conferences gained a throw blanket, then a pillow.

Once Violet started school some part of the rare thing they'd built on Artemesia Drive came with her, and his office became an extension of their home. He'd initially given her the extra key to his office so she could drop off books between classes or use his printer, but then he started finding her there at unexpected times. If things were tense at home or something had happened between her and her mother, Arthur could reliably find Violet hiding out in his office, often working, occasionally curled into the fetal position, as she was now, frowning in a fitful sleep.

He put his bag down gently to keep from startling her and flicked on the overhead lights. Violet groaned, tried to cover her eyes from the harsh light, and untucked her legs from the chair.

"No overheads," she mumbled into the crook of her arm. "Fluorescence is death."

Arthur went over to his desk, tapped on the floor lamps Violet had insisted on, and switched off the overheads. She uncurled and rubbed her face. Her eyes were red and there was a small pile of balled-up tissues tucked under one of her legs.

"See your mother today?" he asked.

"Is it obvious?" She groaned.

"You know she's under a lot of stress right now, trying to finish—" Arthur stopped short when he saw Violet's chin start to quiver. He pulled up his chair and kicked the door to the office closed.

"Lettie, what happened?" he asked.

Violet dropped her gaze to her hands and slowly shook her head. Arthur sat back and waited. He kept his body facing his daughter, so she knew he was there for her. He kept his eyes on the bookshelf behind her, so she didn't feel pressured. He was patient and he waited. After her breath evened out again, she started to speak.

"I don't know how much longer I can do this with her," she said in a small voice. Arthur resisted the urge to give her a hug right then. She sounded so much like she had when she was little and the girls at school were being mean.

"I try to talk to her, and it's like . . . It's like I can't remember who I am anymore or why I'm there. I went to her studio, the other studio, to ask her one thing. Then we got into it and . . ." Violet squinted. "I start in one place and then I wind up somewhere else, and I don't know how I got there. And I feel awful afterward. It feels so bad I carry it around in my chest, it's like this weight right here"—she pressed a hand on her sternum—"and nothing gets rid of it except crying. And sometimes it can take days for me to cry. I can't just make it happen and then get over it. It sits and gets heavier, and I just have to wait until it breaks open."

Arthur waited, listening to the small tic of the seconds on his wristwatch, and when he was sure she was finished he began.

"I know it's hard on you. On you and your sister. Your mother is an intense person. And she's intense right away, with all her feelings up front, and then once she feels them they go away, poof, like they were never even there. And you're more like me."

Violet nodded and her face crumbled as she started crying again. Arthur picked up the tissue box from the floor and handed it back to her.

"Okay, so what is it that's upsetting you now?"

Violet shook her head. Arthur sighed and said the same thing he'd been saying to Violet since she was old enough to speak.

"If you don't tell me what's wrong," he said, "I can't help you."

"Marigold heard some of the art students talking," she started slowly, keeping her eyes down, "and apparently Gabriel Grant has some of Mom's work."

Arthur jerked back in surprise.

"And I went to her," Violet started speaking faster, "and I asked her if that was true, if she'd taken money from him—"

Arthur winced at her phrasing, imagining his wife's reaction.

"—but then she got all pissed that I was trying to tell her who she could sell art to, which I wasn't really saying at all. Then I just wanted to make sure she hadn't sold him one of her early works, because the idea that he could have picture of me hanging up on his wall, and that he could look at it every day, and I wouldn't even know or be able to stop it is just—

"It's just—" she tried and failed again. Arthur reached out and took her frantic hands in his.

"Okay," he said. "It's okay, I get it."

"I can't keep doing this with her, Dad, I can't keep being the wrong one. Revolving everything around her, always understanding, always taking whatever she gives and never pushing back."

"I know it's tough, but your mother loves you so much."

"Stop!" she shouted and jerked her hands away from his. "I'm sorry," she said, "but what does that have to do with anything? Every time Goldie or I bring something up it always ends up with 'I love you' like that's supposed to be the answer to everything, and it's not."

"But it is the answer to everything for her," Arthur tried to explain. "Your mother had a rough time as a child, she never had what we have, she never had a real family. So, when you get upset with her that is all that matters to her. That she loves you and you love her."

"But then, that's it? That's all we get? Her parents fucked her up and now we just take what we can get?"

Arthur took a deep breath to stall for time while he thought of a way to handle this. Because he did agree with Violet. The idea of Grant having a painting of his daughter was repulsive. But then the part of his brain he called logical would step in and argue the alternate point. Grant was her biological father. He hadn't really made that much of a mess of their lives. Not as much as he could have. So what if Alice had sold a painting of Violet to him, or even given it to him? What was that small thing in the face of the whole life they had built together? Every hurt was so great and damning to Violet, the way it always was to a child. *But,* he reminded himself, *she's not really a child anymore.*

"Fine," Arthur said, leaning back in his chair. "You're an adult now. Let's discuss this like adults. This is what I do when I'm dealing with something someone has said that's hurt me. Your mother actually taught me this technique, so it might give you a little insight. In one sentence, say what it is you want to happen in that relationship. What do you want from your mother?"

"I want her to stop doing things that make people gossip about us," Violet tried to sum up.

"Alright, what else?"

"I want her to stop having anything to do with Gabriel Grant," she said more definitely.

"What else?"

"I want . . ." Violet searched the ceiling while she thought it through. "I want her to ask permission before she uses my face in her art," she stated. "And if I say no, I want her to take it as a no. And

I want her to say thank you. For all the years I helped her and all the hours I put in that she never paid me for or mentioned at all. I want a thank-you."

Arthur nodded seriously.

"That all?" he asked.

"I want everyone—"

"Let's just stick with her for right now," he interrupted.

"Okay. I want her to stop lying about important things?" she said cautiously, hazarding quick sideways glances at him.

He coached himself not to react to the implication of her words. *Just say it*, he thought. *Just say, 'I'm his biological daughter.' The door is right there, walk through it.* It was clear she knew. *But was this really the right time?* The logical part started counterarguing again. It was supposed to be a controlled conversation. It was supposed to be him and Alice sitting her down together and going through everything. Alice would be furious if they had this talk without her. He could hear it now. Her accusations that he went behind her back, poisoned her child against her. And without being a witness she might accuse him of saying horrible things about her behind her back, like she'd done in the past. And as much as he wanted in that moment to just give Violet the truth she clearly needed, he'd still made a promise with his wife that they'd talk to her together.

"Okay, that's enough," he said. "You would be happier with these changes?"

"Yes." Violet nodded, the weight on her sternum listing just an inch from having said all of it aloud.

"Well, everything you said, all these things you want." Arthur looked at her steadily. "None of it is ever going to happen."

He watched his words land with a pang. He wished he didn't have to do this. But she had to learn.

"That's the truth," he continued. "Your mother will never do any of those things. And nothing you do, or I do, will ever make her do those things. So, the only person that can change here is you." Arthur pulled at his beard. "You think in twenty years of marriage there weren't things I wish were different? Of course I do. But I can't blame your mother for those things, and I can't hold her responsible for something I feel. Do you get that? I don't have to keep being married to her the same way she doesn't have to keep being married to me. We stay here because we both choose to stay. She told me when she first moved into our home that the living room would have to be turned into a painting studio, and I dealt with that. I told her to stop using you girls as models when you were young and she dealt with that. I found somewhere else to watch TV, she found somewhere else to paint. You could have left when you were eighteen, moved out, left us behind, but you didn't. You could have gone to another school—sure, you would have had to take out loans, but you could have done it. No one here is making you stay. You said you wanted to stop sharing a room with Goldie and Mom gave you her office. She dealt with it. And now what? You're mad that she found another place to work?"

Violet leaned back in her chair and nodded like a child receiving a scolding. And really, wasn't it the same thing?

"I know this is hard to hear. But you're not a child anymore. You're so upset about what you mother does, how she acts, and you keep acting like your pain is her fault but really, Violet." Arthur knocked his knee into hers to get her to meet his eye, which she did. "The only person making you miserable is you. You have to *decide* to stop being miserable. That's being a grown-up. The only person in the world who can make you feel any better about all of this is you. Not your mother, not me, not Grant, not your sister. It's just you."

Violet nodded again as she digested his words.

BACKSTITCH

The Transformation of the Dioscuri by Zeus
2016

Alice Snyder
American, 1974–2017

Marigold had checked and double-checked with her sister which day Violet meant to have "the talk" with their parents to be sure she wouldn't be interrupted. She needed a stretch of time long enough to see to her own plans. It wasn't that Marigold didn't appreciate Violet's efforts, it was that she believed her sister's approach to be inherently flawed. Yes, confronting their parents about the state of their family was the obvious choice, even the logical one, but down in the human realm where people often act illogically and against their own best interests, down in the realm where Marigold lived, she knew the one with all the power was Gabriel Grant.

He was the unknown agent. The outlier. And even Marigold could see, plain as day on their faces, no matter how much she may like to ignore it, how much he'd contributed to the biological reality of her sister. He was free of all the ties that bound the Snyder family. Gabriel Grant was the man her mother hadn't married and the father her sister had never had. He, out of all of them, was the easiest to get rid of.

Marigold got his address from the same girl who'd seen her mother's art on the walls. Marigold didn't want to give him time to call their mother, so she just turned up to his apartment unannounced. There was a moment, after she signed in with the security guard but before she got to his door, where she realized she hadn't actually considered if he would be there when she arrived. But then she knocked, she heard the muffled call of "Coming," and the last of her nerves fell away. The door swung open, and Gabriel just stood there for a moment, blinking in confusion.

"Oh," he said eventually. "It's you."

"Are you expecting someone?"

"I just thought, when Roger called up and said Ms. Snyder . . ."

"You thought I was my mother." Marigold fought the urge to look away in discomfort. "Well, I'm not. I'm me. Can I come in?"

"Um." Gabriel stepped back just enough for Marigold to make her way past him into the room. The apartment was awful. Clearly decorated by a professional, every surface oozing the same bland smell of wealth she'd seen sometimes when she helped her mother deliver art to buyers. No personal pictures, no clutter, no soul. She clocked the two wineglasses he'd pulled out and left on the kitchen counter despite it being the middle of the day. *This is what his girls see,* she couldn't help thinking. *This is what my mother sees.* The moment she heard the front door click closed, Marigold was ready to begin.

"I want you to stay away from my family," she said. Gabriel paused again, considered, then breezed past her on his way to the kitchen.

"You've known my mom a long time, you've worked together, you've dated. But that was a long time ago. That was before she had us. She doesn't need you anymore."

Gabriel laughed at that. Not a mean laugh, a sort of sad one. Marigold wondered if maybe this wasn't the first time he'd heard a speech like this. He went to his fridge and pulled out a sweating bottle of red wine. He poured himself a glass, and after a glance at his unexpected guest, poured another.

"I'm serious." Marigold hated to hear her voice faltering. "I am. You being here is bad for her reputation. People are gossiping, they're making it out like you two—"

"Like we two are what?" he asked. He tasted from his own glass, seemed to approve, then carried both back to face her. He offered Marigold hers and when she made no move to take it, he sighed and placed it on the side table nearest her.

"People are gossiping," he repeated. "They're making it out like we are—what? Having an affair? Is that so strange? Even if we didn't have the past we have, any man and any woman spending any considerable amount of time together in this city will get people talking. It's the national pastime."

"They're making it out like you're paying for all her work," Marigold tried to specify. "Like you're paying for her studio space, like she's this, this kept woman who—"

"Isn't she?" he cut her off. "Isn't that exactly what your mother is? And why is that so bad? She married your father because he could provide for her. She takes my money because—"

"You don't know anything about my father," Marigold spat.

Gabriel just studied her, took another sip, and studied her again. She wanted to knock the glass out of his hand. Just the idea of seeing it shatter on the floor was enough to calm her down a bit.

"You don't know anything," he said snidely. "About why they got married."

It's bait, Marigold reminded herself while she fought the urge to get into an argument with him. *It's the only card he has to play.*

"I want you to leave her alone," she said, trying to get back on track.

"Ah, so at first I was supposed to stay away from the whole family, but now it's just your mother?"

"My mother is the only one you ever bothered with."

He pulled a cartoonishly doubtful face.

"I'm not so sure about that," he said. "I am supposed to have certain rights."

"Violet is over eighteen."

"So you do know." His eyes lit up with interest. "I was never sure what they told you. Your mother made it *very* clear I was never supposed to even ask about you, let alone meet you. I guess she didn't think you'd come here yourself."

Everything in her told her to go. The tightness in her belly, the rising heat in her face, the itch of her scalp. They were all her body's way of telling her things she already knew but fought against anyway. He was right. She shouldn't be the one to come here. It should have been her mother doing the right thing. But she also knew her mother was off somewhere with Lettie, ignoring her sister's pleas, pretending that nothing was wrong. Marigold assessed the man in front of her. He seemed a lot sadder than she thought he'd be. And all alone in this ugly apartment, she thought, it must be lonely. Waiting and waiting for someone to come up and help him mark the passing of the day. Having to rely on other people's minds to have something to say, and on other people's bodies to make any art of worth.

"You know, I find it hard to believe you're my sister's father." She couldn't help herself. Marigold made her voice cold and crisp just like her mother did when she was saying something cruel. "My sister is brilliant and you're so . . . *uninteresting*. So why keep bothering with my mother? Out of boredom?" Marigold asked. "You can't love her, so why—"

"Why can't I love her?" He kept his voice casual and his eyes direct.

The thought made Marigold feel sick. Being here, listening to this, actually meeting him, she could feel it working on her, tricking her into doubting herself. She tried to hold on to some bit of high ground. She fought the whispering voice that suggested he might, even just a little, have his own version of things.

"She's outgrown you," Marigold said, hoping it was the right jab to throw.

Gabriel nodded slowly. "But she still comes back, doesn't she?" He brought his glass up to his lips, smiled, then knocked back the remaining quarter of wine. He turned back to the kitchen before Marigold could think of something to say.

"I just think—" She felt forced to walk after him, trying another kind of appeal. "I mean, I think it would be better for *everyone* involved. Because it's a lot of people at this point. It's her family, and all your . . . models. And you're right that people like to talk so why not just stop giving them things to talk about and let them—"

Marigold came up short as something off to her right caught her eye. At the end of a short hallway, given pride of place on its back wall, was a copy of *The Escape*. Marigold lost her train of thought and went down the hallway. She drew up close to the work and with the gentlest possible touch, she trailed her fingers along the edge of her sister's purple skirt. She felt the place where paint met fabric. Not a print then, this was the original.

Marigold stepped back. Her mother's hand was everywhere, not just in the painting, but in the staging as well. It was hung lower than one might expect so that the main figure was eye-to-eye with the beholder. The wall behind it wasn't exactly white, but a very pale blue to better contrast the darkness within the frame. It was lit from above using her mother's favorite kind of track lighting. Marigold had bought that lighting system before. She'd installed it and focused it per her mother's precise instructions. Her mother hadn't just given him *The Escape*, gifted or sold, she didn't care, but she'd installed it here for him, too.

She was here. Her mother and Violet. They were both here with him all the time, to look at any time he wanted.

"You know, I don't think I get enough credit for making her what she is today," Gabriel said from just behind her. Marigold jumped in surprise and knocked the new glass of red wine in his hand back, spilling all over his shirt.

"Shit!" he yelled. He backed away in shock. In a flash his surprise switched to fury.

"Shit!" he yelled again. Marigold flinched and backed farther into a corner of the hallway. "What the fuck is wrong with you?!" Gabriel threw his empty glass at the wall just behind Marigold's head. She ducked as it shattered over her head.

"Fuck!" he yelled one last time before storming off to another room and slamming the door behind him. Marigold sat crouched in the corner until she heard more small banging from the door he'd disappeared into. *He's changing his shirt,* she thought. *Go now,* she thought. She stood and shook the glass off her shoulders and paused. Leaving *The Escape* felt like leaving a part of Violet, and she couldn't do that. Marigold wrapped her arms around the painting, chest against paint, and heaved it up and off its hooks. She sped back out of the apartment, down the stairs and through the front door before she even had the cohesive thought: *I am going to steal this painting,* at which point her thought was wrong because she had already stolen the painting.

No one ran after her yelling. No one stopped her. No one even looked twice. Marigold didn't even have time to react until she was halfway back to her home. She was sitting in traffic trying to figure out where she could hide a painting without her mother seeing, when quite inexplicably, she began to laugh.

MARIAN MITCHELL DONAHUE

Castor Watches Her Sister Pollux
Train in the Boxing Ring
2016

Alice Snyder
American, 1974–2017

As Marigold turned off the paved road and onto the rocky, curving path that took her to her sister, she started to calm down. The gravel driveway was lined with low rods glowing red in the blue evening light. It was so dark in this part of town, still spared the source of streetlamps, she'd had to find the entrance to this place by driving very slowly and looking for the dull white lettering that read: KENNING UNIVERSITY SATELLITE CAMPUS: OBSERVATORY. She turned off whatever pop song had been playing and rolled down her windows to let in the sounds of the trees and the crunch of gravel under her tires. Marigold leaned forward in her seat and tried to look up.

The trees were close together on the main road, looming black figures, but as Marigold followed the road to the left the trees gave away in a sudden release of wide-open sky. The low buildings that made up the observatory were off to her right, hugging the gentle slope of the ground. One long, white trailer on a cinder block foundation, one white painted brick room where the main office was, then the high concrete walls that protected the telescopes ending in a small white cap where they stored the gear. Marigold avoided visiting her sister when she had nights at the observatory even though Violet often pushed the option. Although it was only fifteen minutes from their house, this small, preserved world felt like another planet. It was too far removed, too enclosed. Even the open stretch of sky didn't feel right to her because she knew that it wasn't really open. That sky was actually so full her meager human eye barely saw any of it. But Marigold knew, from her father and her sister, how much was out there, and it unnerved her, this reminder that her beautiful sky was really a silent, endless vacuum.

She parked next to her sister's Corolla with the mismatched doors and the peeling paint job. The crickets and hawk calls were almost as loud as the gravel when she opened her car door. A constant, pulsing screech going on and on like the heartbeat of the trees. Marigold gave herself a thorough going-over with bug spray, checked the tarp she'd thrown over the stolen painting, then started loading herself up with supplies. A large white paper bag with spicy chicken sandwiches and fries from Wendy's, two large Cokes, a plastic bag from 7-Eleven with water, candy, and a pack of those oil blotting sheets for Violet's forehead. She took a breath before stepping under the floodlight outside the front door where the flies were swarming. She kicked the bottom of the flimsy door twice in lieu of knocking. To her right the tops of some telescopes peeked up above the line of the concrete wall. She never called Violet's time at the observatory "homework," and Violet never called her art "assignments." It was all just work to them.

The door swung open.

"What happened?" Violet demanded.

"Surprise! I brought dinner!" Marigold could hear the too-high squeak in her voice but charged into the room anyway before she swallowed a mouthful of bugs. Violet closed the door behind her and swatted at some errant flies that managed to get in.

"Hungry?" Marigold asked as she looked for a place to put down the bags. It was a tight space. Violet squeezed back around to the other side of a large desk and started cleaning. It all seemed to Marigold to be a concentrated version of their father's office back home. There were the same seventies metal cabinets in the corner, the same newer monitors, though not as nice as the ones on campus, paired with old keyboards and promotional mouse pads from the 1998 *Godzilla* movie. On the back wall was a line of clocks with names underneath marking the current time of the major observation sites around the world. Not that this little trailer park observatory ever actually talked to them. That bit was for the tours opened to the public every other Sunday during the summer for community outreach.

Undergrads weren't usually allowed to be here alone, but Violet was. It wasn't just that her father was two years into a three-year stint as chair of the physics department, though that surely helped. It was Violet herself. She'd taken six classes a year her whole freshman year so that now, as a junior, she was allowed into the introductory graduate courses. She was always on the honor roll, usually at the top of the list, and had even been hired as a research assistant for her mentor, Dr. Ng. On the outside, Violet was ideal. Even their parents had bragged about how solid Violet was, but Marigold had her suspicions. She saw how little she ate, noticed how little she slept. Marigold had heard her sister crying through the thin wall that separated their bedrooms. The cracks in each other's perfectly painted veneers were another thing they both knew of each other without ever having to say it aloud.

The L-shaped desk Violet had been working on was covered in papers. Unlike the haphazard piles on Marigold's desk at home where there was order to things only Marigold could see, here it was two neat rows of stacked piles each labeled with a yellow Post-it note under headers like *ANTHRO-First Section Sources*, *PHYS101-Quiz*, and *PHYS301-Lab Reports*. Violet gathered them, turning each small pile ninety degrees each time so that she could lay them out again easily. As she went, Marigold followed behind her, replacing the stacks with napkins, divvying out each person's meal. By the time they sat down to start eating Violet had a giddy smile on her face.

"What?' Marigold asked, expecting a joke.

"I just can't believe you brought me dinner," she said. "It's really nice!"

"Well, good." Marigold tried to ignore the dread she felt, knowing that she'd have to tell Violet everything she'd just done. "I'm glad," she kept going. "I'm happy that you're happy."

She bit into her sandwich to keep from rambling on. There wasn't much need for Marigold to be worried. Violet launched into an account of everything she'd been up to that day with only a "wow" or "who's that again?" from Marigold to keep her going.

Such a night owl, Marigold thought.

It wasn't until they were throwing their crumpled-up wrappers into a bag that Violet asked Marigold a question.

"So how about the sculpture? How's it coming?"

"Good actually," Marigold said. "Almost done. The night you helped was a big turning point. Feels like I've been coasting on momentum since that."

"Good." Violet seemed to deflate. "I'm glad I was useful. And I'm glad you've had enough time to work on it. I know Mom's thing has been pretty demanding."

Marigold put down her soda and mentally braced for a disagreement. The "thing" Violet was referring to wasn't just any "thing." It wasn't just a new piece or a more involved commission for a private client. It was their mother's next big thing. It was a project so large and complicated she'd even confessed to Marigold, one morning when she'd been assisting her before school, that she'd imagined it for years before even attempting to make it. Silently, just to herself, Marigold referred to the nameless work as the magnum opus because that was what it felt like they were doing. They were making her greatest work so far.

And Violet, for some reason, was increasingly prickly about it. Always calling it "Mom's thing" or "the monster in the living room" due to its size. True, their mother seemed more affected by this one than usual. She was more withdrawn, more prone to trailing off mid-sentence or even walking out of the room mid-conversation to go work on it without any recognition of the family she'd just been talking to. But to Marigold that was more proof to support her theory, that this work was the great work, and so required the greatest attention and energy for its creator.

"It hasn't been taking up that much time," Marigold addressed her sister's usual complaints. "And I've gotten her to stick to a regular schedule so no more last-minute all-nighters or sudden calls in the middle of class."

"I just . . ." Violet sighed to let out her agitation. "I just don't want her taking advantage of you."

"I *offered* to help."

"All this time and work and it's not even your piece." Violet pulled the 7-Eleven bag out and dumped it between them. "You don't even get credit."

"Assistants never get credit, they're always invisible." Marigold tore open her bag of Skittles and started picking out the red ones. "I'll have an assistant one day, and I won't be expected to credit them. That's how it works. You put in your years in the background supporting others until you can take control, and then you get supported."

"It just doesn't seem fair." Violet sighed again. Marigold began getting annoyed.

"You know," she said to Violet, "you don't really have a leg to stand on here."

"Hunh?" Violet looked genuinely confused. "I haven't worked with Mom since—"

"No, I mean with Dad." Marigold nodded to the stack of papers her sister had cleared from the desk. "You mean, if I looked in there

I wouldn't see a bunch of Dad's Intro to Physics grading? You haven't been helping him out?"

Violet rolled her eyes.

"That's different," she said.

"No, it isn't. You're not his TA. You're not getting paid, but every time he's behind on his grading you step in."

"It's just some quizzes."

"And you help keep him on track."

"He's slammed with meetings now that he's chair. And he gave up his TA so that Dr. Myerhoff could have one because he has that gallbladder thing he has to deal with. He's *so* stressed, all the time, and it's just easier this way."

"It's easier to just do the work for him and keep him happy, right? Keep him moving forward?" Marigold sat back in her chair. "That's all I'm saying."

Violet seemed to turn that over.

"It isn't *exactly* the same," she mumbled in defeat. "I'm correcting math, making some notes. I'm not actually assigning them grades. Dad does that."

"But you have done grades before." Marigold felt the immature impulse to annoy her into a play fight creep up on her. Violet hated being wrong. Always made the same face, like she was sucking on a lemon wedge.

"I've only actually written grades for the nonjudgment stuff. Multiple choice, calculations. Dad says I'm too harsh on the other stuff. Apparently, too much criticism is 'demoralizing.' I think he's too easy on them."

"You're going to be one of those teachers everyone is afraid of," Marigold said, grinning. She could imagine the hush that would fall over the students when her sister walked to the front of the class with a stack of graded blue books in her arms and a grimace where a smile should be. But then Violet laughed, popping the bubble of her vision.

"I'm not becoming a teacher," she said. "Absolutely not."

"Then what?" Marigold asked. The image of her sister in front of a classroom faded.

"I want to actually be in it, you know?" Violet leaned forward on the desk and looked off into the middle space. "I want to be in the lab, doing research, asking the next big questions."

"So, what does that mean, exactly?"

"I think I want to help push the big questions. The origins of the universe. The moments after the Big Bang. I feel like that's where we're going, you know? The beginning of everything. That's the place I should be."

Marigold made a small noncommittal noise.

"The James Webb Space Telescope is supposed to launch in 2019," Violet continued, looking over at her sister. "If I can do my PhD in five or six years, I can be working by the time the first images come up. I mean, I'll just be starting, but still."

"And where would you need to be to do that?" Marigold asked. *How far away will you have to be?*

"Oh, probably just up in Baltimore," Violet said. Marigold relaxed her shoulders. "I'm interested in the science, not the actual building of the thing. If I can get in with the Space Telescope Science Institute up there, then I'd be happy. Plus, you know, it's an easy drive back down here, I could come back for all the major holidays and birthdays. And you can come up and visit me." Violet smiled at her sister.

"Perfect, yes, you do that." Marigold laughed in relief. "I was scared you were going to tell me you had to go live in Antarctica or something and I'd never see you again."

"God no." Violet laughed with her. "Can you imagine having to fly to see each other? Sounds awful."

They lapsed into silence. The relief of hearing her sister's plans would have been a buoy any other day, but Marigold could not accept the good news until she had finally confessed. She thought of that moment just after Gabriel had gone to change his shirt when her arms had reached out to take the painting before she'd even had the conscious thought of taking it. Her vision changed every time she tried to imagine the repercussions. She saw herself returning it, apologizing. She saw herself keeping it. Saw it in her father's office hanging above his desk. Saw her mother taking it from her. She saw Violet pouring turpentine on it and setting it on fire in the backyard just to be sure no one would ever own her again. This last vision, that of chemical fire and revenge, felt so real to Marigold her eyes welled up and her throat tightened as she imagined it. Just when she felt sure she would whine aloud from the violence in that future, she opened her mouth to confess everything to her sister.

"Lettie, I need to—"

Violet perked up suddenly and cut her off.

"Do you want to meet the telescopes? Sorry," she said catching up with herself. "What were you saying?"

"Telescopes?" Marigold repeated. Her mind was so far in another place she was having trouble orienting herself back into this moment. Here she was. Violet. Dinner. Observatory. Night.

"Yeah, you've never visited me here. I need to give you the tour!" Violet stood, rounded the desk, and went for the door off to their left. Marigold followed her out to the annex. Stepping from the meager air-conditioning of the office to the thick, humid air outside was enough to make both girls cough. The ground was crowded with machinery and the ceiling had been retracted to give a full view of the sky. Marigold could see the black lace of the tree line creep up over the edges of the high concrete walls. The brightest stars were showing but the sky didn't have the inky, matte quality yet.

"It doesn't look dark enough yet," Marigold said.

"It's not going to be," Violet said looking up, hands on her hips, frowning like a disapproving teacher.

"The university golf course is close enough to give us *just* enough darkness to still see things," she explained, "but everything else is getting too built up. Apartment complexes, that downtown thing they're trying to build in College Park. Soon the light pollution will be too bright, and we'll be blinded."

"So, they'll build a new observatory?"

"Maybe." Violet pulled out a rolling metal step stool with a bad wheel that scraped against the concrete floor as she dragged it. She pulled up next to one of the larger telescopes and climbed up. It had a solid white base, and the optical tube was longer and narrower than the others. It was set up to look out over the clearing to their right. Violet punched in something on its keypad and the tube moved slightly.

"D.C. is getting too big in general," Violet said. "Schools around here, the ones that still have astronomy programs, are buying land in places like Texas. Kenning might be able to afford something up in Pennsylvania, maybe upstate New York. Most likely they'll just let this place go and stop requiring observatory hours. Send people out to other places, share resources, something like that."

Violet pressed her eye to the telescope's eyepiece. She straightened, punched in another code, and looked again.

"What kind is that one?" Marigold asked. She used to know the differences between machines like these. Years ago, when her father took them both stargazing and taught them both the names of things.

"Fourteen-inch refracting. She's my favorite." Violet lifted her head and grinned at Marigold. "You want to see something cool?"

Marigold grinned back, letting her sister's good mood lift her own for a moment. Violet checked the eyepiece one more time before stepping down and beckoning Marigold to step up and look. The stool creaked under her weight, and the angle was awkward. Marigold had to lean over the telescope to line up with the eyepiece. Her right hand kept wanting to reach out and touch the instrument, to place her hand at the bottom of the tube and her left on the eyepiece, but she couldn't. This wasn't her world. Maybe she'd had access to it once, but at some unremarked-upon moment she'd gone one way with her mother, and Violet and her father had gone another. Her swaying weight, the ache in her back from leaning over, all of it told her how much she did not belong here, acting like one of them.

"Can you see it?" Violet asked, squinting off in the same direction. Marigold looked again. She joined her hands behind her back and held them tight to keep from touching. Inside she could see two points of light lined up at a forty-degree angle. She looked up from the telescope and saw only one.

"How is it . . . ?" she asked.

"They're called binary stars." Violet smiled. She pointed to the single point of visible light. "You see that star there?"

Marigold nodded and looked in the eyepiece again. Just as before, she saw twins. One a little brighter than the other, but still, two distinct points of light.

"It's two stars revolving around a common center. They're so close they look like a single star in the sky, which makes them visual doubles as well. I love showing them to people," Violet's voice went soft. "When I do the tours, people always expect to see the planets.

Venus, Mars. Sometimes even Jupiter's Spot on a good day, but no one's expecting the binary stars. When people look at the planets, they just see a closer version of what's out there, but with these two they get to see in a way they just can't by themselves."

"You seem happy," Marigold said.

"I guess so." Violet laughed it off. "I know it's not a *real* observatory, but it's better than trying to work at home and dealing with Mom's moods."

Marigold felt a trickle of sweat run down her side. She tasted the dew in the air. She watched her sister watch the sky, her face more relaxed than she'd seen it in days. Her graduation was so close. Then she'd be off to grad school, and it'd just be her and their parents left. She knew it would never be like this again. The world would never be this complete again. She tried to find the words to tell Violet what happened but there was nothing there, just a vast expanse of nothing hanging over this small bubble of their lives.

"I need to go," Marigold said, her voice small in the symphony of crickets all around them. Violet heard her anyway.

"You sure?" Her face fell a little. "You can work here if you want. No one's really going to check."

"No, I need to go do something—get a book. I need to pick up a book from my friend." She stepped down carefully from the stool and went to go gather her things.

The parting was brief and strange. Even the hug they shared was off, but Violet didn't ask her to stay again, and Marigold didn't offer. It wasn't until she was in her car, the shadow of the painting looming at her back, watching the floodlights of the office recede into the darkness as she drove away, that Marigold noticed how much calmer, and how much lonelier, she felt.

The Fire at Artemesia Drive

2017

Various

Photo array

Here is a full photographic account of the fire on Artemesia Drive at Snyder's home in May 2017. Gathered here are photos from local newspapers, from the family's personal collection, and from the neighbors and bystanders who were present that day to witness the tragedy. We thank the Photo Editorial team at the *Hyattsville Gazette* for gathering and arranging these images.

    The official account is this: Gabriel Grant entered the property sometime around three p.m. and less than an hour later smoke began to pour out of the front windows of the house. Firefighters arrived quickly but had trouble containing the blaze due to the amount of chemicals and flammable elements inside. They managed to enter the property and retrieve the unconscious Gabriel Grant, who was then rushed to the hospital and later revived. At some point in this same time frame Alice Snyder managed to enter the property in an attempt to save her newly finished magnum opus, *The Alice Tapestry*. She barely made it to her studio before passing out from the noxious air. She, too, was quickly retrieved and rushed to the hospital, but died from suffocation en route.

Here is the truth of it: When Gabriel Grant pulled up to the house on Artemesia Drive, he thought the empty house was just a sign of his good timing. The unlocked back door was a sign of his good luck. He'd have all the time and space he needed to finish his fifth of vodka and find his missing painting. He didn't expect to see Alice's great work just hanging there like it was waiting for him, but this, too, must have been a sign of fate.

The embroidery was hung against the wall, and the curtains were pulled back to let in the light. It was a long strip of linen, and on it was the story of her life. At first, he thought she'd left it there for him. It was finished, finally finished, this secret thing she'd been making for years and would not tell him about. This thing that consumed her time, pulled her focus, called her attention away even when it was just the two of them in his apartment talking. The whole life of a red-haired woman fabricated; a story told in thread. When he first saw it, he thought, *She left this here for me.*

He sat on the floor in front of it like a child, all elbows and knees. He lit a cigarette. Read the images. Lit another. Found the continuation of her story piled in the corner. He unwound it and kept reading. He went forward, then he looped back, searching for a sign of himself, but all he found was his absence. Events he didn't recognize. When had she gone to the beach? When had she ever gone to church? He noticed the dress she was wearing in the tapestry was wrong. She should have been wearing the white thing he'd put her in for *Ophelia*. That was her dress. That was the marker of herself in her art. Portrait after portrait, she always kept his mark on her. Here, in front of him now, was some other white dress he'd never seen. He assumed it was the one she wore to marry the astronomer.

Alice wore green when she married Arthur. She was already

showing when they scheduled the date with the courthouse and white felt like a lie she didn't care enough to tell.

Here is the truth of it: The figure he was staring at wasn't Alice, it was her mother, Rose. Her story didn't start with her own birth; it started with her mother.

Gabriel didn't remember knocking over his vodka bottle, but he did. He didn't remember throwing his still-lit stub into the puddle, but he did. He remembered his surprise when it went up, remembered how pretty he thought the flames were. He said it was ridiculous to claim that he would sit there watching as the fire started licking the hanging tapestry. He said he wouldn't have done that to her, wouldn't destroy the thing she had made just because she left him out of it. But even he knew that he did.

The beauty was spoiled by the smell. It went out in all directions, up the embroidery, across his shoes, over to her workspace. The fire found paint, thinners, primers—chemicals that sprang and sputtered when lit. Chemicals that burned his throat, watered his eyes, poisoned the air. The danger to himself felt far away, he remembered. All his life he had thought it would end in water.

He grew up by the water. He was Joseph Turner then. He had a brother then. His brother's name was David.

Joseph had never liked Annapolis. He'd always felt misplaced there. He hated the summer months everyone else lived for. His skin didn't darken in the sun; it burned and peeled. His clothes never fit right, they hung from his frame like rags. The only thing he remembered liking were the hours he spent with David and their father out on the boat, barely talking, sipping warm beer, spotting each other when they took a piss off the side.

When David went to do lacrosse drills at the park with his friends, he let Joe carry his bag there and back. Joe's favorite memory came from that summer. David and the others ran laps as a warm-up while Joe sat on a bench nearby doing his summer reading. As they passed him, he heard one mutter "fag" and a few others snickered. Joe had been perfectly fine to let it slide. He was pale and thin and unathletic, so he'd gotten used to that kind of thing. But before they'd made it any farther David suddenly turned mid-run and tripped up someone in the middle of the pack. The guy fell, rolling in the dirt to protect his ankle while the rest of them kept jogging. There was even more snickering. Joe looked to his brother. David ran backward for a few steps, nodded to him, then turned to fall back in line with the others. Joe could have cried. He didn't, of course—that would have undone everything. But he held on to that beautiful, sterling memory: the breaking of the ranks, the puff of dust as the anonymous boy fell, the nod.

The room grew warm. Gabriel took off his shirt. He balled it up and put it under his head as he laid down on the floor. The smoke swirled on the ceiling like ink in water. The light outside the bay window was dimming. Storm clouds pressing in, pressure aching in his head.

The day David died there was a sudden summer storm. It was a Friday in that perfect month after David had come home from school and Joe was ill. He'd been up all night hacking built-up phlegm into tissues and sweating through his bedsheets. His mother wouldn't let him go with them that day, sure that if he had just one more day of absolute rest, he'd be able to shake it. He remembered hating her a little after David left with their father for the marina. He still hated her a little for that.

Joe got the details from a news article in the *Capital Gazette*. For some reason never explained to him, their father decided to take out his friend's multi-sail Bermuda sloop instead of their own, simpler, Jamaican sloop. The wind was strong, and it was just the two of them out there on an unfamiliar boat. It capsized and David went with it. For a young man of such promising athletic ability, the article theorized, he must have been injured during the accident because once he was under, he didn't surface again. There was no sign of a fight. He was there. He went under. He was gone.

The article left out that their father hadn't manned a Bermuda sloop since college, that they'd had beers with the unnamed owner of the sloop for an hour before they went out. It left out that when a nearby deck boat dragged their father out of the water it took three men to pin him to keep him from diving back in to find his son. There was a picture of the wrecked boat next to David's yearbook photo. He was smiling.

The curtains caught easily. They were heavy, but they'd spent years taking on paint splatters and thinner fumes. They were imbedded with flammable chemicals. They burned so prettily.

Joseph first met Alice during a fire drill their freshman year at Kenning University. At 11:50 a.m. the fire alarm went off and he filed outside into the warm fall afternoon with the rest of the occupants of the art building. The clouds were dark, but sparse. The dappled light made people squint and cover their eyes.

Alice was sitting on top of a splintering wooden picnic table with a group of other art students Joe didn't recognize. He didn't see them. All he saw that first moment was her red hair, and a moment after that her face. She didn't look right in modern clothes. Her dark eyes and strong features made her look displaced in time.

A stranger squealed. People looked to the girl covering her head and then looked to the sky. A sun shower. Joe felt a few heavy droplets hit his head and then everyone seemed to move at once. Most of the students ran to the next building. A few huddled under the awning on the front of the art building but didn't go back in. Some started twirling and dancing around. Some just turned and started walking away. Joe tucked his camera into his jacket and ran under the tree. The red-haired girl was still on the bench, abandoned by her classmates. Her face was turned up to the sky and there was an easy, peaceful grin on her face. He took the first few shots without thinking, protected from the rain by the intertwined branches of the tree.

She opened her eyes and turned to him, surprised. They caught on each other—his pale brown eyes and her dark ones. She swung her body toward him and assumed the same pose. Hands up, eyes closed. The happiness was brighter. Her cheeks glistened with rain like she'd been crying. He started taking more, stepping side to side to find the right angles for her cheeks. The sun was coming in sideways under the storm clouds, so the shadows were contrasting in a way he'd never captured before. She went through some simple motions. Hands clasped together in front of her chest. Eyes open but squinting. Some sitting up straight, some leaning back on her hands. She broke suddenly, shaking the water off her face and laughing.

She pulled the elastic free at the end of her hair and unwound her braid. She combed through her hair with damp fingers. It sat flat from the water. As she ran her hands through it, Joe commenced taking pictures. He scooted as far to the side as he could go without risking getting water on his camera. The last picture was her in profile, looking out in the distance while she raked her long hair back and over to the other side of her head with both hands.

Burned faces were black. Drowned faces were blue. It wasn't how he'd want it, but this was where he was. This burning room. He took deeper breaths and willed his body to give up. He wanted to be asleep when he caught fire.

People thought he could not see a version of her life that did not begin and end with him.

Here is the truth of it: He would not see a version of his life that did not begin and end with her.

The first and last time Arthur Snyder saw the house on Artemesia Drive that would contain all the best years of his life, he thought of a poem he'd had to memorize in school. He'd carried it out with him in his mind like a toddler carrying a handful of wet sand from the tide back to the castle it builds on dry sand. Less and less with every step forward, water streaming out between desperate fingers. He'd known the whole thing once, but all he had left were the words *a habitation marvelously planned.*

Arthur's father had been upstairs destroying all the glassware when Arthur had memorized the poem. His voice had risen and fallen with the thump of furniture being thrown or overturned, like the afterburner of fireworks, when a bit of porcelain or glass met the wall.

Bored of the task in front of him, a sliver of Arthur's mind had separated itself and tried to estimate the total number, in dollars, what it would cost to fix the damage upstairs just based on the noise. His mother, to his knowledge, only ever bought the nice stuff and the nice stuff shattered when it hit the wall.

Every time she needed to order more they'd make a day of it in the city. Shopping at Woodward and Lothrop, always with the woman who ran the crystal department, always the same quantity, always with delivery. When they left his mother would lean down and say, "She looks *just like* Deborah Kerr." Then they'd ride the elevator down to the café on the bottom floor where his mother would drink a tiny coffee and he would order a croque monsieur. He would offer to split it with her three times, always three, so that on the third one she could say, "Oh if you insist!" and then proceed to eat most of it.

When the boxes arrived, she'd unpack the fresh glasses carefully, only ever touching the stems to avoid fingerprints, like she didn't already know that when his father went for them, he scooped them from the cabinet, sweating palm flat on glass-cut bowl, and hurled them at the wall.

Here is the truth of it: Mr. Snyder never hit his wife or son. He only hit things around them, and that was a very different thing.

When they'd gone to Woodies this last time his mother had let him pick and he'd gone with one of the bestsellers. The Lismore line. Deborah Kerr had made a comically appreciative face and told his mother that he had good taste. He'd been happy to be included, but there were unintended consequences. He'd never seen the price tags before.

Each glass was twenty-one dollars and fifty-one cents. Each sound was twenty-one dollars and fifty-one cents.

Huge Ocean shows, within his yellow strand,

Twenty-one dollars and fifty-one cents.

Times two is forty-three and two.

A habitation marvelously planned

Arthur had often wished his father would just hit him one day and get it over with. So much less property damage that way. And he was sure he could take it. If he'd ever been given the choice between the glass and himself, he'd have saved the glass.

The end of everything didn't happen the way he'd thought it would. It wasn't the slow separation of his daughters from himself, it was the ghost of his wife come to haunt the house they'd built, and it was her rushing into a fire to save what she'd built.

He'd tried to comfort himself once, years later, thinking *At least she went back in for her work, and not to save him* but that didn't comfort him much at all.

After the house was all but gone, burned and condemned, waiting to be razed, Arthur went back and pulled out some of the glassware his mother had sent them after they'd gotten married. He stood in the backyard and threw it, pitcher-style, at the brick wall. The breaking didn't make him feel any better, but after, there was a lift in his chest like pleasure when he saw the glittering shards he'd left in the mud.

Here is the truth of it: Arthur was already counting his daughters gone by the time he lost his wife and so it never seemed possible that he could have abandoned them. He stayed just long enough to settle the accounts. He left to a visiting position in Texas, then a year in Hawaii, then when Kenning University demanded he either resign or come back, he resigned. He left his tenure and started taking up jobs wherever he could find them and he refused to look back.

Here is the truth of it: Even when he heard them cry on the phone asking him to fly back, just for a week, just for the weekend, just to see their graduation, just to see their mother's show, even as he heard himself say he would try, he knew he couldn't go.

In the confusion of the day the chronological sequence of events became jumbled. Here is how it actually went: Arthur, Alice, and the girls left Violet's graduation reception early when Arthur got a call from the fire department. On arrival they saw the crowd of their neighbors come to watch the show. They saw the black rising from the windows, felt the heat warn their skin of burning, smelled the reek of wrong things being put alight. Arthur went to the men in uniforms. The girls held on to each other. And not one of them noticed Alice get past the line of hoses and make for the back door of the house, past the EMTs loading Gabriel onto a stretcher on the side of the house, and through the broken open back door with a shawl pressed over her face. The last anyone saw of her conscious, she was fighting her way toward her studio, and they all assumed she was fighting to save her work.

Here is the truth of it: Alice was only in the house for a few minutes before she lost consciousness. It was less than five minutes before a fireman went in and was able to pull her out. Less than an hour before she was dead.

Here is the truth of it: The girls never saw her go in, they only saw her come out, carried in the arms of a stranger, looking peaceful.

She was staring up at the sky and she saw rain clouds forming, pregnant with water, ready to rain. And she was thinking, *It's not enough, it's not enough, it's enough.*

Here is the truth of it: Alice did not go into the fire to save her work. She was not moving toward the studio. She was trying to get to her sewing basket. The box was at the bottom, a matte gold jewelry box. Inside: four sets of embroidered roses, the girls' first attempts on top, then hers, and underneath, her mother's. It was Violet's graduation present. It was supposed to be passed down. It burned.

MARIAN MITCHELL DONAHUE

The Alice Tapestry
(Lost)
2017

Alice Snyder
American, 1974–2017

Embroidery on linen

To your right you may see a full set of plans for *The Alice Tapestry* alongside selections from her personal notebooks, and the few surviving photographs where the tapestry was caught in the background.

    Here, on this wall, we hold a space for what was lost in the fire.

What It Was Like to Be There
2023

Marigold Snyder
American, 1996–

Immersive projections

In conversation with her mother's 2004 piece *Two Girls with Fruit*, here we are invited to experience some version of what it was like to be present for the creation of a piece of art. The artist's daughter created this piece in honor of her mother's legacy and in celebration of her posthumous success. She says:

My mother was always so focused on capturing the quiet moments of life. She was incredibly reflective in her art. I'm not sure she ever realized what an unquiet home she had created. I wanted especially to make something related to her earliest work, back when my sister and I were young and before she had an audience. Back when it was just us and the images and the work.

The piece runs for three minutes from beginning to end and marks the end of the exhibit.

The entrance to the final room was in the back corner, marked only by the text on the wall finally catching up in time and place to where she was at that moment. Violet hoped she never would never lose the clench of pride she felt every time she saw her sister's name in print like this. There was a young attendant at the wall overlap, headset chirping and stopwatch in her hand. Violet peeked around the corner and saw the shadows and moving lights of what would come next. There was sound, too, something rhythmic, then a woman's voice, but she couldn't make out anything in particular. A couple lined up behind her, then another stranger, then another. The group built up, and then when the moving shadows in the next room stilled and faded back to black the attendant gestured for them to enter, and they walked into the room in single file like mourners in a procession.

Violet could only see by the light of the LED strips lining the path and the bright red EXIT sign over the far corner where just a sliver of daylight spilled in through the overlapping walls. There was a figure already in the room that Violet recognized immediately as her sister. She went over to stand by her, and in the scant light she saw Marigold nod in greeting, then turn her face up to the wall for the next rotation of the show. Violet did the same.

It started with a sound in darkness. Wood sliding against wood, metal clicking into place, a clatter—paintbrushes, Violet recognized, a clatter of wood-handled paintbrushes rolling onto their mother's cart. The sounds began to overlap as a dim gray light rose onto each of the four walls with four clear black lines shaping each into a canvas. There was the turn of metal tops off their containers—paints and thinners—the run of the kitchen tap for her water glasses, and behind it all a mechanical sound Violet hadn't heard in years but knew could only be her mother's percolator making coffee at every hour of the day and night. Then came the brushes, the sound of wet fox fur sweeping against a canvas as the first brushstrokes appeared on the walls. They were wide and aggressive at first, then they narrowed and became more detailed. Two figures began taking shape, one immediately recognizable as a girl standing and one short and malformed—no, not malformed, just sitting. The lines came in cleaner, and the malformation became just a girl in a chair. The colors stayed muted as the picture became composed, but it was not a mistake. *It was a technique, it was . . .* Violet thought. *What was the word for it?* She dredged her memories and came back with the answer: the underpainting, the invisible structure that supported the finished image. This was an underpainting, and just as she thought this the colors changed and became brighter as it moved into the next phase. *The overpainting.*

Cue their mother's voice saying, *Stand still, almost there, just one more, one more minute.* Violet felt a rush of blood to her face, and she struggled to keep her breath even. How had Marigold gotten this voice? There was no way she could have had a recording. Violet turned to her sister for an answer, but Marigold was focused on some minute detail on the lower left corner of one of the projections, no doubt seeing some flaw in her own work no one else would catch. *Stand still, almost there, just one more, one more minute.* Violet tried to stay quiet, to stay still, to let the tears well over and trickle down her hot cheeks. It sounded so like their mother, but no, it wasn't exactly right. It must have been Marigold then, doing an imitation. Pitching her high voice down to match their mother's own. Violet had no idea her sister was even capable of such close mimicry. She'd had no idea.

As the paint strokes calmed and the image of *Two Girls with Fruit* settled into the finished piece she recognized from the very first room, the sounds shifted. Brushstrokes morphed into soft staccato beats with a rushing noise between them: Their mother's embroidery needles punching through linen and running floss through backing. Each sound resonated in clear, even strokes. Violet felt her body sway with the rhythm of it, giving into the movement like she never could when she was posing, letting herself be rocked back into calm by the old lullaby. On the walls the images changed, too. Projections of textured thread appeared in the paint, first in the girls' eyebrows and hair as it was in the original, but then the projections went further. The thread spread to the outline of their bodies, then the shadows, then the main images themselves.

There was a sudden crack of wood splintering. Violet felt the strangers in the room jump in time with her. The neat black lines that kept the image contained crumpled and the faux frames unfurled onto the ceiling and floor, their edges mingling and overlapping. The focus began to close in on details. All the time the spread of thread never stopped. The original halved fruit began sprouting life. Mold, moss, and flowers unfurled from the initial images and spread throughout the room. A visitor laughed and jumped back as the projectors splashed ivy and roses over her shoes. All the strangers instinctively backed up as the light spread, but once they were caught in the middle of the room, they had no choice but to let themselves be submerged in it.

Violet closed her eyes as the line of light rose up her body and slipped over her face like water. Then the images began to move. The fabric flowers swayed in an invisible wind, the ivy climbed up the ceiling, caught on the bodies of the viewers in the room, making them a part of it, catching them in its snare. Above them simple green leaves turned over to become pairs of eyes, brown eyes and hazel ones, hers and her sister's. Violet let her head drop all the way back and her mouth gape open like a fish to watch as the natural forms morphed into ocular ones. This is what was on the posters, she realized. It was these eyes, not the painted ones of her mother, but the new ones her sister had made. This is what had watched her come home.

Violet felt her sister's attention turn on her, Marigold's face full of the unasked question. Did she like it? But that was the wrong question. This thing her sister had created was beyond liking, it was even beyond the usual kind of understanding. They were past those easy questions meant for other people: Did she like it, did she get it? No more of that. Now only: Is it right? Violet looked over at her sister, wiped the meager tears off her face and broke into a wide, sad smile. She reached out to take Marigold's hand just as her little sister did the same. Hand in hand they turned their faces back to the lights.

ACKNOWLEDGMENTS

Many people have helped me get to this moment with this book over the past eight years. Let me begin most recently with my editor and cofounder of Galiot Press, Anjali Duva, who saw the soul of this book right away and helped usher it into its final form. Thank you to Henriette Lazaridis, the other cofounder of Galiot Press, for helping me as I learned the legal and publicity side of publishing for the first time. Thank you to FaceOut Studio for my beautiful cover.

I would not be here without two teachers who helped develop me as a person and thinker years before I started writing: Matt Goyette and Dr. Taryn Okuma. Thank you to my mentors in grad school, especially my thesis advisor, Paul Harding, and my novel teacher, Susan Scarf Merrell. Your support in and out of the classroom has been more precious than I have words for.

I have not been alone in facing down the blank page thanks to my community of writers. Special thanks to Claudia Acevedo-Quiñones, Robert Taylor, Alex Sniatkowski, Grace Dilger, Quinn Adikes, and Max Parker for finding ways to keep creating amidst the horrors of the world. Thank you for reading early versions of this work, telling me what you saw, and cheering me on even when it looked like it would never be seen in print. Thank you to the Church at Sag Harbor for the time to create during their Mixed Media Artists Residency, which gave me the space I needed to reset my brain. I also thank the BookEnds Program, especially my pod mates, Patricia Friedrich and Sally Martell, and my mentor, Robert Lopez.

I am most grateful to my family, both for being a part of Team Donahue and for the years of love and support you've shown me as I've written this book. Thank you.

Galiot's first three books were made possible in part though the support of the following individuals:

Allison Cook & Jack Humphrey
Dena Enos
Marina Hatsopoulos
Bandita Joarder
Breanna Powers Kirk
Erin McKenna
Julia Sullivan
Justine Uhlenbrock

And 295 other contributors to our crowdfunding campaign

For more about the author, additional content, and to look up or purchase additional Galiot books, visit **www.galiotpress.com**

More by Galiot Press:

SEX OF THE MIDWEST by Robyn Ryle In this group of linked stories set in the fictional town of Lanier, Indiana, things get rolling when everyone in town receives an email titled "Sexual Practices in a Small Midwestern Town". A link leads to an extensive survey, but why has Lanier been chosen? And by whom? Street by street and house by house, the email opens up the secret (and not-so-secret) lives of one small Midwestern town grappling with current issues in our post-pandemic world. (Fall 2025)

SWALLOWTAIL by Emily Ross In the gritty seaside town of Quincy, Massachusetts, the killing of a teenager on her daughter's dance team plunges Detective Samantha Star into the trauma of her abduction twenty years before. As clues point to a serial killer obsessed with Surrealism and Greek myth, Sam must unravel the mystery of her own kidnapping to solve the crime—before her daughter is next. At stake are not just the teenagers' lives, but also Sam's identity as a detective and an artist, and a community's chance at healing. (Fall 2025)

THE DAYS OF MIRACLE AND WONDER by Irene Zabytko In 1992, just after the fall of the Soviet Union, a Ukrainian-American woman travels to Ukraine and boards a bus on an unlikely pilgrimage. In a manner reminiscent of the Canterbury Tales, the passengers—a swimmer, an artist, an interrogator, and more—tell extraordinary stories of ordinary people caught between Soviet realities and American dreams. **THE DAYS OF MIRACLE AND WONDER** is a timely glimpse into the complexities of balancing political pressures, collective responsibilities, and individual happiness. **(Spring 2026)**

THE ENDED WORLD by Libbie Grant A young woman's vision over a Quebec lake sends her on a search to understand her relationship to the divine. While she spends years as a cloistered nun, a young boy struggles with his Mormon upbringing and, discovering the internet, grows up to design an AI entity that stuns him by appearing sentient. Embarking on their own separate road trips, these characters unite to face the scope of their responsibilities, their understanding of what's holy, and the very question of what it is to be a human being. Steeped in philosophy, theology, and computer science, **THE ENDED WORLD** is a novel for our times. **(Fall 2026)**

www.ingramcontent.com/pod-product-compliance
Lightning Source LLC
LaVergne TN
LVHW091713070526
838199LV00050B/2378